S.I

some comfort

among us

NDE Publishing
2004

Some Comfort Among Us

By S.P. Hozy

Cover and title page illustrations by François Thisdale © 2004

© 2004 by S.P. Hozy

© 2004 by NDE Publishing

Elena Mazour, Publisher

NDE Publishing

15-30 Wertheim Court

Richmond Hill, ON L4B 1B9

tel: 905-731-1288

toll free: 800-675-1263

fax: 905-731-5744

e-mail: info@ndepublishing.com

url: www.ndepublishing.com

National Library of Canada Cataloguing in Publication

Hozy, Penny, 1947-

    Some comfort among us / S.P. Hozy ; François Thisdale, illustrator.

ISBN 1-55321-108-1

    I. Title.

PS8615.O99S64 2004   C813'.6   C2004-902395-0

Printed in Canada

NDE Publishing is a trademark of NDE Canada Corp.

For Sylvia and Gerry Enjoy!.

S.P. HOZY

some comfort among us

S.P. Hozy

"penny"

NDE Publishing
2004

chapter one

March 1, 1987

"Dear Stephie,

I wish you could see this place,*" Ann wrote to her daughter a month after her arrival. *"India is not what you think it is, it's much, much more. I never thought it would be so beautiful. Listening to your father all those years talking about the Raj and his ancestors and all that British pomp and circumstance, I pictured it frozen in time a place where lily-complexioned ladies wore white cotton dresses and played croquet on the lawn, and sunburned young men with blond mustaches wore topis and riding breeches and administered justice under the trees in the heat and the dust.*

"The Indians were always incidental, sweeping and serving in the background. And the country itself, the land, was a subtle

and dangerous enemy. It was full of wild animals and poisonous snakes, a breeding ground for fevers, mysterious and deadly diseases that carried off children and young women before they even unpacked their things. The drinking water was poison, the climate was unhealthy and any kind of travel was hazardous.

"I remember your father telling me the story of his grandmother who lost four babies to fever before she died of it herself. And then his father's first wife died in childbirth. I can just picture her coming over on the boat in 1924, a young woman with her hair freshly bobbed, nervous and excited about meeting a young man in the Civil Service or a dashing young soldier to marry.

"But I've seen things that take my breath away, like the silken swaying of sari-clad women. I've heard choruses of songbirds, not just a few, but hundreds at a time; smelt the pungent fragrance of frangipani and tasted the succulence of mangoes. Sometimes I just stop and listen. There's so much life (!) here that it makes up for all those frozen Canadian winters, those dead, hard, gray winters.

"If I seem giddy, it's probably the vegetarian diet and the cleansing of the soul I've been undergoing. They tell me this isn't unusual—it's like waking up from a coma or taking the bandages off after surgery: you've been given a second chance. I know I'll be able to look at things from a totally different perspective from now on and maybe my old hang-ups will simply fall apart like rags. Got to run. Time for massage therapy.

Love,
Mother."

Stephanie closed her eyes and tried to remember the details of her mother's face, the high, slightly prominent cheekbones, the delicately pointed chin, the small lines that appeared around her eyes when she smiled. But all she could think was how naïve her mother was to believe she could solve her problems at an ashram halfway around the world.

"I'm going to find release from the bondage of the self," she had told Stephanie during lunch at a fashionable downtown cafe. "I feel fragmented, unwhole. My body is separate from my mind and they're both separate from the universe. I need to find a way to transcend these earthly bonds and feel at peace with the cosmos. No amount of reading books is enough. I have to go to India where these things happen and find a teacher to show me the way."

"A guru, you mean?" Stephanie had asked, trying not to let her skepticism show.

"Yes, a guru. A person who has experienced enlightenment and will show me the path." Ann wanted her daughter to understand but she knew Stephanie was only pretending to be interested. "I know it's hard for you to take all this seriously but it's very important to me and I want you to know I'm not just going off on a lark. I need to do this."

"I know you do, Mother, and I'm trying to understand, but I really don't know very much about this stuff. I mean, I hope you're not going to join the Hare Krishna."

Her mother had laughed but Stephanie remembered the sadness in her eyes.

"And what if I did join the Hare Krishna? Would you and your father try and get a court order to stop me, or would you give me your blessing and let me go?"

"Don't joke about it. It's not funny."

"No, it's not funny. And I'm glad you don't think it is. I want to be taken seriously, Stephie, especially by my family. I'm not going to come back with my head shaved. I'm going to come back with a deeper understanding and appreciation of the Life Force. I'm going to come back whole."

At that point Stephanie would have said anything just to get out of there. "All right, you can have my blessing if you want it. I hope you find what you're looking for and I hope you bring it back with you."

Afterward, when it was all over and the real anger hit, when all the hurt and confusion and regret surfaced, Stephanie Hobart, young, smart, fearlessly independent, would wonder why she hadn't been better equipped to deal with the events that happened over the next few months. Her memories would be of moving through those days as if on a conveyer belt, accumulating layers of emotion that would eventually suffocate her certainty.

chapter two

Ann's last letter told them she was suffering from headaches and persistent diarrhea so she'd decided to come home and get treatment before it got worse. A local doctor told her she might have an intestinal parasite but he hadn't done a test. "I'd rather go to the Tropical Disease Clinic at Toronto General," she wrote, "and get treated at home."

"Does that mean she's tried all the hocus-pocus remedies and they didn't work?" Stephanie said to her father as they waited for Ann's plane to land. "Don't be unkind," he said. But secretly he agreed with his daughter. Ann had probably been receiving spiritual treatment for what was clearly a physical problem and in the meantime her condition had likely worsened.

For both Stephen Hobart and his twenty-five year old daughter, the habit of protecting Ann and treating her as if she were lacking basic survival skills had started early in Stephanie's childhood. She knew her mother wasn't like the other mothers but she never let anyone know how much it bothered her. While her friends' mothers met in the afternoon to play bridge, Ann went to fortune-tellers and learned to read the future in a deck of cards. And while other mothers examined their children's hands to make sure they were clean, Ann examined the lines in Stephanie's palm and told her she would have a long life. Other mothers painted and decorated their homes, but Stephanie's mother painted canvases with bold strokes and dark colors. Once Ann painted a woman's face with her mouth wide open and told Stephanie it was every woman's cry for help.

Ann was always studying some new philosophy or occult belief system that would lead her closer to the meaning of life. She wanted to understand why things happened. Ann looked to the beginning of things to find explanations for them—astrological birth charts, childhood relationships, prenatal life. Her husband Stephen, an economist with the Bank of Canada, looked at the consequences to understand the reason for things. It was a fundamental difference between them. To him it didn't matter if you were the seventh son of a seventh son. What mattered was what you did with the resources you had.

Their daughter was like him, impatient and striving, but with a contemplative side that came from her mother. Stephanie was interested in theories and ideas. She had studied political science at university and landed a job as a researcher for a television newsmagazine program. She told her father that someday she would produce her own shows. Research, she told him, was the quickest route to the top.

"She'll probably be the last one off," said Stephen, as they watched the first weary travelers from the Bombay flight straggle out the automatic doors of the arrivals gate.

Ann was always the last one off a plane, the last one out of a theater. "Why get pushed around by all these people?" she would say. "Why not just wait a few more minutes and leave at our own pace?"

Because there won't be any taxis left or the restaurant will give away our reservation, Stephen would say. What he meant was, because I don't want to be last, I want to be first. But that impulse didn't exist in Ann. It never bothered her to wait for things. She always found something to occupy her mind, something to talk about or just think to herself about if he didn't feel like talking.

Stephanie and her father watched the last passengers emerge from the arrivals gate pushing overloaded luggage carts, but Ann wasn't among them.

"Just give her a few more minutes," Stephanie said. "She's probably still clearing customs."

"Maybe she's ill," said Stephen. He started jingling the coins in his pocket to keep his hands busy. "Maybe she needs help."

"I'm sure they'd page us if that were true." Stephanie refused to worry. Her mother was just taking a long time to do a simple thing, as usual.

"I'm going to ask someone," Stephen finally said, looking around for an Air India uniform. "She should have been out by now."

They caught up with a young woman just as she was closing down the Air India counter. "Everyone is off the plane," she said. "I'm quite certain of it."

They insisted she check again. Knowing they wouldn't give up, she went off in the direction of the arrivals gate. When she returned a few minutes later, their fears were confirmed. Then she checked the computer. "It would appear that Mrs. Hobart was not on the airplane when it left Bombay," she finally said, looking at them over the top of the computer terminal. "I'm sorry, that's all I can tell you. Her ticket was not used."

chapter three

Stephanie saw the worry lines forming around her father's eyes. His handsome face appeared to cave in on itself as the lines around his mouth deepened. "Maybe she got sick again and decided not to leave," she said, trying to reassure him. "It's a long flight. Maybe she just wasn't up to it."

Stephen's frown told her he wasn't convinced. Normally he would assume Ann had missed her flight. It had happened before. But the fact that she was suffering from some undiagnosed tropical disease in a place like India was worrying. What if she was delirious with fever in a strange place and couldn't get help? He kept fiddling with the change in his pockets, wishing he had a cigarette. But it had been seven months since he'd quit and he never carried them anymore. Why had he ever agreed to let her make that godforsaken trip alone? Why hadn't he insisted she take a friend along? He would gladly have paid the expenses. Now he cursed himself for being so stupid. He should have known it would turn out badly.

"Come on, let's get back to the house," said Stephanie. "I'll bet there's a telegram waiting for us." Stephen allowed her to take the lead as they headed for the parking garage. He walked half a pace behind his tall, attractive daughter and saw why people always said how much she was like him. She was five feet eight to his six foot two, with wide shoulders and slim hips. She was large-boned and strong like her father and she walked with an athletic grace that came from years of dance classes and figure skating lessons. Able, smart and needing to be in charge, she preferred solitary activities like walking, swimming and climbing. Her hair was the color his had once been before it had turned silver, the color of teak after it's been polished to a glossy sheen, a color that was almost identically matched in her eyes, with tiny green flecks that flashed when she was angry or excited. Stephanie's ruddy complexion came from her mother, however, giving her a perpetually healthy glow so unlike the elegant pallor of her father's skin.

If it had been anyone else they had come to meet Stephen would have taken control of the situation in just the same way. Said something practical. Kept things moving. But this time it was different. This time it was Ann. She had missed planes before, but she always called. Ann had some strange ideas, but she wouldn't make him worry like this. If she had just missed the plane–who knew what could happen in a place like India; the traffic must be dreadful–there was probably a telegram waiting for them right now.

Stephanie walked over to the driver's side of the car and put her hand out for the keys. "Let me drive. I know you're worried and I don't want you driving through a red light."

"I've never driven through a red light in my life, young lady," said Stephen, clenching and unclenching a fistful of coins in his pocket.

"I know, but if I drive, you can think of a plan." Stephen reluctantly handed over the keys and climbed into the passenger seat. He didn't have the energy to argue with her.

It was nearly midnight and even though traffic in Toronto seemed to be increasing every day, it parted mercifully for them as they merged easily onto the express lanes of the freeway. Once off the highway, Stephanie headed south to the prosperous neighborhood her parents had lived in since she was a child. Ten minutes later she swung the car onto the circular driveway of the large two-story brick home and eased to a stop beside her own Honda Prelude. Her father was out of the car and unlocking the front door before she'd turned off the engine.

Stephanie followed him into the library and sat on the leather sofa. Stephen was already dialing the phone.

"Who are you calling?"

"CN/CP to see if there's been a cable."

When he asked them to double check, Stephanie knew there had been no telegram. Stephen began immediately dialing another number.

"Who are you phoning now?"

"Arthur Ross in Ottawa. Maybe he can get someone at the Embassy in New Delhi to make some calls or get someone to go to that ashram and find out what's going on."

"But the ashram's a long way from Delhi," she reminded him. "It could take days."

"I know, but it's a start. They've got more contacts over there than I have. There's no phone at that damn place. The fastest way is to get someone to go there." He held up his hand to stop her from speaking. "Hello Arthur," he said into the phone. "Arthur, I'm sorry to call you at this hour, but–he listened to the voice at the other end–"Yes, it's me, Stephen. Look Arthur, I'm sorry to call so late, but Ann was supposed to be on a plane from Bombay tonight and she never showed up. Apparently she never got on the plane. In her last letter she said she hadn't been feeling well –I don't know what–something tropical. I'm extremely worried. This is just not like her. Is there any way you can contact the Embassy and get a runner to go out there and find out if she's okay?"

Stephanie watched her father as he listened to his old school friend and fraternity brother. Arthur Ross, External Affairs mandarin, was probably wearing pinstripe pajamas, standing barefoot in the front hall of his Ottawa mansion while he reassured his former classmate he would do everything he could to locate his wife. The old boys' network, she thought. That was how things really got done. Forget about protocol and regulations and a level playing field. You weren't even in the running unless you'd paid your dues at Upper Canada College, the elite private school for the sons of the rich and powerful. She wondered if she would ever be able to pick up the phone and dial her way into the higher echelons of power.

"Arthur says it could take two or three days," she heard her father say and realized he was no longer on the phone. "They can try and get someone there through the Red Cross, but if the village is off the beaten track, there's no quick way in."

They looked at each other for a moment as they slowly realized what was happening. Stephanie could hear the grandfather clock in the hall chiming the quarter hour. She couldn't stand the thought of waiting two or three days. And what if her mother had already left the ashram and was stuck in Bombay too sick to travel? They might never find her if they had to go through official channels.

"I'm going to go and get her myself," she heard herself say. "Even if we hear something in a couple of days, we still won't be able to do anything. If I'm over there or on my way, at least I can bring her home."

She waited for her father to protest, to argue with her, to tell her she wasn't capable enough. Instead he said, "So then I can worry about both of you."

"Dad," she said, knowing he could be persuaded, "maybe it's not such a big deal. Maybe she has a bad case of the runs and can't deal with a twenty-hour flight by herself. Not just that, don't forget, she has to get to Bombay first by bus and train."

Stephen looked at his daughter and knew she was right. "I don't like the idea of you going alone, Steph. I have a conference in Ottawa in three days with the Germans and I can't get out of it. See if Paul can go with you. Tell him I'll pay."

"For God's sake, she's not in the jungle. This isn't *Heart of Darkness.*" Stephanie heard the annoyance in her voice. She took a deep breath. "I can handle it," she said quietly. "I'm not a child."

"Oh you can handle it, can you? India isn't like France, you know." But Stephen knew she'd made up her mind. "That's exactly what your mother said just before she got on the plane. 'Don't worry. I can handle it.'"

"I don't need to ask your permission," Stephanie reminded him. "I'm going and I'm going alone."

chapter four

tephanie spent the night in her old room sleeping fitfully, wakened several times by the now unfamiliar sounds of the house. She had been on her own for four years, living in a small second-floor apartment in Toronto's trendy Annex neighborhood close to the university. She hadn't had any trouble adjusting to the confined quarters of an Edwardian-style rooming house after the spacious luxury of her parents' Forest Hill mansion. She relished her independence and the freedom to come and go as she pleased. Besides, she spent more time away from her apartment than in it, often using it just to sleep or change her clothes. Her job kept her busy and the days were long, but whenever she had any time off, she'd drive to her parents' cottage in Muskoka, a habit that had lapsed during her university years. They referred to it as "the cottage," but it was, in fact, a substantial second home on Lake Joseph. Often when she made the three-hour drive on a Friday night, her father would already be there, smoking his pipe and reading an English mystery novel.

Her mother came only during the summer to escape the humidity and oppressive heat of the city. Ann had never been keen on water sports and boating, but she loved the cool breezes that came off the lake and the smell of logs burning at night to take the chill out of the air. She had planted a wild and fragrant herb garden between the huge jutting rocks that gave the property its most characteristic feature. Everywhere birch and pine grew tall and flourished, the base of their trunks emerging from a floor of fern and wild strawberry. Stephanie would often find her mother sitting perfectly still on one of the wooden Muskoka chairs, staring out at the deep blue water as if hypnotized by the dancing fragments of sunlight on the lake's surface. For her mother, life was a sensuous experience of smells and tastes and sounds. She always associated places she'd been with the meal she'd eaten or the smell of the air.

Ann Hobart's life was formed of concentric circles that rippled and occasionally merged like the ripples that formed on the lake in front of the cottage. But for Steph and her father, life was a series of conquests that moved in a slowly ascending straight line. They liked things clear-cut and defined. Life became bothersome and messy when things overlapped too much.

Steph woke up the next morning at eight o'clock and knew her father would already be at his Bay Street office. He was an early riser and was usually at work by 7:30. Steph and her mother were the night birds in the family, as her father called them, always staying up to watch Johnny Carson or a late movie, no matter how bad it was. Anything to avoid going to sleep. Always afraid they might miss something. Before going to bed, Stephen had made a reservation for her on the night flight to Bombay and promised to make some phone calls and arrange a last-minute visa. He was still not convinced she should be going with so little preparation, but Stephanie was determined and he knew she would not change her mind. For her, this would become a mission, and she wouldn't rest until she'd brought her mother home.

She had an almost frightening ability to focus her energy, but he had seen the vulnerability to failure that lay beneath her drive to success. And he worried she might get hurt because in the fierceness of her ambition she would refuse to acknowledge danger.

Stephanie showered and dressed quickly and debated whether she should stop off at her apartment and change her clothes. She decided not to bother, knowing that if she did, she would get caught up in worrying about what to pack for the trip and whether she had enough clean clothes. This way, if she left it to the last minute, she would have no choice. She would take what was there and that would be it.

Stephanie made sure the door of her parents' empty house was locked and climbed into her car, a gift from her father on her twenty-fifth birthday. She noticed that the buds on the trees were beginning to open even though it was just the end of April. It was the time of year when Canadians began to shake off their winter moodiness and cautiously admit to themselves that summer might happen again. But this year it had been a cool spring, until a week ago when a seven-day heat wave sent the temperature climbing into the high eighties. Winter-weary Torontonians, their blood thick and sluggish from months of freezing temperatures, had suffered through the unseasonal heat in a state of shock. Their bodies told them it felt like July, but their eyes saw no leaves on the trees and grass still brown from winter's deep freeze. Some relished the arrival of an early summer, while others complained of missing spring. But this week the temperature had returned to normal and people put on jackets and sweaters with a certain relief that nature had righted herself and the rhythm of the seasons had been restored.

I'd better check the weather report in India, Stephanie thought as she maneuvered her way through downtown traffic to the CBC building. She made a quick stop at a photo shop and had the pictures taken, arranging for them to be sent collect to her father's office as soon as they were ready. She pulled into the CBC parking lot at 9:25. When she stepped off the elevator she found Dave Abbot, her producer, by the coffee machine.

"I need to talk to you, Dave. Can you give me a couple of minutes?"

"Sure Steph. Come into my office and we can split a donut. But two minutes is all I've got. I'm half a day behind and losing ground fast."

Dave was always half a day behind and, considering he usually put in a fourteen-hour day, there was little chance he'd ever catch up. World events always had a way of overtaking him. He blamed it all on fax machines and satellites, saying they accelerated the present and turned everything into instant history.

Dave was the same height as Stephanie and weighed maybe fifteen pounds more, but he always looked as if he'd just lost twenty-five pounds and hadn't had time to buy a new wardrobe. Even his horn-rimmed glasses seemed to have been made for a larger face and were always perched halfway down his ski-slope of a nose. His hair was thick and dark and naturally curly, so it always looked unkempt, and his blue eyes, with their long curled lashes, gave his angular face a softness it didn't deserve.

"I have to fly to India tonight," Steph told him as soon as they were in his office. "My mother was supposed to be on a plane from Bombay last night but she never showed up. My father and I are worried; we think she might be sick. I'm going over to bring her home."

"Oh yeah," said Dave, "she's on some kind of guru trip over there, isn't she?"

"She's on an ashram," Stephanie said impatiently, washing down a hunk of donut with what tasted like yesterday's coffee. "She's been doing meditation and yoga or something, to find her center. It's a spiritual thing she wanted to do. Anyway, I shouldn't be more than a week, maybe not even that long."

"Look, Steph, I know you have to go and I know I can't stop you, but let me remind you that the Meech Lake Accord thing is happening, like, right now. We are up to our eyeballs in this shit and it's only going to get deeper. This is the biggest thing that's happened in this country since the repatriation of the Constitution."

"I know Dave, I know. And believe me, I don't want to miss it. But I have to do this. I'd never forgive myself if anything happened to her."

She could feel the pressure of the production office around her, the sound of the phones ringing and people's voices seeping through the thin walls of Dave's office. She thrived on the excitement and the tension, the unpredictability of events. She knew her parents, accustomed to the thickly carpeted halls of wealth and power, didn't understand the appeal of this daily frenzy, couldn't comprehend the physical high she got when a story started to come together. She couldn't wait to be a producer, calling the shots, deciding the priorities, shaping the stories. In the meantime, she was satisfied to be part of the scene, scoring points, making contacts.

"Okay," said Dave, "I'll get a freelancer in until you get back. Too bad you can't do something for us while you're over there, but nothing's going to overshadow this Meech Lake thing. Except maybe an assassination. I mean, the Cold War's old news now that Gorbachev's talking glasnost. What's left, for God's sake?"

She had to laugh at Dave. He had such a pragmatic way of looking at world events. They were either newsworthy or they were not. There was no such thing as a human interest story or point-of-view documentary for him. There was news or there was no news. Everything else was just filling time until something happened.

"Via con Dios," he said, "and get back fast."

"Thanks Dave," she said, tossing her styrofoam cup in the garbage. "See you in a week."

chapter five

I'd better find Paul and let him know, Stephanie thought as she emerged from Dave's office. If he hears it from someone else he'll be annoyed.

Stephanie had met Paul Anderson during her last year at university. She was majoring in political science and Paul was pre-med. At the end of their final semester, Paul had decided not to go to medical school. He and Stephanie both applied to the CBC and he was now a full-time researcher/writer for a weekly nature series. Paul had asked Stephanie to marry him twice now and both times she'd refused. They hadn't broken off their relationship but continued in a wait-and-see pattern.

As she took the elevator down to the fourth floor, Stephanie tried to anticipate Paul's objections to her going to India. Her father's suggestion that Paul go with her irritated her. She didn't need protecting like her mother. She knew she could handle it on her own. Now she was preparing to defend her decision to Paul.

She tracked him down in one of the editing rooms where he

was timing the film for a script on the reproductive life of puffins.

"Come on in," he said when he saw her. "What brings you down to the humble world of science and nature?"

"I wanted to talk to you," she said, sitting down beside him. He turned off the machine he was using and smiled at her expectantly. Paul always seemed so relaxed to Stephanie, so reliable. But underneath the casual, amiable surface, was a tension, a muscularity that had always appealed to her. He had a predatory awareness that was only partly concealed behind his easy manner. He reminded her of a lion. His straight blond hair had fallen across his forehead and he ran his fingers through it to push it back. He leaned back in the armless chair, stretching his long legs in front of him and clasping his slim, strong fingers behind his head. His gray eyes watched her affectionately and his slightly lopsided smile revealed straight, even teeth.

"I'm flying to India tonight to bring my mother back. We had a letter from her saying she was sick and would be on a flight from Bombay arriving last night. But she never got on the plane and Dad and I are afraid she might be too sick to travel alone." She was conscious of the fact that she was speaking a little too quickly and hoped Paul wouldn't think it was because she was anxious about making the trip. He might insist on going with her and she was determined to go alone.

"Did she say what the problem was?" Paul liked Ann Hobart, even though she had some funny ideas. Ann wanted Stephanie to marry Paul. She thought he was sensitive and caring and would make a good husband. Stephanie agreed with her mother that Paul was all those things, but she wasn't sure she wanted or needed a husband.

"She said she had diarrhea, nausea and headaches but wasn't tested for anything specific."

"It could be dysentery or an intestinal parasite, I suppose," said Paul, "or it could be gastritis or even food poisoning. Whatever it is, she should get treatment fast because she could become dehydrated and weaken quickly if it's left too long."

"That's why Dad and I felt it would be better all round if I just went over and got her. If she's too sick to travel alone, it's the fastest way to get her home," Stephanie lied, hoping Paul wouldn't hear her father's slightly different version, at least not before she left.

"Maybe I should go with you," he said, sitting up straight in his chair and bending towards her. "It would be an advantage to have a man along, especially if she needs to be carried."

"No Paul, I'm sure it won't be necessary. I'll be able to manage. Besides, it's too expensive." Please God, don't strike me dead for that one, she thought.

"Never mind the expense," he said. "I'm not broke, you know." Paul always overreacted when she mentioned money because he knew he would never be able to give her the kind of life her parents had given her. Although his own parents weren't rich, they made a comfortable living between them. His father was a high school principal a few years away from retirement and his mother an administrator with the Board of Education. They had been disappointed when Paul decided against medical school, but they had two other sons in university and were firm believers in education for its own sake. If Paul wanted to do television work, they had no objection.

"Let's not get into any of that right now," she said. "I just wanted you to know what I was doing so you wouldn't worry."

"You know I'll worry about you every minute you're away, Steph. I love you and whether or not you love me doesn't seem to make any difference. I can't change my feelings for you." He knew this wasn't the time to say it all again but he could feel her pushing him away, denying him access to her innermost thoughts and feelings. He knew she wasn't being completely honest with him, that there was more to this trip to India than a desire to bring her mother back. Her absolute insistence on going alone was what worried him. It was as if she were putting a wall between them that he would have to dismantle brick by brick, but it would always be a row of bricks more than he could tear down.

She seemed to resist him constantly. Not physically, because she never refused to go to bed with him, but emotionally, mentally, spiritually, whatever other dimension there was to resist him on. He knew she would never give in. She believed if she allowed herself to be vulnerable to him even for a short while, it meant giving in to him forever. She was so afraid to risk it she would rather gamble on a lifetime alone. He had done everything to gain her trust but he could never get close to her. Her mother knew that about her. Ann told him that even as a child Stephanie had been distant, not liking to be held or coddled. She's like her father, Ann said. They were born standing up. None of that being carried or crawling around on their hands and knees stuff for them.

And now he could feel her taking another step away from him. "Just come back safe," he said. "You and Ann both. I'll be here when you need me."

chapter six

Stephen insisted on driving his daughter to the airport, but when Stephanie opened the apartment door it wasn't her father standing there but Jay, her mother's brother. "Come on kiddo," he said, "let's get this show on the road."

"Uncle Jay!" she yelled, throwing her arms around him and squeezing hard. "What are you doing here?"

"If you thought you were going to sneak out of the country without my knowing it, you were sadly mistaken, my dear." Jay had always had a soft spot in his heart for his only niece and lavished attention and affection on her.

"Actually, if the truth be known, I happened to call your Dad today about a small matter between us and he told me what was up."

James Joseph Stewart was Ann's younger brother. He had been named James Stewart for the actor with Joseph added for his father. That had soon been shortened to J.J. and with time he became Jay. He had never grown up, never settled down, never got married, never done any of the things everybody thought he should do. Jay was always turning up on Ann and Stephen's doorstep looking for a little cash between ventures, and they tolerated him because he was well intentioned and he always managed to pay them back. Stephanie adored him and looked forward to his visits with childish excitement.

Jay was everything his sister Ann was not. She was petite and graceful, while he was tall and awkward, even clumsy. Her coloring was dark, his was fair. While she was serious and superstitious, he could be counted on to be lighthearted and even silly. And while Ann seemed to spend her life searching for meaning, Jay led an apparently meaningless and frivolous existence. For Stephanie, he had always been a ray of sunshine in her solitary and often lonely childhood, the older brother she never had, the playmate she wished for.

"What? No matched set of luggage?" said Jay, spotting her canvas carryall. "Your father won't like that."

"Jay," she said sternly, "that's mean. Daddy has never disapproved of the way I do things. It's only you he disapproves of."

"All right, all right. Score one for you. But I just want you to know that he and I do agree on one thing. We don't like the idea of you going over there on your own."

She started to protest as she had with her father, but he stopped her. "Now I'm not going to give you a Stephen Hobart lecture, but I want you to remember that the people who love you the most are trusting that you'll do the smart and sensible thing and not cause them any more worry than they already have. Am I getting my point across?" She nodded, knowing he didn't say things like this very often.

"Okay. I'm not going to get sloppy on you, but just remember, your father and I will be at the other end of a phone the whole time you're gone." He reached for her bag. "Now let's get going or he'll be up here blaming me for wasting time."

Stephen had waited in the car while Jay went up and got Stephanie. His brother-in-law insisted on going to the airport and, knowing how much he cared for Stephanie, Stephen didn't have the heart to say no. Besides, he knew Steph would be more inclined to take her uncle's warnings to heart than his own. On the way over he'd told Jay he objected to her going alone.

"If you can think of a way to stop her, I'll be glad to hear it," Stephen said. "But you know what she's like. She has the determination of a bulldog. I don't know where she gets that stubborn streak of hers." Jay had looked at him and laughed. "You don't, eh? Seems to me it runs in the family," he'd said, turning his head and looking out the passenger window of the car. He didn't have to see Stephen's face to know what his reaction would be.

Stephen drove to the airport in silence while Stephanie and her uncle chatted comfortably and caught up with each other's news.

"How's Paul?" Jay asked. "I bet he's not too happy you're going off like this."

"No, he's not. But tell me something," Stephanie said, kissing her uncle on the cheek, "why is it that all the men in my life seem to think I can't take care of myself and handle this mission without them? I mean, is there no such thing as a competent female in your world? Must we always be treated as helpless weaklings or can some of us be allowed to go out and flex some muscle once in a while?"

She saw her father take a breath and open his mouth to speak, but before any words came out Jay said, "Flex some muscle! Now if that isn't a New Woman talking. I've got nothing against muscular women, believe me. If Joanie isn't the most competent female I've ever met, then I don't know who is." Joanie had been Jay's girlfriend for the last twelve years. She was divorced and raising her two children alone. Jay seemed to be in no hurry to marry her and she stuck with him because he was good to her kids. Jay was still talking: "But you can't expect men to roll over and play dead just because Margaret Thatcher's Prime Minister of England! I mean–" he ducked to avoid Stephanie's mock punch "I mean, where will it end? Is there no safe place for men in this world?"

"Give me a break," said Stephanie, knowing they could spar like this for hours. "You men have done such a bad job of things, you should all just lay down your arms and surrender."

"Oh, I surrendered a long time ago, my little pumpkin," said Jay. "I know when I'm beat."

"You two are giving me a headache," said Stephen as he wheeled the car into a parking space. "Stephanie, it's time to get serious. Are you sure you have all your documents and the list of phone numbers I gave you?" She nodded. "Show me," her father said.

"Relax, Dad. I've got everything." But she reached into her bag and pulled out the sheaf of papers and her passport.

"Good," he said, opening the car door. "And don't forget what I said about the water. Only drink it if you see them boil it. Don't just take their word for it. Come on. Let's go."

It took no time at all to check her in and send her bag off on the conveyer belt. Then it was just the three of them standing there with too much to say and not enough time to say it. "Remember," said her father, putting his arms around her, "call me as soon as you can and if you can't call, send a telegram."

"I promise," she said, kissing him on the cheek. "And try not to worry too much. Everything will be all right." She turned to her uncle.

"And you," she said, hugging him, "don't make a big deal of it. I'll be back before you even miss me."

"Sure kid," he said. "I don't miss you already." He winked and touched the side of her face in a mock punch.

She walked toward the departure lounge and turned to wave to them as they stood watching her, two tall, big-boned men who could have been brothers they were physically so similar, but who were so different in every other way, they wouldn't have spent five minutes in each other's company had they not been bound by family ties.

Stephanie settled into one of the uncomfortable seats in the departure lounge to wait for her flight to be called. She'd brought along a book on India's political history that her father recommended but she couldn't seem to focus on the words. Her mind was a jumble of instructions, do's and don'ts from everyone she'd talked to since announcing her plan to go to India and bring her mother back.

She'd remembered to check on the climate of the region she was going to and was relieved to discover that the monsoon season didn't occur until the end of the hot months of June and July. In fact, the climate she could anticipate in early May would be a lot like a typical Canadian summer, in the high eighties during the day and dropping about twenty degrees at night. She could also expect mosquitoes, which apparently couldn't survive the hotter weather, but which thrived during the cooler months. The ashram where her mother was staying was located south and east of Bombay, close to the center of the subcontinent. The climate there would probably be more tolerable because it was a couple of thousand feet above sea level.

If she hadn't been concerned about her mother Stephanie might have been eagerly looking forward to her first trip to India. She'd been listening to stories about her family's history in that exotic land for as long as she could remember. But, until now, she'd resisted absorbing much of it. Her father had tried to interest her but as a teenager she thought it was boring that her grandfather had been born in India and that her great-grandfather was an engineer during the Survey of India. Now she wished she could remember more of their stories.

Stephanie smiled, remembering how her father read Kipling to her while she'd been more interested in the Brady Bunch. She would make up for it, she promised herself, as soon as she got back. She'd read Kipling and everything else in her father's library. In the meantime, she had to be practical. The glory days of the British Empire were long past. The jewel in the crown was now a place that proudly called itself the largest democracy in the world, whose fight for independence had been bloody and hard won. She knew she would probably see unspeakable poverty and encounter unfamiliar religious and social customs, and she hadn't had time to prepare for any of it.

I have to be ready for anything, she thought. I won't let myself be caught off-guard or let anyone think I'm afraid. If I go in feeling confident, people will take me seriously. Stephanie had always believed that you could pull off anything if you acted as if you had a right to do it. People had perpetrated incredible scams because no one ever challenged their credentials. She would refuse to be intimidated.

What a difference from her mother's attitude, she thought. To Ann, India was a spiritual place, a country of holy men and flourishing religious practice. She had gone to India seeking some kind of spiritual harmony between herself and her surroundings. She had been eager to go, believing the ashram and its followers were going to give her the peace she was unable to find within herself. But for Stephanie India represented a battle zone, a place where she would have to be vigilant and strong.

chapter seven

have come here," Ann wrote to Stephanie shortly after arriving at the ashram, *"to find a way to live in the world. I don't expect you to understand why I have to do this. I only ask that you accept it. I don't know why I experience life so differently from you. I have spent most of my life trying to figure that out. I do know that I cannot just put one foot in front of the other like you and your father and get on with it. Getting on with it doesn't work for me. I have to know the reason for the journey. I have to know if there is more than one possible destination. I can't accept things the way they are just because they are that way and yet, I'm asking you to do that for me. So please, Steph, find it in your heart to be patient and not pass judgment on me. When I get back, we'll sit down and figure it all out together. I promise."*

Here we go again, Stephanie had thought, suddenly feeling tired. Ann was always asking for something. As a kid, Stephanie couldn't bring her friends into the house because they might make it dirty. Everything always had to be perfect or Ann would get one of her headaches. And then you couldn't talk to her or make a sound because the slightest thing could put her off. And it was always someone else's fault–usually Stephanie's–when Ann was having one of her spells. Like the time she and Rosemary from across the street had decided to play dress-up. Rosemary's mother had given them a couple of her old dresses and some scarves, and they had gone into Ann's cupboard to borrow some high heels. Stephanie loved the red pair with the puffy leather bow on the toe, and they also borrowed the black suede pair with the sparkly clips. And yes, they had tried on a few more pairs and left them on the bedroom floor, not neatly lined up in the cupboard, but was that such a big deal? "I can't cope with this," Ann had said. "I have so much to do and now I can't do any of it. You've ruined my day."

It wasn't that Stephanie didn't love her mother. Of course she loved her. But it was getting harder and harder to be patient with Ann. Sometimes she just wanted to scream at her, "Grow up! I've had to grow up. I've had to take responsibility for my life. Why can't you?" How many times, thought Steph, had Ann asked her to be patient, to try and understand? For Stephen, the last straw had been his wife's immersion in the occult, which had become a huge source of embarrassment. When Ann started consulting psychics and astrologers, holding séances at the house and, finally, wearing kaftans, people had started to talk. For Steph, by the time she was hitting her teens it was all too much.

Stephanie was glad she had taken a window seat on the plane. She could turn her back to the rest of the passengers and read her mother's letters that she had stuffed into her bag at the last minute. The man and woman who had taken the seats next to her were an older Sikh couple who apparently didn't speak much English and she was grateful they weren't interested in making conversation. The woman, who was sitting next to Stephanie, had already fallen asleep and was snoring lightly in a pattern that blended easily with the sound of the plane's engines.

"Now that I've had a chance to settle in, I can see that I was right to come here. Guru Father and Deva Mother, as they are called (although to my knowledge there is no relationship between them—she seems to be responsible for the day-to-day running of the ashram), have taken me into their hearts and made me feel welcome and needed. We spend a lot of time meditating, which I am learning to do—it's not as easy as it sounds; you have to learn to clear your mind completely, but Guru Father tells me to be patient and it will come—and I take classes in yoga, Sanskrit, reflexology, massage therapy and Chakra balancing. And there's a wonderful Tibetan humming technique called 'Nadabrahma' that causes your whole body to vibrate but leaves you with such a feeling of peace! I've found something here that's good for me."

Ann's early life did not suggest that she would someday seek her spiritual consciousness on an ashram in the heart of India. Born in Winnipeg, she had been raised in a strict Christian home where the emphasis had been on hard work, cleanliness, good deeds and charity. Her father Joe had joined the RAF at the start of World War II just after Ann was born and had gone overseas before the birth of her brother Jay two years later. Ann's mother Althea had worn the mantle of both motherhood and fatherhood and believed she had a sacred trust with God to raise her children to be obedient and respectful and to keep them safe until their father returned. And if that meant the occasional beating, Althea did what she believed she had to do. Joe took up his old job as a public school teacher after the war and Althea handed control back to him. But the damage had been done. Ann rarely spoke of her childhood, and when she did, there was a knife-like edge in her voice. She had refused to attend her mother's funeral.

"It's not all meditation and classes, of course. There's work and lots of it. Deva Mother, who, I think has been here from the beginning, manages things with incredible efficiency. There's gardening–vegetables and flowers–spinning and weaving, cooking, sweeping and cleaning. I'm up at 5 every morning and don't lay my head on the pillow until 9 or 10 at night. I'm sure you wouldn't recognize your mother cheerfully performing such dreary tasks! I could lose track of time here; each day slips so easily into the next."

Ann had been a serious child who loved her books and even before she could read them would sit turning the pages and making up stories to go with the pictures she saw. Make-believe played a large role in her childhood. Growing up in the flat expanses of Manitoba, she had imagined tall, snow-capped mountains and splendid green forests. Forced to play indoors during the long, harsh winters, she had pretended to be a captive princess, held prisoner in the steaming jungle. Jay was often her only playmate and together they would be orphans in the forest, like Hansel and Gretel, hiding under the dining room table where the wicked witch wouldn't find them.

The wicked witch, thought Stephanie. Gramma Althea. What a terror she'd been. But it was a little too easy to blame Gramma Althea for all of Ann's problems. They were a mismatch as mother and daughter, one of nature's cruel jokes. Gramma Althea could no more understand her daughter's needs than fly to the moon. Ann had learned to keep things inside from a very young age and blamed Gramma Althea for all the pain and unhappiness she had suffered as a child. "Your grandmother was a cruel woman," she told Stephanie. "She destroyed people. She called herself a Christian, yet she destroyed souls. You know she once made me eat bread and water for a week? A whole week! I was seven years old and had refused to eat something she had cooked–if you can call what she did to food cooking–and so she said, 'Fine, young lady, if that isn't good enough for Your Highness, see how you like this.' She put a piece of white bread in a bowl and filled the bowl with warm tap water and made me eat it before I could leave the table. And I got the same thing for breakfast, lunch and dinner for the next seven days.

"Luckily Jay sneaked me some real food occasionally, an apple or a single sparerib that he pulled out of his pocket and picked the lint off so I wouldn't starve to death. I was near fainting by the end of the fourth day. But she wouldn't relent. She would not relent. She would pray to God for my soul and all the time she was destroying it."

The trouble was, Stephanie had liked her grandmother. Gramma Althea was a no-nonsense, what-you-see-is-what-you-get kind of woman and Stephanie had to admire that. Gramma Althea knew what she believed and she was living proof of it in everything she did. What she believed might have been a little twisted and harsh, but she went with it all the way. Ann, on the other hand, never seemed to know what she believed. She lived in some airy-fairy world where everyone was supposed to be nice to everyone else. She thought Gramma Althea was an aberration, a monster. Stephanie thought Gramma Althea was just doing her best to make good on her promises to God. Ann wanted God to intervene and save her and then when He didn't, she added another stone to the pile of resentment that was building up inside her. Gramma Althea didn't expect anything from life and she wasn't disappointed. Ann expected to be happy and disappointment grew on her like another skin until she absorbed heartbreak through every pore into the deepest part of her nature. And because she was disappointed, she blamed everyone but herself for the unhappiness she didn't deserve.

"I have even begun to like the food, although it's strictly veg-etarian and consists of only things grown on the ashram, so the variety is limited. And everything is curried, which I don't mind too much, although sometimes it gives me a bit of indigestion. I sometimes long for a nice thin slice of roast beef (rare, please) or a nice chicken divan the way Lili makes it, with that yummy cheese sauce. Sometimes before I go to sleep, I can actually imagine the taste and I treat myself to a good cup of coffee after-wards (in my head, of course!). I told Guru Father and he laughed. 'I expect that's because you're human,' he said. 'You must give it time. A man does not lose his skin though he may try to scrub it off. Nor does he become a king because he imag-ines it.'"

When Ann moved to Toronto to attend Teachers' College, she made friends with Lili Hobart. She met Lili's older brother Stephen at a Christmas party later that same year and they began to date. Stephen was in his last year of Economics at the univer-sity. They became engaged the following year and were married soon after Ann got her first job teaching primary school. She quit her job tree years later, five months before Stephanie was born, when the pregnancy was starting to show. Motherhood wasn't easy for Ann. She was depressed after the baby came home and was consumed by the enormity of the task before her. She was fearful and fretted she would not be able to raise her child. There was so much to do. Was she up to it? She didn't even know where to begin. Ann had long ago rejected her own moth-er as a role model and was determined not to be like her. It meant she was starting with a lot of "do nots" and a copy of Dr. Spock to guide her.

"I remember when you were born you were so fierce and alive I was a little afraid of you! Your father was so proud. 'Look

how strong she is!' he'd say. 'She'll be able to take care of herself.'
And Jay–you'd think he'd given birth to you himself! He was the
only one you'd let carry you around. I'd be at my wit's end and
I'd say to your father, 'Call Jay. I can't get her to sleep.' And he'd
drop everything and come running over and hold you and walk
around, singing stupid things like 'Nellie's in the barn with her
pants down and Jake just wants to make hay!' And you would
finally fall asleep."

To listen to Ann tell it, you'd think they'd been a normal,
happy family just like the ones on TV. The one's that didn't really exist except on TV. She omitted the parts where she cried for
most of the day and Stephen would come home to find Stephanie
in a dirty diaper in her crib, a cold bottle of formula sitting on the
table beside the rocking chair. Ann hadn't been able to breastfeed.
It was too painful and the doctor told her she didn't have enough
milk. Another stone to add to the overwhelming pile of disappointments.

Ann had become interested in the occult a year after Stephanie's
birth. She was having dreams that troubled her and she became
convinced they were cognitive and that she was being sent messages she couldn't understand. She started reading books on
dream interpretation and parapsychology. When she dreamed
about her new baby she'd wake up in a cold sweat, believing it
meant the baby was going to die. She would look out the window for hours, losing track of time, thinking she had fed the
baby, not remembering she hadn't bathed her.

By now Stephen's star was rising at the Bank of Canada, and
he asked her if she would like him to hire a nanny to help look
after the baby. He knew something was wrong, knew the baby
wasn't being properly cared for. Ann was furious. It was her baby
and she would look after it. It took time to settle into a routine,
that's all. She just hadn't worked out a routine yet. Her mood

swings began to alarm Stephen, but he didn't know what to do. He didn't think she would harm the child; it was more a case of neglect than anything else. Maybe Ann was right. She just needed to work out a routine.

And eventually she did. Her depression began to recede and she was able to cope with the mornings. She would bathe and feed the baby, put her in the carriage and take a walk to the store and back. But the afternoons were still difficult. She would pull the drapes and lie on the sofa, and try to shut out the baby's crying. Listening to Bach helped, but she was so tired she couldn't get up and get the baby's afternoon bottle. Stephen finally asked Lili to drop around once in a while, just to check. And Lili would heat the baby's bottle and give it to her while Ann lay on the sofa with her eyes closed, shutting out the world and listening to Bach.

Then, one day Ann picked up a book about astrology and it intrigued her enough to get her horoscope done. She was astonished by what a perfect stranger was able to tell her about herself simply by determining the configuration of the planets at the time of her birth. For the first time she had a picture of herself as an individual who did things for reasons that were beyond her control. It wasn't her fault that the planets were lined up a certain way. She now had a way of explaining the world to herself that absolved her of responsibility. Her moon was in the twelfth house of secret sorrows. And it was in Scorpio, a water sign, so it meant the sorrow was profound and deep within her. It was all she could do to manage her own burden of sorrow, let alone manage a house and a baby.

Stephen would have to do more to help, she decided. She didn't want strangers in her house touching things and putting things out of order. She didn't want strangers raising her child. But she couldn't do it alone. Stephen would have to do more. Stephen learned to recognize when Ann had reached her limit. He got so he could hear it in her voice, even over the phone. He knew the exact second when she switched from being capable and on top of things, to being suddenly overwhelmed and completely unable to cope. Not one more thing, her tone of voice would say, I can't do one more thing. She was like a piece of glass about to shatter. One second she would be whole, and the next she would be in fragments.

Soon Ann was studying astrology and learning to cast charts. She took to calling Stephanie "my little Libra" which Stephen asked her not to do, so she only did it when he wasn't around. Astrology led to an interest in numerology and then palmistry. Séances followed and card readings, all of which Stephen tried to discourage, possibly because he saw how much she was changing and he couldn't understand her anymore. Or because he was afraid she was going to a place she would not be able to return from. There was also the fact that her conversation at cocktail parties was becoming increasingly bizarre and people didn't know whether to take her seriously or not. She began to ask people what sign they were, long before it became fashionable. She offered to do their horoscope, or their children's horoscopes but they would politely decline and walk away. She couldn't see that her obsession was scaring people, that it was too personal. She was showing her vulnerability, exposing herself and offering to expose them as well.

Of course to Stephanie Ann was just her mother, which meant this was all normal, until the first time one of her friends said, "Your mother's weird, isn't she?" She hadn't noticed up until then, but she began to notice after that. She began to notice other things too. Like the way her father would sometimes use a certain tone of voice with her mother, especially when they were going out. His warning voice, Stephanie used to call it. He used it with her sometimes too. Like when he didn't want her to behave a certain way. "Take your fingers out of your mouth, Stephanie. You're not a baby." He would say to Ann, "Don't talk about that occult stuff with these people. They don't want to hear it. And they'll think you're crazy." He started using the word crazy, which he had avoided doing for so long. He didn't really think Ann was crazy, but people might think she was because she sometimes said crazy things. My crazy mother, thought Stephanie.

Stephanie slept for a while, lulled by the steady drone of the plane's engines. She had taken some wine with her dinner and her head felt heavy. It would be hours before they landed in Bombay and she would need her wits about her. The droning vibration of the aircraft and the contorted sleeping position kept her muscles tense and her mind just on the edge of consciousness. Her mouth was dry and she dreamed she was walking down a dirt road dragging her canvas carryall behind her. Whenever she saw someone, she asked if they had any boiled water. They all shook their heads and kept walking. Each person she encountered was wearing the brightly colored, tightly wound turban of a Sikh. When I get to Bombay, she thought, I'll be able to get boiled water.

And then she was in a garden, hoeing between rows of vegetables. The earth was dry and dusty and badly needed water. There was another woman working with her and when she turned her head, she saw it was her mother.

"Stephanie," her mother said, "the roots in this garden go very deep. There are hidden springs far beneath this parched surface that nourish these plants and keep them alive. If you keep digging, you will eventually discover the Life Force."

Stephanie awoke with a start and realized the old woman sitting next to her had nudged her gently. The woman nodded her head toward the waiting flight attendant.

"Would you like some breakfast, Ma'am?"

"Oh, uh, yes, please," Stephanie mumbled, her mouth parched, her tongue thick.

chapter eight

The plane landed in Bombay ninety minutes later and it seemed like another ninety minutes before Stephanie found herself in the terminal. She was surrounded by a mob of small, dark men wearing bright red turbans, asking to carry her bag. She wasn't about to give up her carryall to anyone, so she just kept saying "No thank you" over and over while she pushed her way through the chattering mob. Once outside the terminal she spotted the long row of identical black and yellow taxis and headed for the end of the lineup.

The noise! she thought. Why is everybody shouting? And why do they have to honk their horns so much? Nobody's even paying attention.

Women and children sat on piles of luggage while men bartered and argued with taxi drivers. Red-turbaned bearers balancing suitcases stacked on their heads, or bending under the weight of heavy trunks on their backs, poured out of the airport, struggling to keep up with the multitude of passengers anxious to get taxis into the city.

Stephanie's pulse pounded as anger and adrenalin pumped through her body. She thought she would explode if it didn't all stop instantly. It's making me crazy, she thought. I can't stand it! She squeezed her eyes shut and willed herself not to hear it. Wait, wait, slow down. You're overreacting. It's culture shock, that's all. Pull yourself together. You can deal with it. Just tune it out. That's right. It's just cars and people. Nothing unusual. Just a lot of cars and a lot of people. Jesus Christ and we aren't even out of the airport yet.

Finally the next cab was hers. She threw her carryall onto the back seat and climbed in after it. "Railway Station," she said, enunciating clearly and speaking loudly.

"Which railway station, memsah'b?" the driver asked. Oh good, she thought, he speaks English.

"Victoria Terminus," she said, not quite as loud as before.

She settled back and watched in fascination as the driver maneuvered the car along a narrow, ill-defined road where it wasn't clear who had the right of way. Everything seemed to be happening right in the middle. People carrying large bundles on their heads walked down the middle. Large animals like water buffalo and cows were led down the middle of the road by skinny young boys wielding sticks that they frequently used on the animals' rumps to keep them moving. Women wearing gauzy and colorful saris, their thick black hair braided down their backs, walked down the middle, deep in conversation. Through it all, the driver swerved and leaned on the horn, never cursing or yelling at people, as if it were all a matter of course. Stephanie couldn't believe they hadn't figured out how much easier it would be for everybody if the people walked on the side of the road and the cars drove down the middle.

After what seemed like an eternity they reached the outskirts of Bombay and she saw that things were getting progressively worse. Now there were bullock carts as well as pedestrians, scooters, bicycles, pushcarts and all manner of transport known to man. Trucks jockeyed with buses, rickshaws maneuvered around scrawny men carrying enormous loads on their turbaned heads. The constant noise continued like a steady rain of pebbles pouring down on the city from above.

After what seemed like hours, they pulled up to a gigantic Victorian wedding cake of a building, extravagantly ornamented and trimmed, several floors high, and containing so many wings that Stephanie thought it must surely be the Houses of Parliament.

"Victoria Station," said the cab driver, when she didn't move.

"You're kidding. This is the Railway Station?"

"Yes, memsah'b. Railway Stay-shun. Fifty rupees."

Oh my God, she thought, I forgot to change money at the airport. "Uh, I uh–"

"You need change money, memsah'b?" the driver asked.

"Yes. Do you know where I can do it?"

"I can change," he said. "How much you want change? Fifty dollar? One hundred dollar?"

"You can change that much?" she asked, amazed at the ease with which things were happening.

He nodded his head from side to side and she took this to mean yes.

"What rate will you give me for one hundred dollars, U.S.?" she asked, thinking how horrified her father would be to see this.

"Cash or traveler check?" he asked.

"Cash."

"Cash, very good rate. Twelve rupee, one dollar. Best rate."

"Okay. Show me your money."

Besides her traveler's checks, Stephanie had five American hundred-dollar bills and she was about to part with one of them. If this is a scam, she thought, I'm dead. But something told her this was the way things were done. She remembered hearing a cameraman from the news crew say that the easiest way to change money anywhere was to ask a cab driver. They always had a little black market cash on them. Well, here goes, she thought, handing over the hundred in exchange for a fat wad of flimsy paper bills about two-thirds the size of the American bills.

"Thank you," she said, handing the driver five ten-rupee notes. No need to tip, she thought. He's probably just made a bundle. She hauled herself and her carryall out of the cab and headed into the station.

Once inside, Stephanie found herself stepping between and around people and piles of luggage, suitcases and trunks, boxes tied with rope, and even bundles wrapped in cloth. She'd never seen so many people lying on the ground like this. Could they all be waiting for trains?

The interior of the station was another sea of noise. This just keeps getting worse, she thought. The airport was bad but it was nothing compared to this. How could they stand it?

She made her way to a ticket window, fending off beggars and porters as if she had been doing it all her life.

This isn't really happening, she thought. I'm still on the plane. I'm dreaming. The plane hasn't landed yet. It's not going to be anything like this.

"I need a ticket to Hyderabad," she told the man at the wicket.

"Second class, second class sleeper, first class or air-conditioned?"

"How much is air-conditioned?"

"Very expensive. Four hundred fifty rupees."

"How much is first class?" He quoted her a figure half as much.

"I'll take first class," she said, wondering why she was trying to save money when it was only a matter of twenty dollars.

"When does the train leave?"

"Three hours," he said. "Seven p.m. on track eleven."

Three hours, she thought. Now what?

chapter nine

Ma Vera rose at 5 a.m. as usual. She'd slept fitfully on her rope bed. As she threw aside the rough cotton coverlet and put her feet on the smooth cement floor of her cell, she had a feeling of apprehension, the same tension behind her eyes she had felt the night before. This day will not be like other days. Things will never be the same again, she thought. But I must put these thoughts from my mind.

She heard the stirrings of other devotees as they rose to perform their morning rituals. Ma Vera walked along the second-floor corridor to the bathroom where she proceeded to bathe herself, as she did every day, by dipping a metal cup into the cistern and splashing cold water over her body. She rubbed herself down with an oblong of coarse, hand-woven cotton and mechanically wrapped her sari of white homespun around her stout body with the ease of long years of practice.

Ma Vera was an Englishwoman who had been born in a village fifty miles outside of London in 1920 and had lived in India since Partition in 1947. She had come to the ashram in 1964 when she decided she no longer wanted to belong to the world of men and their institutions. She was now the longest-standing member of the ashram, except for Guru Father and Deva Mother, of course.

Ma Vera made her way to the temple that stood in the south-east corner of the ashram compound. There, she and the other devotees would meditate for an hour before beginning their morning chores. I must clear my mind, she thought. I must not let these thoughts mar the spirit of devotion. She inhaled deeply and smelled the damp early morning air, a mixture of incense, dry cow dung and burning wood, mingled with the soft, moist earth beneath her feet and the slightly fetid smell of the river. She could no longer remember what the air in England smelled like, but believed in her mind it had been green, perfumed by flowers and grass, while this air was brown, seeping from the earth and commingling with every living and non-living thing it encountered. There were no gentle, fragrant breezes in India. The air here was a constant reminder of the relentless struggle between life and death, between the living and the dying.

It doesn't get any easier, she realized. Even after twenty-three years, it still requires all my energy, all my concentration. She knew what Guru Father would say: We are still human, my friend. Enlightenment is not a locked room you enter and then throw away the key. It requires constant vigilance, alertness and a willingness to accept change.

Change. She hated that word. Why did things always have to change? And so fast? Even in this remote corner of India she had been unable, for any sustained period of time, to keep things the same. It was all too true what Guru Father said—life must always change and seek new directions. That is its energy. If you wish stillness, you must find it within yourself, but you must realize that it is the same energy—the divine, or God principle—that governs all life.

I will dig, she thought, as she nodded in silent greeting to her fellow sannyasins. I will dig in the garden until my bones are aching. I will not look up from the earth until my head is clear and my thoughts are pure.

Stephanie awoke with a jolt, the sound of iron wheels on iron rails grating in her ears. She was lying on her back, staring at the green ceiling of the first-class railway compartment, thinking: That's right. I'm on the upper berth and I've been on this train for the last twelve hours. She turned on her side and saw that the three people sharing the compartment with her, a young couple and an older woman traveling together, were up and seated, the opposite berth having been cleared of its bedding, the luggage replaced neatly. She smiled and nodded; they smiled and nodded back.

I hope they don't expect me to get up, she thought. There's still another five hours before we reach Hyderabad. She remembered her first impressions of Bombay and the walk she had taken through the neighborhood around the railway station.

It had been impossible to walk on the sidewalk because of the number of squatters who had set up housekeeping there. Some had erected shelters of corrugated metal and cardboard; others had draped a tattered sari over a couple of sticks to demarcate the boundaries of their dwelling. The repeated cry of "Ma! Ma!" reached her ears and whenever she looked over she saw a thin, dark face, its large black eyes appealing to her and a bony hand and scrawny arm reaching out to her beseechingly. She started handing out small coins, but in a few minutes she was surrounded by beggars. She pulled her bag close to her body and tried to make her way past the grasping hands. She finally managed to push through the crowd and ran to the next street, which was the same as the one she had just left.

After a while, she pretended she didn't hear them, pretended she didn't see the half-starved children with their protruding bellies and twiggy limbs. Looking over the top of the makeshift lean-to's and ragged tents, she saw she was actually in a fairly prosperous neighborhood of solid homes, whitewashed and painted in pastel yellows and pinks, set well back from the four-foot high cement walls that lined the crowded street.

Further down the street she saw a number of people gathered around a water tap mounted on a three-foot pipe that emerged from the sidewalk. Some were filling battered tin cups and jars; others were scrubbing and wringing out rags that were probably used as clothing. One woman squatted close to the ground and vigorously scrubbed her small, protesting child. Further on Stephanie noticed someone eating something white and mushy off a banana leaf, using his fingers to form lumps of the stuff and stick it in his mouth. Once in a while he would shove one of the lumps into the mouth of a child squatting beside him.

Stephanie walked for several blocks but the scene didn't change. Several sharp smells combined to assault her nose, including urine and an acrid, smoky smell from the occasional cooking fire. She was getting used to the constant chatter of human voices and she became aware of another layer of sound–the constant cawing and chirping of birds that filled the trees and perched on every wall and post. Most were big black birds, like crows, only smaller. The trees were laden with the most colorful birds, finches and bright green parakeets. Not once did she see someone enter or leave one of the permanent homes on the street, even though it was the end of the work day, the hour when you would expect to see them hurrying home for dinner. Maybe there are secret passages under the street, she thought. Or maybe they're all stuck in the endless traffic that never seems to let up, not even for five minutes.

Stephanie walked for several more blocks, always making sure she made right turns so she could find her way back to the station. To get back to the station she had to cross the four-lane road that ran in front of it, dodging the constant stream of taxis and buses and scooters that passed up and down. She walked past a number of makeshift kiosks along the road and slowed to look more closely. Most of the goods looked like they'd been salvaged from flooded or burned-out warehouses. The packaging was faded and limp or non-existent. Most vendors sold a selection of razor blades, soap, toothpaste and cigarettes, which apparently could be purchased individually rather than by the pack, and one or two had a selection of magazines and newspapers. Anything a hurried traveler might need.

There were food vendors as well, peddling soupy lentil concoctions and fried flatbreads, tea in small, disposable clay cups, or soda pop in a range of colors from bright orange, red and yellow, to dark amber and cola. Some of the bottles were labeled, others were not. Although she was hungry and thirsty, there was nothing here that appealed to her. She looked at her watch and saw that it was quarter to six, just time to grab a quick meal at the station dining room and find her seat on the train.

Inside the station, Stephanie walked past the second-class waiting room, the second-class dining room, the first-class waiting room for Ladies, and the first-class waiting room for Gentlemen, until she came to the first-class dining room. Nobody questioned her right to be there or asked to see her ticket. She found a small table off to the side and picked up the menu. The choice was between mutton curry, chicken curry, vegetable curry and omelette. What the heck, she thought, and ordered the chicken curry.

The curry came with a lump of white rice and a small dish of finely sliced sweet red onion. There were a few pieces of chicken still attached to the bone sitting in a spicy, rather tasty, she had to admit, caramel-colored sauce. Stephanie had eaten enough Indian food in Toronto to know that this was very plain fare, somewhere between soup kitchen and diner caliber. But she was hungry enough not to mind. She washed it down with a bottle of orange soda pop called Fanta–something she would never dream of doing back home–and went off to claim her luggage and find her train.

The train was already sitting on track eleven when she got there and the second-class coaches were filled to overflowing with people hanging out the windows and lounging on the luggage racks. It suddenly occurred to her that if she hadn't had a reservation, she would never have got a seat on this train. She found a conductor in a faded and shabby Indian Railways uniform–probably going back to the Raj–and he helped her find her coach. Her three fellow passengers were already settled in and they nodded in silent acknowledgement when she entered the compartment.

The train jolted to a stop and Stephanie looked at her watch. Nine o'clock already. Only three more hours. She wondered if this was the stop the breakfast trays would be brought on. They had given their orders the night before to a porter who had taken two rupees from each of them. She found her receipt in her handbag and carefully lowered herself to the floor. She was starving.

Ma Vera was on her knees pulling at weeds with her bare hands. Occasionally a bead of sweat from her brow would drop onto the soil and she would reach up and pass her forearm across her eyes. Don't think. Just work. She repeated the words to herself as if they were a mantra. Once she heard a voice call to her: "Why don't you use a hoe, Ma Vera. It would be much easier." She looked up and saw Ashok Anand.

"If I wanted it to be easy, I'd get you to do it, little brother!" she called back, and Ashok laughed. Ma Vera was known for her wit.

She worked her way slowly along the row of green beans, stuffing the weeds into a sack as she went. Hard work is good for the soul, she told herself. It helps to dull the pain. Or maybe it just gives you an aching back and that's what takes your mind off your troubles.

Her mother used to say that, she remembered. She hadn't thought about her mother in a very long time. Probably a good thing. Her mother had never forgiven her for living with those heathen Hindoos, as she called them. On her deathbed she had said, Tell Margaret (she was born Margaret Evans) I cannot forgive her and I die sinning against God because of her. May God have mercy on my soul.

A dramatic end for an unkind, selfish woman, thought Ma Vera. Stop, she told herself. Stop. Stop. Stop. Enough of these poisoned thoughts. Concentrate on the dirt and the weeds. Huh! That's probably what made me think of Mother! And she laughed in spite of her foul mood.

To Stephanie's surprise, the train pulled into the Hyderabad station on time. Almost on time. Within ten minutes. That meant she would have time to catch the bus to Midnapor. The porter told her where she could catch it and estimated the trip would take two hours. From there she would have to get a taxi or local bus for the remaining thirteen miles to the ashram. No wonder her mother hadn't been able to face the trip, she thought. You had to be in top form and even then it was no picnic to travel for more than thirty-six hours straight through God knew how many time zones. She could have stopped and spent the night in a hotel, but she was anxious to get to the ashram and see her mother. She had to make sure she was all right.

The bus ride to Midnapor was not unlike the taxi ride from the airport to Bombay. It was a swing-and-sway affair as the bus swerved to avoid pedestrians, animals and vehicles of every description, horn trumpeting full blast the whole way. Stephanie was hot and exhausted by the time the bus pulled into the center of town and discharged its load of passengers and cargo. Thirteen more miles, she thought. I'm almost there.

Ma Vera kept pulling weeds right through lunch, stopping only occasionally to drink water offered by concerned ashramites. Some of them wondered if they should speak to Guru Father about Ma Vera's strange behavior. After all, she wasn't so young anymore. When Manu asked if she could help her with the weeds, Ma Vera said no. I just need to be left alone to work. It's good for the soul.

It was after four o'clock in the afternoon when she finished the last row and slowly and painfully got to her feet. She had filled five sacks to bursting. She had pains shooting up her back and her knees felt like someone had driven spikes into them. The pain behind her eyes was still there.

Ma Vera slowly hobbled along the path to the main residence and watched a taxi pull up to the front entrance. A tall young woman emerged from the back seat pulling a large shapeless travel bag behind her. Ma Vera stepped off the stone path and started walking on the grass toward the young woman who had already spotted her and waved. Nobody else was around.

Stephanie put her carryall down and walked toward the woman, who was limping, her left hand on her back as if she were in pain. As she got closer, Stephanie saw that the woman was in her late sixties, not very tall, a little stout, with very short but thick salt-and-pepper hair. Her ruddy skin was lined from years of exposure to the sun. Her dark eyes glowed like coals under straight black brows. Her square face was streaked with mud beside her short, broad nose. Even her lips had mud on them, as if she'd been eating dirt. Stephanie also noticed that the woman had slim ankles and very small hands and feet, giving the impression despite her stocky build that she could easily be toppled by a gentle push or a gust of wind.

"Hello," she said to the woman when they had reached each other. "I'm looking for Ann Hobart. Do you know where I can find her?"

Ma Vera stood as if turned to stone, her heart skipping a beat.

"Dear God, you've come," she whispered.

"Yes, I have and it hasn't been easy." Stephanie smiled at the woman and waited for her to tell her where Ann was. But the woman just stood there looking at her, her mud-smudged face creased with pain.

"I'm so sorry, my dear," she said hoarsely. "Ann died two days ago."

chapter ten

When Stephanie woke up it took a few minutes to remember where she was. She was lying on a bed, the single piece of furniture other than a wooden chair, in a small, plain room that resembled a prison cell. Then it came back to her. She was at the ashram. Her head was throbbing and every muscle in her body ached. A young woman, seated in a chair next to the bed, was watching her anxiously. "Would you like some water?" she asked, her voice soft as rain.

"Is it boiled?" Stephanie barely recognized her own voice it seemed to come from so far away.

"Yes, it's boiled. But anyway we have a good well here. Come. Drink." She helped Stephanie sit up and take a drink from a cool, metal cup. After a few sips Stephanie lay back down on the bed.

"I am Manu," the young woman said. "Are you Stephanie, Ann's daughter?"

Stephanie nodded and felt her eyes fill with tears. She let the deep, wretched sobs roll over her like a wave, turning her face to the wall and pulling her knees into her chest as if to form a container for her grief.

"Yes, you must cry," said Manu softly. "There is nothing else to do."

After a while Stephanie slept again, her exhaustion so profound it was as if she were under anesthesia. When she awoke, she emerged from blackness, struggling to find her way to the top of the deep pool she had been submerged in. She was still facing the wall. She had not moved.

"Are you awake, my dear?" She heard a woman's husky voice and slowly turned over onto her back.

"Yes," she said, but her voice sounded strange, toneless. She turned her head to see who was sitting in the chair and realized it was the same woman she had met on her arrival.

"Good morning, Stephanie. I am Ma Vera. I was a friend of your mother's."

Stephanie nodded. "Is it morning?"

"Yes," replied Ma Vera. "You have been sleeping for twelve hours."

Allan Lloyd sat in the lotus position, his head bowed, the thumb and fingertips of each hand touching to form a circle of energy, and chanted to himself: *Ram Nam Sat Hai*; The Name of God is Truth. He had been at the ashram for nearly six months and soon he would have to decide if he was going to take the vow of *Sannyasa,* a vow of poverty, chastity and obedience, and become initiated into a life of *bhakti*, devotion and *arati*, worship service. He would have to undergo a purification ceremony and receive his new spiritual name. He would be born again to journey on the lifelong path to *Brahman.*

He was certain in his mind that he would do this, despite what his parents and his brother thought. Allan came from a family of doctors. The town where he was born, Shackleton, Oregon, even had a hospital named after his grandfather, Henry

Hudson Lloyd. He didn't like to break with tradition; he had nothing but respect and love for his family. But ever since Barbara had been killed in a motorcycle accident he hadn't been able to concentrate on his medical studies, hadn't had the heart to complete them. He couldn't even face being in Shackleton any more, the memories crowding in on him, all the landmarks in their relationship haunting him, increasing his despair.

He had wanted to get as far away from it all as possible. And so he had come to India and found the ashram on the outskirts of a village that didn't even have electricity. And surprisingly, he had found a kind of peace here. The pain was still there; he didn't expect that would ever go away, but he had felt love again in his heart. Not love for a woman, the way he had felt about Barbara, but a love of God and nature and the power of life. He had everything he needed here as well as a sense of purpose. He began to see that a life of devotion and worship was a way of justifying his existence, a way of enduring the fact that he had lived and Barbara had died.

He heard the low hum of *Om* being chanted by the fifteen other devotees around him signaling the end of devotion, and he joined in, feeling his heart lift and his energy surge. Soon the rich deep humming filled the room and the collective sound vibrated from body to body.

Leaving the temple, he remembered the events of the previous evening. Ann's daughter had arrived in the afternoon unaware that her mother was dead. She was exhausted from her journey and had cried when Ma Vera told her. Ma Vera had persuaded her to spend the night at the ashram and asked Allan to carry her bag upstairs to one of the guest rooms. Her name was Stephanie and she was very different from her mother. She was tall and athletic-looking with large hands and feet and thick, dark auburn hair.

Allan thought about the first time he had seen Ann, remembering the sense of recognition he had felt, knowing they were spiritual kin, brother and sister in their search for liberation from their own turbulent thoughts and emotions. They were attending a yoga session, learning the art of breathing through one nostril and then the other, which for the novice produced a kind of high that was both exhilarating and purifying. All new-comers to the ashram were required to practice the Hatha Yoga techniques to improve their posture and physical strength before embarking on the more strenuous road to spiritual liberation. Only when the mind and body were disciplined, they were taught, could the veritable Essence be experienced.

Allan had been at the ashram just three months when Ann arrived. His emotions still raw and vulnerable, he had avoided the other novices and devotees, not wanting to get close to any-one until he felt more in control of himself. He was still experi-encing culture shock, he believed, and was not comfortable with the climate or the food or the degree of devotion required to get through the day before falling into an exhausted and often rest-less sleep at night.

In Ann he recognized the same kind of vulnerability, the same uncertainties, the same fears that he was experiencing. He knew instinctively he could trust her not to betray him. He felt it was important that the others not perceive him as weak or frightened. Yet at the same time, it frustrated him to know that exposing his insecurity would be the best way of dealing with it. He was part of a community here and he would have to learn to feel safe in it. Ann was the first person he had been able to reach out to and he would always be grateful for the friendship they had shared. He had been closer to her in many ways than to Barbara, despite the generation difference in their ages. They seemed to have reached the same point in their lives, but by very different routes.

"You're my spiritual twin," Ann had said to him after one of their conversations. "Just knowing you're on the earth some-where, even if we're miles apart, will save me from ever being alone again."

But Ann had died, like Barbara, much too soon and for no reason. Maybe I'm meant to be alone, he thought. Maybe that's the lesson I have to learn in this life, that to form earthly attachments is to lose them. That these bonds are an unreliable means to peace and happiness. That the soul is the only deliverance from pain and sorrow.

"I have to contact my father," Stephanie said, sitting on the edge of the bed, trying to find the energy to stand up.

"That will be difficult," said Ma Vera. "There's no phone here or in the village. You must go by bus or taxi to Midnapor and phone from there. But your father must have received the telegram we sent the day after your mother's death. He would have received it by the time you landed in Bombay."

"I still have to talk to him. He'll be frantic with worry and I can't imagine what he must be going through right now. He'll be waiting to hear from me." She struggled to her feet and felt a rush of lightheadedness. She realized she hadn't eaten since the previous morning on the train. She steadied herself by reaching for Ma Vera's outstretched arm, refusing to give in to the impulse to sit down again. "Where is my mother now? I'd like to see her."

"I'm afraid that won't be possible," Ma Vera said gently. "Ann's earthly remains were cremated yesterday morning in the Hindu tradition." She waited for Stephanie to react and saw the young woman's face turn red with anger.

"How could you do that?" she demanded, feeling a sudden surge of energy. "Without our permission? We would never have agreed to that."

"It would be best if you talked to Deva Mother," Ma Vera said, before Stephanie could continue. "She's in charge of administration."

Stephanie pulled herself together on the walk across the courtyard to Deva Mother's office. Stepping outside into the hot, bright sunlight, smelling the dry, baked earth and feeling the warmth of the air touching her skin brought her back to reality and reminded her where she was and why she was here. The same cawing and chirping birds she had heard in Bombay were overhead, but the constant keening of people and traffic was missing. This place was quieter and cleaner, as if all the beggars had crept away and all the vehicles had run out of gas while she slept. It felt like Sunday, a welcome break from life's normal rhythms.

Deva Mother's office was on the main floor of the ashram building, a spacious and sunny room with two sets of open French doors revealing a small patio with a wicker table and chairs. The late morning sun shone down hotly on the white painted furniture. It seemed a small luxury in an otherwise sparsely furnished environment.

"You're English," were Stephanie's first words on being greeted by the tall, angular woman who administered the affairs of the ashram and was often referred to as The Mother.

"By birth, yes," she responded in a cool, upper-class accent. "But I have not lived there for many years." She indicated a chair and Stephanie sat down. She had been prepared to raise the roof with Deva Mother, but the Englishwoman was clearly used to being in control.

"Let me say how terribly sorry I am about your mother's death. We're all saddened by this tragic and sudden loss. Our only comfort is that Ann is in a better place and that her soul is at peace."

Stephanie kept her eyes on Deva Mother's face. She was aware of the hum of a ceiling fan overhead, gently moving the warm, dry air around and delicately lifting the hairs on her bare arms.

"I wanted to talk to you about my mother's remains," Stephanie said, surprised at how calm her voice sounded. She remembered her vow to act with confidence. "How dare you cremate someone without the family's permission. My father and I would never have agreed to it."

Deva Mother raised her eyebrows slightly. She was about the

same age as Ma Vera, but she was much taller and her bones were visible beneath the skin. The folds of her pale blue sari did nothing to soften the angularity of her appearance. Unlike Ma Vera, Deva Mother's skin had retained some of its English creaminess. Her pale hair was streaked with gray and pulled back from her face in a knot at the nape of her neck. Her eyebrows were thin and delicately arched and the eyes beneath them were a cool blue washed with gray. She had probably been strikingly beautiful when she was young, an icy blonde with good bones.

"Your mother gave her permission before she died," she told Stephanie. "We acted in accordance with her wishes."

chapter eleven

The Mother agreed that Stephanie should go into town and telephone her father. It wasn't possible to get a taxi, but there was a bus that passed on the main road every two hours. There was time for her to have some lunch before catching the next one. The Mother insisted that someone accompany Stephanie to town and asked Ma Vera to assign the task to Manu. The Mother told Stephanie she was welcome to stay at the ashram until she felt ready to travel again. She hoped Stephanie would find comfort at the ashram while she was there. She encouraged her to take part in any activities that might provide some comfort, or at least a distraction.

Ma Vera took Stephanie around to the east side of the main ashram building where the large cafeteria-style dining room was located. It was here that Stephanie finally realized that the ashram was filled with people and wasn't the deserted sanctuary it had at first seemed. The large oblong room was furnished with folding tables and chairs, the kind used in high school gymnasiums and church bazaars. There must have been close to forty people assembled for the noon meal. At each table an assortment of people of various nationalities and races sat eating from what looked like aluminum pie plates. Conversation was sporadic and muted but an occasional burst of laughter would make its way to the surface, relieving the sense of solemnity that filled the air like the oppressive heat.

Stephanie and Ma Vera took tin plates and had them filled with steaming rice and vegetables, thick slices of fresh bread and hunks of fruit. They sat across from each other at the end of one of the long tables and began to eat. Stephanie found the food mildly curried and not very interesting, but it was fresh and filling and satisfied her hunger. Ma Vera took their empty plates back to the food counter and came back with two mugs of hot herbal tea.

"I hope you'll consider staying with us for a while, my dear," she said, sipping her tea. "I'm sure you're anxious to get home to your father, I can understand that, but you've had a terrible shock and it may not be wise to undertake the journey so soon." She watched Stephanie over the rim of her cup and waited for her to respond.

"Thank you," Stephanie said, "but I'm sure I'm strong enough for the trip. At least I'll know what to expect this time."

"Physically, perhaps you're strong enough, but are you sure you won't break down emotionally on the way." Ma Vera's concern was genuine but Stephanie wondered why she should care about what happened to her.

As if sensing her confusion, Ma Vera said, "We feel responsible for you in a way. Ann was a part of our family and so are you. If you were my daughter, I wouldn't want you traveling in your present state."

"In my present state?"

"The full force of your mother's death may not have hit you yet. Believe me, I'm only saying to you what I believe Ann would say if she were here."

"If she were here," said Stephanie, "we wouldn't be having this conversation."

"She's not here in the flesh," Ma Vera said gently, "but her spirit is here. If you let yourself, perhaps you will be able to feel it. It may comfort you."

Is she for real? thought Stephanie. She had to admit, though, it was exactly the kind of thing Ann would say.

"I realize you're not like your mother," Ma Vera went on, "and I sense you're a person who chooses action over contemplation, but this place can offer you a chance to understand what your mother was trying to do with her life, and you may find some peace in that understanding."

Stephanie finished her tea in silence. Ma Vera took the mugs back to the counter and recommended they find Manu so she and Stephanie could catch the bus to town.

"She's probably in the spinning room," said Ma Vera. Stephanie envisioned one of those centrifugal force rotor rides at a carnival, where the room rotates like the spin cycle of a washing machine and the floor drops away, leaving everybody stuck to the wall. She followed Ma Vera along a pathway that pointed northeast from the main building and ended a couple of hundred yards later at a rectangular-shaped whitewashed building measuring about thirty by fifteen feet. The window openings were framed by wooden shutters painted green and half of them were closed against the fierce rays of the midday sun. Inside, the air was cool and slightly moist. Water had recently been sprinkled on the hard earth floor to keep the dust down and when Stephanie's eyes adjusted to the dimness, she saw that the room was filled with piles of yarn, raw cotton and homespun. There were a couple of spinning wheels and a large wooden loom in the center. Manu was sitting in the far corner sorting and cleaning a pile of raw cotton.

"Manu!" Ma Vera called, her deep-throated voice carrying easily across the room. "The Mother has asked that you accompany Stephanie to town so she can telephone her father. The bus will be passing within a quarter of an hour."

Manu set aside what she was doing and walked quickly towards Stephanie and Ma Vera. She was a graceful young woman, about twenty years old, with a perfectly shaped oval face and thick black hair that was pulled loosely back from her face in a long, fat braid. Her skin was the highly prized fair skin of an upper caste Brahmin and her figure had the softly rounded plumpness of a young woman raised in a prosperous Indian home. Stephanie fleetingly wondered why she was living at the ashram.

Ma Vera reached into the folds of her sari and pulled out some crumpled rupee notes. "Here is money for your tickets," she said to Manu. "Take Stephanie to the P.T.T. and make sure they do their utmost to put the call through. Don't allow any shenanigans."

"I have money," Stephanie protested, but Ma Vera waved her hand and said, "No, no, not this time. Now go quickly. You don't want to miss the bus."

Manu and Stephanie took the path back to the main building, skirting the perimeter and picking up another path on the west side that led to the main road. This was the road Stephanie had taken on her arrival, when she first saw Ma Vera.

The bus came in five or six minutes and they boarded quickly to escape the dust and exhaust fumes that billowed from its hot underside. It was a rickety affair, similar to a school bus. The seats were plastic, the floors wooden. Stephanie and Manu managed to find a seat near the back and grabbed for it amidst the lurching and grinding of gears.

"What luck," said Manu. "Often we must stand, but I guess because it's just after lunch there are not so many people. In India people are always going somewhere. The trains and buses are always full. Why they travel so, I do not know. One town is much like the next."

"Perhaps they're curious," replied Stephanie. "How can you

know what things are like unless you go and look for yourself?"

"I suppose," said Manu, "but I think people must keep moving because they fear that if they stop they will have to face themselves and the emptiness of their lives. If you think about it, must you see every tree in order to know what a tree is? Or is it better to know one tree very well to understand the essence of trees?"

Stephanie smiled. "You've been studying philosophy," she said. "Those are questions without answers, designed to drive a person crazy. I prefer to deal in facts, things I can see with my own eyes."

"Ah," said Manu, enjoying herself, "even facts are *maya*, illusion. What is a fact for you, may not even exist for me."

Stephanie relinquished the argument with a shrug and turned to look out the window. She was tired and hot and the noise and the dust were not conducive to conversation. Manu didn't seem to be affected by it and smiled contentedly as the bus jolted and swerved toward its destination.

Everywhere she looked, Stephanie saw bright green rice fields in various stages of cultivation. Occasionally she noticed a small figure in a vividly colored sari bent over a patch of green, or a swaying cluster of muddy-looking water buffalo lounging in a swampy enclave. Once, she saw a brilliantly plumed bird swoop towards the earth like a swatch of turquoise silk caught by the wind. This was not the India of teeming masses she had been led to expect. There was a timeless tranquility about the place that transcended even the gnashing mechanics of the ancient bus.

This place is beautiful, she thought. It's so full of contradictions. Then she remembered that several generations of her father's family had been born here. And died here. How many Hobart graves must there be scattered across this vast and unforgiving land, she wondered. Babies and children killed by fever and dysentery. Young women dying in childbirth. Soldiers on the battlefield. And old men with nothing left but memories. They could fill volumes with their stories of the beauty and the horror of this place. Maybe it was fitting that she had come to India because of sickness and death. It was almost like a family legacy.

After a while, she became aware of increased activity on the roadway as people and vehicles began to converge on the outskirts of the town. She turned to Manu.

"How did my mother die?"

Manu, startled by the suddenness of the question, seemed to pale and shrink from her directness.

"I–I don't really know," she replied, her voice muffled as if her throat were full of dust.

"You don't know?" said Stephanie, ignoring Manu's discomfort. "Did she have a fever? Was she in pain?" Suddenly it seemed imperative to know these things.

"Well," Manu began slowly, "I think she had dysentery for a few weeks and then she developed a fever." She didn't look at Stephanie, but kept her eyes on her hands, which were clutching the bar on the back of the seat in front of her.

"Did she have pain?" asked Stephanie, more gently, but still urgently. No one had talked to her about it yet and Stephanie needed to hear it.

"Yes, she had pain," whispered Manu, blinking back her tears. "You should talk to Ma Vera. She was with her." She looked at Stephanie, a look that pleaded with her to stop.

"Did anyone else have the same illness?" she asked, wondering why it was so difficult for Manu to answer her questions.

"No. No one," said Manu, her voice a strangled sob. And then Stephanie saw the tiny spark of fear in Manu's eyes before she blinked and turned away.

chapter twelve

The day began early at the ashram. Before sunrise, Stephanie heard the quiet patter of rubber flip-flops on the stone floors as people rose, bathed and dressed for morning worship. Ma Vera had told her to stay in bed and she would come and get her for the morning meal. She seemed pleased that Stephanie had decided to stay for a few days and told her she shouldn't feel compelled to take part in the devotions. Stephanie remembered the trip into town with Manu the previous afternoon. Manu had behaved so strangely when she asked about Ann, like a mouse suddenly running smack into the cat. She refused to say any more and they had walked to the Post Office in silence. They were unable to place the phone call, despite Manu's determination to avoid any "shenanigans," because of an inability to connect with an overseas line. Quite common, apparently, but annoying and upsetting for Stephanie. She finally agreed to leave a cable message to be transmitted when the lines were clear.

Am well cared for. Staying a few days to clear details. Love you. Don't worry.

Breakfast consisted of thick porridge and curds, a dense yogurt made from rich buffalo milk. Herb tea and fresh, warm bread were also available, along with stubby, sweet bananas and foot-long slices of papaya.

She and Ma Vera were joined at their table by a blind man and his wife who were introduced as Werner and Else. Werner was about five foot eight, with a medium build and brown hair that was a mass of unkempt curls. In contrast, his carefully clipped beard and mustache were a rich shiny black that drew attention to the lower half of his face and away from the asymmetrical stare of his pale green eyes.

Else had the robust good looks of a woman who had been raised in the country and fed plenty of fresh milk and eggs. She was a couple of inches shorter than her husband but probably matched him in weight. Her arms and hands looked strong, like those of someone used to lifting heavy objects. Her figure was well proportioned and unfashionably voluptuous. Golden blonde hair, short and fine, framed her face in straight lines like a paper cutout.

Werner had been blind from the age of sixteen and Else had been his guide for the twelve years of their marriage. They spoke English with a German accent but were in fact from Austria, a distinction they made clear from the outset.

"Austria is different from Germany," Else said, "much as I'm sure Canada is different from the United States and Sweden is different from Denmark." Else kept up a steady stream of patter, interrupting herself occasionally to describe something to Werner. "Oh look, Werner," she'd say, as if he could see, "there's Manfred and he's sitting beside Lisette, that little French girl I told you about, the one with the shaved head like a Hare Krishna. I think

Manfred has a crush on her, poor boy. I'm sure she can't see him for a hill of beans." Werner nodded his head in agreement, his blind gaze staring far beyond the walls of the cafeteria. He smiled contentedly and Else continued chattering.

"They say he went crazy last year in Colombo and set fire to a hotel," she said to Stephanie, nodding her head in Manfred's direction. "Drugs," she whispered knowingly. "I'm sure of it."

"Else," Ma Vera said disapprovingly, "that's gossip and you're repeating it to someone who's never even met Manfred. You do a disservice to both of them. It's uncharitable."

Stephanie heard a low chuckle emerge from Werner's throat. "You are fighting a losing battle, Ma Vera, if you think you can change her. She is an incorrigible dramatizer who refuses to stick to the facts." He turned his unfocused gaze in Stephanie's direction. "Manfred is the son of a prominent Berlin doctor whom he firmly believes was a member of Hitler's S.S. Manfred feels it is his social responsibility to be a rebel. German youth carry a tremendous burden of guilt because of the war. Their parents refuse to talk about it and so the children often imagine the worst. Manfred is an extreme example of this, but how do you think he is able to afford to travel the world?" He looked around the table.

"His father sends him checks, that's how," said Else, a hint of righteous indignation in her voice.

"Yes, absolutely," said Werner. "You have a word for that in English, when someone is paid by his parents to stay away from home."

"Remittance man," volunteered Ma Vera.

"Remittance man, yes," said Werner. "Manfred is a remittance man." He chuckled again and settled back in his chair.

Else took this as her cue to speak again and she launched, for no apparent reason, into the topic of vitamin therapy, quoting everyone from Adelle Davis to Linus Pauling.

She's like a bird on a wire, thought Stephanie, and the wire has an electric current zinging through it that charges her with a kind of manic energy. Else drew Werner into the conversation every chance she got, yet he seemed very undemanding and content. She's so diligent, thought Stephanie, as if she has some kind of mission in life. If she wasn't married to a blind man, she'd probably be married to a paraplegic.

"I told them they should give your mother Beta-carotene for her immune system," Else was saying, "but they wouldn't listen to me."

"What did you say?" asked Stephanie, who had been absorbed in her own thoughts while Else chattered.

"I told them to give your mother Beta-carotene but they wouldn't listen," Else repeated.

"Why should they have given her Beta-carotene?" Stephanie asked, suddenly interested in what Else had to say.

"Beta-carotene strengthens the immune system. Her white blood cell count was down because of the poisons in her system."

"What poisons?" asked Stephanie.

"From her illness, you know," Else said patiently. "She was getting weaker and weaker and she couldn't fight the illness any longer."

"What was done for my mother?" Stephanie demanded, turning to Ma Vera.

"Everything was done, my dear, I assure you," she replied, in a soothing tone. "If Beta-carotene would have helped, I'm sure we would have given it to her." She looked at Else sternly but the younger woman continued to talk.

"But they could have tried it," said Else indignantly. "They should have learned after Vishnu died so suddenly that you can't take any chances."

"Vishnu?" asked Stephanie.

"Vishnu was here for a while to help with the accounting," Ma Vera said quickly, before Else had a chance to reply. "He took ill quite suddenly and died within forty-eight hours. Very sad. It happens like that sometimes in this part of the world."

At that point, Stephanie heard Werner say something to Else in German. She uttered a long "Ohhh" and turned to Stephanie.

"I am so sorry," she said. "I have been careless to talk in this way to you, Stephanie. Please forgive me. I sometimes talk too much without thinking." She turned to Werner as if seeking his approval but he spoke to Stephanie.

"Please accept our condolences, Stephanie. It was not appropriate for us to speak of these things. Now Else," he said, pushing back his chair, "we must go. It is time for music therapy."

When they were out of earshot, Ma Vera said to Stephanie, "You shouldn't pay any mind to Else. She tends to dither sometimes and get caught up in her own thoughts. She's a good person, really. It mustn't be easy guiding a blind man around India. She has to look out for the both of them."

Stephanie said nothing. She was thinking about what Else had said about her mother's illness and the "poisons" in her body. Was she referring to an infection, or to something more specific? Stephanie wondered who had diagnosed Ann's illness and who had prescribed treatment.

"You were with my mother when she died, weren't you?" she asked Ma Vera. The older woman nodded. "What can you tell me? What exactly did she die of?"

"I'm not a doctor, my dear, so I can't really say." Ma Vera's discomfort reminded Stephanie of Manu's reaction on the bus.

"But surely somebody knew what she had," Stephanie persisted. "Wasn't a doctor called in?"

"Yes, your mother saw a doctor," said Ma Vera slowly, as if by drawing out her answer they might run out of time.

"Well, what did he say?"

"He wanted to do some tests before he could be sure of a diagnosis." Ma Vera seemed determined not to volunteer anything.

"But did he have any idea what it might be? He must have thought something."

"You know how doctors are, my dear. They rarely offer a guess in case they're wrong."

"Did he do the tests? Were there any results?" Stephanie didn't like prodding Ma Vera, but her reluctance to answer made Stephanie more stubborn and she persisted.

"Only a blood test. Unfortunately your mother felt she was too ill to undergo any further tests. She would have had to travel to town, you see, and she wanted to wait until she felt stronger. She clearly felt she would get better."

But she didn't, thought Stephanie. Had they really done everything possible for her or had they drastically miscalculated the extent of her illness and let her die through sheer negligence? And who was this Vishnu that Else had mentioned? Had he died of the same thing? Manu hadn't said anything about him; in fact, she had stated that no one else had the same illness as Ann. Why were they so reluctant to give her the facts?

"What was the name of the doctor?" she asked Ma Vera, as they rose to leave.

Ma Vera felt old and tired all of a sudden, as if she had lived too long. "Dr. Gopal Singh," she said. "He has a private practice in town."

chapter thirteen

It was already too hot to take the bus into town, so Stephanie decided to wait until after lunch to speak to Dr. Gopal Singh. She spent the rest of the morning checking out the ashram's facilities, hoping the time would pass more quickly. The main building resembled an ancient southern mansion built around an inner courtyard. It was white, a combination of wood and stucco with dark green shutters and doors. She walked around the perimeter of the courtyard, glancing occasionally through the unshuttered windows on the ground floor to watch a class or therapy session in progress. There were no more than half a dozen people involved in any one gathering and the disconnected sounds of chanting and individual instruction mingled in the air with the sound of sitar music. The sense of activity was muted as if it were happening far away and in slow motion. The dense heat stifled the energy of the morning.

The upper two floors of the main building consisted of small sleeping rooms and bathrooms that opened onto the common balcony overlooking the courtyard. The dining room was on the east side of the building, but the kitchen, Stephanie discovered, was in a separate bungalow twenty feet behind the main building. Beyond the cookhouse were the outdoor ovens, fueled by wood fires, and used for baking bread and slow cooking. The well was a good twenty-five feet to the south of the cookhouse. A bank of trees defined the boundaries of the property at its furthest eastern reaches.

Stephanie followed the trees in a southerly direction and passed what looked like a temple on her right. It was a simple wooden structure but its roof was a series of ornately carved layers stacked like a wedding cake and topped with a circular golden dome. The structure itself was whitewashed and its flat, grainy surface contrasted with the glinting gold of the dome.

The southern perimeter of the property was defined by a river that clearly was running at less than full capacity. No doubt the rains, when they came, would quickly submerge the smooth white stones that lay on the river's banks. She could almost smell the stones baking in the sun like little hot biscuits on a metal pan. At the same time, the river had its own smell, like a thin soup with all the flavor boiled out of it.

The vegetable garden was planted close to the river, probably to enable watering and irrigation, and Stephanie was surprised to see row upon row of vines and stalks, onions, eggplants, gourds, carrots, beans, peas, tomatoes, all immaculately planted, labeled, staked and weeded, their leaves spotted brown by the unforgiving sun. A few trees provided shade during the long afternoon, but most of the western half of the ashram consisted of grassy areas and footpaths edged with bushes and tall, spiky plants that required little water to sustain life.

The main road to town ran along the western edge of the ashram. Stephanie walked toward the north end, past the main entrance, noting the abundantly planted flowerbeds that hugged the corners of the building. Here and there she would spot a white-clad figure in a straw hat, indistinguishable as male or female, crouched over a section of the garden, carefully tending the plants. Presumably, they were assigned these tasks. Stephanie didn't believe such order could be maintained on a voluntary basis.

At the north end of the property were the stables and hen house, also shaded from the afternoon sun by a few trees. Between the stables and the main building was another white bungalow that Stephanie discovered was for casting clay pots. Again, the baking oven was outside the pottery house. The spinning room Ma Vera had taken her to the previous day was directly east of this. Looking around, Stephanie figured the ashram property to be somewhere between eight and ten acres.

She slipped through the main building into the courtyard, catching a glimpse of Manfred, the young man Else had been talking about, climbing the stairs to the second floor balcony. Three more people emerged from one of the classrooms and crossed the quadrangle to another. It reminded Stephanie of her university days, people moving silently from class to class, deep in thought, carrying notebooks. But instead of blue jeans and sweaters, these students wore baggy homespun pants and loose shirts that protected them from the sun.

Stephanie decided to write a letter to her father before the midday meal. She would use the excuse of mailing the letter to make the trip into town to find Dr. Gopal Singh.

"Dear Dad," she wrote, when she was back in her room on the top floor, "Please don't be too upset with me for not coming straight home to be with you. I arrived here two days ago to find that Mother had died and you had already been notified by cable. I was upset and exhausted and they put me straight to bed. I think someone was with me the whole time. They have been extremely kind, especially an older woman who calls herself Ma Vera, and a young Indian woman called Manu. I have met Deva Mother (both she and Ma Vera are English, by the way, in their sixties) but I have not seen the Guru Father yet. Ma Vera worked very hard to persuade me to stay a few days and rest up before I travel again. She seems to have been very fond of Mother and feels responsible for me, I think. They've given me the run of the place, lots to eat and a little room to sleep in. I will offer to pay, but if they refuse, I'll leave a donation to the ashram.

"I've been trying to find out exactly what happened to Mother, but everyone seems reluctant to talk about it. There's no easy way to tell you this, but they cremated her remains before I got here. I couldn't believe it and was going to raise a stink, but Deva Mother told me that it was what Mom had requested. I'll see about bringing her ashes back with me so we can have a memorial service and a proper burial. This afternoon I'm going to town to mail this letter and I'll talk to the doctor who treated her. He prescribed some tests but she wasn't feeling up to them. That must have been when she decided to try and come home.

"I can see how she might have been happy here. The ashram is a nice place, simple and a bit remote, but well tended and peaceful. There are quite a few Europeans here (and probably some North Americans, but I haven't met any yet). They seem to take classes and meditate most of the time. I've also seen them gardening, weaving and making clay pots. The place seems pretty self-sufficient, supplying most of its own food as far as I can see. I assume they must buy rice, flour and sugar and other staples from the town.

"There's no car here, just some ancient-looking bicycles. You have to catch a bus, which passes on the main road every couple of hours, to get to town. You can get a taxi back, but it costs quite a bit unless you can guarantee a return fare.

"Please don't worry about me, Dad. I'm fine and will probably be home before this letter gets to you. I tried to reach you by phone yesterday but it was impossible to get an overseas line, so I sent you a cable (which I hope you have by now). I will try again to phone you and will wire you as soon as I am on my way home. All my love, Steph."

She caught the bus right after lunch, reassuring Ma Vera she was just going to mail a letter and would have no trouble. She knew the way now and there was no possible way she could get lost. The ride was as rough as the day before, but this time she noticed that the other passengers stared at her most of the time, something she hadn't been aware of when she'd been with Manu. Staring at foreigners seemed to be a favorite preoccupation in India. She'd been aware of it in Bombay as well, on the street, at the station, wherever the train stopped. She must have looked a lot stranger to them than they looked to her. For the most part she ignored them. It was hopeless to try and outstare them. Their fascination was boundless; they never tired of looking at her.

The post office was only two blocks from the bus terminal and Stephanie took her time, stopping to look at the storefronts and stalls that sold rice, vegetables, sweets, fried snacks, fabrics of astonishing color and variety, silver jewelry and plastic bangles. Midnapor was built like a frontier town, rough and tumble, vendors staking a claim to a piece of turf and then throwing a couple of walls and a roof on it. It looked like a shantytown that had established itself and now nobody questioned its right to be there. No doubt a complicated system of rents and taxes had evolved over time and probably no one questioned that either.

Stephanie mailed her letter and then followed the same procedure as the previous day to put a call through on the telephone. This time the call went through but the phone on the other end rang several times without being picked up. Then she remembered that her father was at a conference in Ottawa. He might not even know yet that Ann was dead. He had given Stephanie a list of phone numbers, but she had forgotten all about them. They were probably somewhere in the bottom of her big handbag that was hanging on the back of the door in her room at the ashram.

Damn, she thought. I should have remembered. She couldn't even call his office because it would be the middle of the night over there. She decided there was nothing she could do for the moment. She went back to the counter and asked the clerk if he knew where she could find Dr. Gopal Singh. He knew the doctor and gave her directions to his office, which was only three blocks beyond the post office.

Dr. Gopal Singh's office was in a bungalow of whitewashed stucco that he shared with a dentist and another doctor who, according to his shingle, specialized in the "homeopathic treatment of childbirth and internal diseases, male and female." Dr. Gopal Singh advertised himself as a General Practitioner.

She opened the door with his name on it and poked her head in, expecting to see a nurse or receptionist. Instead she saw a clean-shaven man, middle-aged, with short, thick, wavy black hair combed straight back from his face, wearing a white lab coat over a blue shirt and a black necktie. He was sitting behind a very old wooden desk, making notes from an open file in front of him. He looked up as she entered the room and smiled. "Can I help you?" he said.

"I'm looking for Dr. Gopal Singh."

"I am he."

"Oh," she said quickly, "I'm sorry, I thought you might be–that is, I uh, expected to find a nurse."

"Is it a medical matter you wish to see me about?" Dr. Gopal Singh asked, ignoring her discomfort. "I am a professional doctor. I assure you, there is nothing to be concerned about."

"Oh, no, it's nothing like that," said Stephanie, feeling foolish. "I wanted to talk to you about my mother. She was staying at the ashram. I'm Stephanie Hobart and my mother was Ann Hobart. They told me you were called in to see her."

"Ah, yes, I remember her," the doctor said, indicating that Stephanie should sit on the chair in front of his desk. "What was it you wanted to know?"

"I wanted to know what your diagnosis was and whether or not you prescribed any treatment."

"Well," he said, looking at the wall behind Stephanie as if he were consulting a chart there, "it was difficult to make a diagnosis without some tests I wanted Mrs. Hobart to have. She was reluctant to leave the ashram as she was already very weak by the time I saw her. I offered to take her to the clinic in my own car–I really felt it imperative that treatment should start immediately–but she refused. Perhaps she felt it would do no good, that our facilities were too primitive. I can't be certain, you see, as to why she refused, but she said she was already making arrangements to go home to Canada. I tried to dissuade her by telling her I didn't feel she was up to it, but she only thanked me for my concern and said she would be fine." He smiled at Stephanie as if to say, I tried.

"Why did you advise against traveling?" asked Stephanie. "Did she have a high fever?"

"There was fever, yes, and vomiting," the doctor was tapping the tips of his fingers together, forming a pyramid with his hands, "but it was her irregular heart rate that I was most concerned about. It was inconsistent with the other symptoms. That was why I wanted her to have the tests."

"What do you mean inconsistent?" Stephanie asked. "What did you think might be the matter?"

"The fever, the stomach pains, the vomiting, were all consistent with a possible gastro-intestinal disorder," he explained. "That could be anything from gastritis to food poisoning. Some kind of inflammation was indicated by the tenderness and pain in the abdominal area. But an irregular heartbeat is not usual in these cases. Her fever was not that high and she had not had any convulsions, or at least, that is what I was told. I was quite anxious about this."

"What would an irregular heartbeat indicate?"

"Some kind of heart disease, most likely. A blockage, perhaps. Did your mother have any history of heart problems?"

"No, she didn't," said Stephanie, trying to remember if her mother had ever mentioned such a thing. "I'm sure she didn't." Ann wouldn't have kept something like that a secret.

The doctor continued to tap his fingertips together, waiting for Stephanie to continue. She kept her eyes focused on the big toe of her right foot, trying to put the pieces together in her mind.

"What did she die of?" she asked, finally.

The doctor sat forward in his chair and rested his elbows on the desk. "I had to put cardiac arrest on the death certificate," he said. "Without an autopsy, it is impossible to know what the exact cause of death was."

"Cardiac arrest?" said Stephanie, showing her surprise.

"Yes, Miss Hobart. Her heart stopped."

Stephanie wasn't sure what she had expected to hear, but it definitely wasn't cardiac arrest. "Did you say you signed a death certificate?"

"Yes, it is required by law. The Mother sent a messenger to me," he continued, "and told me the lady from Canada had died and would I come to sign the certificate. This is normal practice."

"Did they tell you what happened?"

"Only that Mrs. Hobart had taken a turn for the worse, that her fever had risen dramatically and that she had expired suddenly," he said in even, measured tones.

"Do you think her death could have been prevented if she had been properly diagnosed and treated?"

He looked at Stephanie and hunched his shoulders, letting out a long breath. "It is impossible to know that and I would be foolish to speculate," he said. "As a professional, however, it is frustrating not to have been able to try and save her life and also not to be able to tie her symptoms together into a single diagnosis." He wasn't prepared to say any more than that.

"Do you know anything about the man named Vishnu? The one who also died at the ashram?"

"Why do you want to know?" he asked cautiously.

"I'm wondering if he had the same thing as my mother."

"No, I don't think so," Dr. Gopal Singh said slowly. "This man Vishnu died very suddenly. He was apparently not ill until a few hours before his death."

That was all the doctor seemed prepared to say and Stephanie didn't want to push her luck.

"I appreciate your talking to me so frankly, Doctor Gopal Singh," she said, rising to go.

chapter fourteen

On the bus ride back to the ashram Stephanie didn't notice the swerving and swaying so much, as if she had acquired her "sea legs" and could roll with the lurching vehicle instead of being tossed around by it. She had a lot on her mind. The suggestion that her mother might have had some sort of heart disease was completely unexpected. It was as if they had been discussing a stranger. Ann had gone to the doctor and had her cholesterol tested before her trip. She had been pleased that the reading was well below average. So what could have happened between then and now? It had been less than six months.

Back at the ashram, Stephanie went to speak to Deva Mother about the arrangements for taking Ann's ashes back to Canada. Deva Mother's secretary, a young Indian woman named Samina, was seated at a desk in the anteroom adjoining the office and smiled when Stephanie walked in. "You wish to see Deva Mother?"

"Yes," said Stephanie, "but I can wait if she's busy."

Samina nodded and said she would see if Deva Mother was

free. She was thin and dark-skinned with enormous black eyes that she rimmed with kohl to make them look even larger. Samina had been shy and awkward all her life and was uncomfortable when people paid any attention to her. She spoke softly and usually had to repeat herself because people didn't hear her. She seemed happiest when she was banging away on the ancient manual typewriter that sat on her desk.

When she returned she said, "Deva Mother says I should offer you some tea while you are waiting. She will see you in a few minutes."

"Thank you," said Stephanie. She was thirsty after the bus ride back from town.

Samina scurried off to get the tea and Stephanie put her head back and closed her eyes. Things just weren't adding up. Nobody seemed convinced of what they were telling her. It was as if they'd all seen a different act of the same play and they were each missing a significant part of the story.

It reminded her of the first time her parents sent her to summer camp. She was eight years old and reluctant to go. She had never been away from her parents and was used to her own company. "Why do I have to go?" she asked. "I'd rather stay here."

"You'll get to meet new people," her mother told her. "You'll make friends and have lots of fun." Her mother's cheerfulness had been edged with a patient firmness and sounded unconvincing to her skeptical daughter.

"You'll learn to ride a horse and paddle a canoe," her father told her. "You'll feel you've accomplished something when you get back. It'll be good for you." Her father's voice had a commanding tone, as if to say, this is what you must do at camp.

Well, she had met new people and learned to ride a horse and paddle a canoe, but she hadn't made friends or felt a sense of accomplishment. Everybody learned to ride and paddle, so it was nothing special. Her parents had conned her. The things they told her about camp were just excuses to get her there.

They had been half-truths, superficial statements that didn't stand up to scrutiny.

She had the same sense about what people were telling her now. They kept talking about symptoms and observations, but none of their stories had a beginning, middle or end. They were just words.

Samina returned with the tea and Stephanie sipped on the hot, sweet liquid while she waited for Deva Mother. Samina went back to her typewriter and inserted several sheets of paper with carbons in between and began to pound out a letter. Stephanie wondered what Samina's reaction would be to computers, photocopiers and fax machines. In a few minutes Deva Mother opened the door of her office and signaled for Stephanie to come in.

"Good afternoon, Stephanie," she said graciously, indicating a chair facing her desk. Stephanie thought she looked even thinner than before. But maybe it was just the light.

"Good afternoon," said Stephanie. She felt awkward addressing her as "Mother" so she said nothing. "Thank you for seeing me."

"It's no trouble, I assure you." Deva Mother sat behind her desk, a large, heavy-looking piece of furniture piled with files and bundles of paper tied together with string.

"I'll be going back to Bombay in a couple of days," Stephanie began, "and I want to take my mother's ashes with me, as well as any paperwork, like the death certificate. I also want to pack up her things, if that hasn't already been done."

"Of course," said Deva Mother. "I'll ask Ma Vera to get Ann's belongings for you. I believe she has already put them away for safekeeping." The fingers of Deva Mother's left hand flipped through the pile of papers on her desk.

"As to your mother's ashes," she said, continuing to flip through the papers, "I'm afraid it won't be possible for you to take them with you. You see, it is our custom to give the physical remains back to the earth, so of course we scattered your mother's ashes on the ashram grounds."

It was another piece of the story she hadn't been told. Stephanie's resentment at the way things were being controlled by the ashram went up a notch. Her body tensed. "What?" she said. Her voice sounded loud in the quiet room. "You must be kidding. Surely you knew her family would want a say in all this? You're English. You know the family has certain rights."

"But you misunderstand, Stephanie," Deva Mother continued, patience underscoring the refined tones of her voice. "Ann was part of our family. She had pledged her life to Guru Father. She was planning on taking her vows before she fell ill. So you see, we were acting in accordance with her own wishes."

"What are you saying?" Stephanie was leaning forward and had placed her hands on Deva Mother's desk. "Are you telling me my mother was going to become a monk, or nun, or whatever it is you become here?"

"Yes, that's what I'm saying. Ann was going to take the vows of a sannyasin. She had made up her mind."

"Forgive me if I find that hard to believe," said Stephanie, trying to control the range of emotions she was feeling. "She never mentioned such a thing in her letters and I'm sure she wouldn't have done anything that drastic without speaking to my father about it." Stephanie could hear her heart pounding in her ears and forced herself to calm down.

Deva Mother said nothing for a couple of minutes. She pretended to be reading something on the desk in front of her. When she looked up, Stephanie appeared no calmer. "I didn't mean to upset you," Deva Mother said, gently. "I didn't realize you weren't aware of your mother's plans." When Stephanie didn't reply, Deva Mother went on. "Ann decided at some point to return to Canada, ostensibly for medical tests. Perhaps she planned to tell you and your father of her plans in person. There was also the matter of a transfer of funds."

"Transfer of funds?" echoed Stephanie. "What transfer of funds?"

"Your mother was preparing to donate a large sum of money to the ashram. It was to affirm her commitment and also to divest herself of her worldly goods. That's why I am so certain of her plans. She told me this herself." Deva Mother's eyes were cool and clear as she waited for Stephanie's reaction.

Stephanie's cheeks were stinging and her eyes were smarting, as if someone had slapped her. She swallowed hard before speaking.

"Do you have anything in writing?"

"No," said Deva Mother. "Ann's illness prevented her from carrying out her plans. She was confined to her bed and her condition deteriorated quite rapidly."

"Who was actually looking after her? I've been trying to understand exactly what happened but pieces of the story seem to be missing."

"There are no pieces missing," Deva Mother said firmly. "Ma Vera and I cared for your mother ourselves. We administered cleansing herbs and broth but she continued to lose strength. Dr. Gopal Singh was consulted at Ann's request, but he was unwilling to diagnose without taking some sort of tests, which your mother refused. I assure you, none of us knew she would be taken by this illness. She just seemed suddenly to take a turn for the worse and there was nothing anyone could have done."

Stephanie didn't tell Deva Mother she had been to see Dr. Gopal Singh and that he had told her about Ann's irregular heart rate. If she knew about it, Deva Mother chose not to mention it. "I am sorry, my dear," Deva Mother continued, "but we cannot know what God has decided for us."

A jumble of thoughts were flying around in Stephanie's brain while she tried to make sense of what Deva Mother was saying. Was she lying? She was so cool and controlled. I don't believe her, Stephanie thought. Mother just wouldn't do that. Or would she? Maybe she got so caught up in it all that she really thought she'd found her place in the world. Maybe she did come to believe that this was her destiny. But could she have left Dad and me to come and live on the other side of the world? Was she planning to divorce him and give the settlement to the ashram? Did she think we'd let her go so easily?

Stephanie stood up abruptly. "Would you excuse me please?" she said quickly. "I need to be alone for a while."

"Certainly, my dear," said Deva Mother. "I understand."

Back in her room, Stephanie took out the packet of letters her mother had written during her stay at the ashram. She pored over the words, examining even the handwriting and punctuation for some hint of her mother's intentions. But although Ann had written enthusiastically about every aspect of the place, not one word indicated that she had decided to spend the rest of her life there.

"I have made some new friends here," she wrote, *"and we have long talks about life and love and the universal principle. It is quite wonderful to be with like-minded people and experience all this support and reinforcement of your ideas. Yet, these people are as different from each other as I am from them in terms of life experience, age and reasons for being here. But I guess at some level we're all 'seekers'; we're all looking for something that we feel is missing from our lives.*

"Ma Vera is an Englishwoman in her sixties who's been here for nearly twenty-five years (it's hard to imagine) and this is the only home she has. She has nothing to go back to, hasn't been in England since 1947 when she came here to work on Mountbatten's staff during the independence and partition thing. Fascinating, but she doesn't like to talk about it much. She can be a bit of a curmudgeon but she's so stouthearted and loyal, absolutely devoted to Guru Father.

"And then there's Allan, a young American man from a family of doctors who came here after his girlfriend was killed in a motorcycle accident. He's very sweet and kind, but I know he has a lot of anger to deal with. I think right now he's looking for

something he can believe in that will make sense of the tragedy in his life.

"There's also a young Indian woman, Manu (did you know that was the name of Mahatma Gandhi's niece, the one who was his protégé, and companion?), who appears to be from a good Brahmin family but I haven't figured out why she's here. And of course I'm too polite to ask ... but I'll find out somehow. I see her looking at Allan with a 'moon-June-spoon' look in her eyes and I wonder if he'll ever notice it without someone drawing it to his attention (who, me?).

"Anyway, somehow we've all come to be in the same place needing the same thing: answers. Something that will stay with us forever, wherever we are. I miss you and your old man. Write soon. Love, Mom."

chapter fifteen

llan Lloyd sat alone at the far end of the cafeteria and prodded the hill of brown rice on his plate. Something had been bothering him for days now and the arrival of Ann's daughter at the ashram had forced to the surface thoughts that he had been trying desperately to ignore. Why had Ann died? Her illness didn't seem life threatening; the symptoms appeared to be under control. It should have been a simple matter of the bacteria running its course and her body gradually regaining strength. But the night before she died, he had slipped in to see her and had found her in a great deal of distress.

"My heart feels like it's stuck in my throat and my arms and legs feel like jello," she told him. "I've never felt this way before, Allan."

He had taken her slender wrist in his hand and felt her pulse. It had wobbled erratically as if her heart were fibrillating. "You should be in a hospital," he said. "I'm going to speak to Deva Mother."

"No, no," she had said quickly. "Don't be silly. I'm not that sick. Really. I'm just nervous about being alone. I never liked being left alone when I was sick." She had smiled reassuringly at him and he had sat and held her hand until she fell asleep. But within twenty-four hours she was dead. Had he been negligent in not insisting she be taken to hospital? Would there have been anything they could do to save her anyway?

He had not wanted to ask himself these questions because he knew there were no answers. He wasn't qualified to make a diagnosis and his knowledge of tropical diseases was limited. But something about Ann's fluctuating pulse rate alarmed him. He wished he could have consulted a medical textbook. There was probably some explanation, but he couldn't get at it. I guess that's what they mean by "a little bit of learning is a dangerous thing," he thought, reflecting on his abandoned medical studies.

"Is this a private party or can anyone join in?"

He looked up to see Manu smiling shyly, holding a tray of food. "Yes, please, join me," he said, awkwardly, half rising from his chair as he remembered his grandfather's rule about standing when a lady entered the room.

Manu put her tray down and sat opposite him. She began to eat slowly, noting that his food remained untouched. "Is something bothering you, Allan?" she asked. "You seem sort of distracted." She felt self-conscious asking him this. She was not usually so bold with the young men at the ashram. But his anguish concerned her and she wanted him to talk to her.

"I was thinking about Ann," he said and she saw his eyes glance in the direction of Stephanie, who was eating her dinner with Ma Vera a few tables over.

"What about her?" Manu asked, holding her fork midway between her plate and her mouth.

Allan seemed to be looking straight into Manu's pupils, as if straining to read some message printed at the back of her eyes. Neither of them moved for a long moment, then he blinked and looked down at the now cold food on his plate.

"I was thinking how she shouldn't have died," he said quietly, without looking up.

Her heart had skipped a beat. Manu glanced at the other diners. Nothing in the room had changed. The hum of conversation continued without pause.

"She was very ill," she whispered, but her voice sounded harsh and grating in her ears.

"Yes, she was very ill," he said, "but it was the kind of illness that healthy people survive. And I believe Ann was a healthy person."

He began to shovel the lumpy brown rice into his mouth, taking no notice of its gluey coldness. His eyes seemed to burn with defiance as if he were daring her to contradict him.

"We didn't know her very long. Maybe there was something else wrong," she offered feebly.

"Maybe, but I saw no sign of it."

They continued to eat in silence and when he was done Allan abruptly stood up and excused himself. Manu watched him return his tray to the food counter and walk toward the table where Stephanie and Ma Vera were just finishing their meal.

She wished he had stayed and talked to her a little bit longer. Allan seemed to be trying to resolve something in his mind and she hadn't wanted to annoy him by indulging in small talk. People were often absorbed in their own thoughts at the ashram and Manu found it difficult to engage them in conversation. She thought it was because they didn't take her seriously. Or maybe they didn't think she had anything of value to say. She wasn't very good at getting people's attention, but whenever the opportunity arose, she loved to exchange ideas and discuss theories of perception. Being surrounded by foreigners provided her with a perfect opportunity to study the culturally determined attitudes of her fellow man. What was it Stephanie had said to her on the bus? "Those are questions without answers." Of course the very opposite was true. The questions she asked had as many answers as there were people on the earth. Didn't it all come down to people creating their individual realities in order to comfortably house what they wanted to believe?

Stephanie's insistence on an empirical reality was much like Allan's scientific approach. He felt Ann "shouldn't" have died, that she must have been more ill than they realized. It hadn't occurred to him that possibly Ann's time had come. That God had a reason for taking her now. It was a matter of faith, and even though Allan practiced being devout and desperately wanted to free his spirit from the burdens of an earthly reality, he was still immersed in a perceptual pattern of cause and effect that could be seen and proved. Manu wished she could help him free himself, wished he would let her help. But she knew it wasn't time yet and she would have to be patient. "A mango is ripe when it is ripe," Guru Father once told her, "and you must wait for that moment. Otherwise you will miss the true sweetness of the fruit and must be satisfied with less."

"Good evening, Ma Vera," Allan said to the older woman as she was finishing her meal. Then he turned to Stephanie. "I'm Allan Lloyd. The last time we met you were in a state of shock. I'm very sorry about your mother. She was a friend of mine."

Stephanie looked at the young man standing beside their table. He was about her age and size, with a slim build and broad shoulders. His hair was a dark copper color, in stark contrast to his pale, milky skin, which was almost a match for the natural white homespun of his shirt. But the most distinctive thing about him was the almost transparent quality of his pale blue eyes. He looked as if he had been bleached by the sun, the color leeched out of his features by the elements. The whole effect was of purity and strength, like a starched linen tablecloth laid on a solid oak table.

"Will you come for a walk with me when you've finished your

tea?" he said to Stephanie. "Would you mind, Ma Vera?"

"Of course not, Allan. My knees are still bothering me. I just want to rub some camphor into them and put my feet up. You two go now while it's still light."

Stephanie picked up her tray and took it over to the food counter. She and Allan left the building by the back exit and started walking toward the temple.

"It's nice down by the river at this time of day," he said. "The sound of water is very soothing, don't you think?"

"Yes," said Stephanie, wondering what he wanted to talk to her about.

"I'm sure that must be a universal truth," he said, smiling. "Your mother and I often walked along the river. We used to have long talks. I was very fond of her. She helped me a lot."

Stephanie looked at the pale young man beside her and tried to imagine her mother deep in conversation with him. In the fading light of early evening, his features seemed even less distinguishable than before. The line of his eyebrows was like a shadow on his brow and his lips were only slightly darker than the rest of his face. He appeared fragile, almost translucent, but she could feel the strength of his will the way you feel heat from a fire.

"Will you be staying long?" he asked, as if he were trying to postpone the real conversation.

"A few days," she replied. "I'm just trying to catch my breath before I head back. Ma Vera insisted I rest up before I travel again. She must think I got here by foot, the way she goes on. She's very sweet, really."

He laughed. "The Ma Vera we know and love is not renowned for her sweetness, believe me. She's got a good heart but she's as tough as a Brazil nut." Stephanie smiled, remembering her mother's letter referring to Ma Vera as a bit of a curmudgeon. So far the old woman had been extremely kind to Stephanie, with no hint of the sterner side of her nature.

"I gather you didn't know that Ann had died when you

arrived here," Allan continued, his tone subdued. "It must have been a terrible shock."

"It was. My father and I got a letter telling us she was coming home and what flight she would be on. We were at the airport but she wasn't on the plane. You can imagine how worried we were. We knew she was sick–that's why she was coming home, for tests–so we thought maybe she was too sick to travel. I figured the fastest way to get her home was to come here myself and bring her back."

Allan didn't say anything for a couple of minutes. They had reached the river and were standing on the bank looking across the water. He bent to pick up a stone and began to rub its smooth, dry surface with his fingers. "She gave you an exact date of arrival?" he finally asked.

"Yes, and a flight number." Stephanie slid her feet out of her sandals and dug at the pebbles with her toes.

"That's news to me. She didn't say anything about making the booking, or even about going home, for that matter."

"Deva Mother told me she was planning to go home for medical tests, but that she would be coming back to take her vows. That was news to me. She never mentioned anything about it in her letters."

Allan began to toss and catch the stone he had been holding as if he were trying to guess its weight. "I wonder why she didn't tell me," he said.

"Is that the kind of thing she would have told you?" Stephanie wondered how close her mother had been to this young man.

"Yes, I think she would have." He tossed the stone into the river and it landed with a soft plop that sent a widening circle of ripples across the water. "I was with her the night before she died, you know."

Stephanie knew this was what he wanted to talk to her about and she waited for him to go on.

"I told her she should be in a hospital. I wanted to get Deva

Mother and tell her, but Ann insisted she wasn't that sick. But her pulse rate was erratic and it worried me."

"That's what the doctor told me," Stephanie said. "He wanted her to have tests."

So there *had* been something unusual in the pulse rate, he thought. I wasn't imagining it. "Did he tell you what he thought was wrong with her?"

"He asked me if she had any history of heart disease and I told him I wasn't aware of it. Do you think that's what killed her?"

"I don't know," he said, scooping up a handful of stones and tossing them like a snowball into the water. "I dropped out of med school, so I know a little bit about medicine but not enough to form a diagnosis. I honestly didn't think she was going to die. But I guess things happen that way sometimes."

"Nobody seems to have expected her to die. Least of all my father and me. And now I come here and find that things aren't clear at all. Everyone pokes around it but nobody wants to put their finger on a spot and tell me what happened. It's really pissing me off."

"I guess we're all still in shock."

By this time, they had walked around to the garden in front of the ashram building and Allan indicated a stone bench under an Acacia tree. As the sound of the river diminished, the chatter of insects and the crooning of nesting birds rose like the opening strains of a concerto.

"What do you know about this guy Vishnu who also died suddenly?" she asked when they were seated.

"Who told you about Vishnu?"

"Nobody actually told me about him, but his name came up in conversation with Werner and Else. Else said she thought more care should have been taken about my mother's illness after Vishnu died so suddenly. She seemed to imply that there was some negligence."

"Else's even more insensitive to your feelings than I am," he said with a self-conscious smile, "talking to you like that so soon after Ann's death."

"I'm not thin-skinned, if that's what you're afraid of. You can say what's on your mind and I'll take it my own way." Allan didn't look convinced. "Look, it's like a dance people do when they're getting to know each other. Else and Werner told me what was on their minds and I learned something about Else and Werner. Even Ma Vera revealed something about herself when she tried to smooth things over, telling me not to pay too much attention to what Else said.

"Most people don't want to rock the boat they're so afraid they might offend someone. Then there are a few people who want to stir things up, get everyone worked up and paying attention. They're the shit-disturbers; sometimes they speak the truth and sometimes they don't, but at least they get everybody thinking again. Then there are people like Else who like the sound of their own voice but are careless. They go by some kind of animal instinct; they react to everything in a very visceral way and we usually tune them out and dismiss them as being emotional. But they're really the ones we should listen to because they notice things the rest of us miss. They're very often right, even though they may not know why."

Allan thought for a moment before he spoke. "What line of work are you in that gives you these kinds of insights into people?"

"Current affairs television," she replied.

"Ah," he said, as if that explained everything. "So you see people as a source of information, is that it?"

"Not entirely. I think that the way people deal with information and the way they transmit it reveals a lot about their personality, like their handwriting or the way they dress."

"I hadn't quite thought of it that way. I come from a family of doctors where personality is more a matter of chemistry. In fact, the first thing you learn is that it's important to control your personality."

"Precisely," Stephanie said, "because doctors don't want to reveal anything. They don't want to betray their feelings because they're afraid it will influence how their patients absorb the information they're giving them."

Allan laughed. "I guess it's true," he said. "But unfortunately, that kind of training spills over into every aspect of your life. You get to a point where you don't know what you feel anymore because you've become so adept at concealing it." He was studying the criss-cross pattern of the leather straps on his sandals. Stephanie heard a brief sigh before he spoke again.

"You know, that's why I was attracted to your mother, as a friend, I mean. She wasn't very good at hiding her feelings and what she exposed to the world was what I was trying to bury inside myself."

"Like what?"

"Fear, insecurity, frustration, rage."

"You think my mother felt rage?"

"Oh yes, I think insecure people often feel rage at those they believe are their oppressors. Or if it isn't that specific, they feel it against a system or a world they can't seem to penetrate. I believe that."

She'd never thought of her mother as an angry person. Never showed concern that her mother's life involved a lot of frustration and pain. If anything, she'd been annoyed by it. Hadn't wanted to know about it.

"Where does your rage come from?" she asked him.

He was studying his shoes again as if the answer were hidden somewhere in the convoluted tapestry of the straps. "I think it comes from feeling trapped by a tradition, a family tradition of medicine, that had nothing to do with me personally. That I was caught because of an accident of birth and believed I wasn't free to choose another path. I could have, I suppose, but not without taking on a lot of other baggage, like the hurt and disapproval of my family and even the community. My family has been prominent in that community for a long time. There's even a hospital there named for my grandfather." He smiled half-heartedly and Stephanie saw defeat in his expression. He didn't tell her about Barbara. Maybe this wasn't the time. He'd told Ann but he'd broken down and cried. Ann had absorbed some of his grief and lightened the burden just a little bit. Stephanie seemed very different from her mother. She didn't telegraph her vulnerability the way Ann did. With Ann, the messages were very clear. If you prick me, I'll bleed, she seemed to say. And if you have pain, I'll feel it too.

"Tell me about Vishnu," Stephanie said, bringing the conversation back around.

"Yes, Vishnu," he said, kicking at a small stone that was under his shoe. "Vishnu arrived out of nowhere and very quickly seemed to be involved in the business end of the ashram, which you probably already know is Deva Mother's domain. She's been the business end of things around here for a long time, I understand. Guru Father is strictly spiritual. He's rarely seen anymore and only occasionally gives private audiences. He's quite old now, and they say his health is not so good."

Stephanie nodded and he continued. "Anyway, I don't know what kind of a sales pitch this Vishnu used, but he took over the accounting and books and probably would have ended up running things if he hadn't suddenly died."

"You never found out who he was or where he came from?"

"No, except that he was Anglo-Indian, somewhere in his forties and had the personality of a barracuda."

Stephanie laughed. "You didn't like him?"

Allan shrugged. "I didn't know him well enough to dislike him," he said, "but I had no interest in getting to know him. He seemed a little slick to me. Kind of small and wiry with an aggressive manner. I'm not drawn to pugnacious types."

"What did he die of?" She was getting tired of asking that question and not getting an answer.

"I wish I knew. He didn't seem to be sick, but he definitely ended up dead. One of those tropical fevers, I guess. My knowledge of diseases specific to this kind of climate is limited, I'm afraid. Nobody seemed to think too much of it. Although I must say, it made me uneasy and it really seemed to upset your mother."

"Really? How?"

"Well, she didn't sleep too well after it happened. Said she was having nightmares. Maybe she was afraid what he had was contagious."

"Do you think she had the same thing?"

"Well, if she did, it wasn't as virulent, obviously. It came on very slowly and she was sick for nearly two weeks before it took her. The symptoms just intensified, but " he hesitated before going on "maybe I shouldn't say this to you. Maybe it isn't fair. But–"

"Say it," said Stephanie.

It was almost dark and Stephanie could barely see his features, but she was aware of his clear, light eyes focused on her face like two intense beams from a pair of distant headlights.

"I don't think she should have died," he said, the force behind his words doubling the impact of the words themselves. He held her gaze for one long moment and she heard her own voice from a very long way off saying, "That's what I think, too."

chapter sixteen

When Stephanie awoke the next morning, her fourth day since arriving at the ashram, she knew she would have to make a decision. She must either finalize the arrangements and begin her journey back to Canada, or she must settle the mystery that had been growing in her mind about her mother's death. There was no question now that things were not what they seemed. Either the severity of Ann's illness had been underestimated, or the ashram had been negligent in caring for her. Worst of all was the suspicion that the ashram had somehow been the reason for her death and some of its members were deliberately trying to hide that fact.

Stephanie could hear the gentle footfall of rising ashramites as they headed for the bathrooms to perform the morning ritual. She would wait until they were all at their sunrise meditation before getting out of bed and dressing. Her eyes were burning from too little sleep and she tried to cool the closed lids by gently pressing them with her fingertips. Maybe she would sleep a little more. No need to be up before breakfast.

Stephanie carefully balanced her tray to keep the tea from spilling while at the same time tracking the room with her eyes until she spotted Werner and Else sitting side by side at one of the long wooden tables. She headed for the empty seat opposite them and lowered the tray onto the table.

"May I?" she asked, before taking a seat.

"Of course," said Else with apparent pleasure. "Look who it is, Werner. Stephanie has joined us for breakfast."

"Ah, good morning Stephanie," he said with courteous cheerfulness. "And how are you today?"

"Good morning, Werner. I'm very well, thank you. And you?" It was impossible to be anything less than cordial with Werner, he exuded such a gracious sense of refinement. Else, on the other hand, was all exuberant vulgarity. If Werner was a shiny, unpeeled and well-formed persimmon, Else could be compared to a fresh fig, pliant and bursting with ribald fleshiness. It's sex she exudes, thought Stephanie, and Werner doesn't have to see it, he can feel it like an electric charge in the air around her. The dynamic between her tension and his responsiveness was so vital they seemed to operate as a single unit. Each needed what the other had. And each was incomplete without the other.

"I am well, thank you," said Werner. "Else and I were just discussing the practice of Karma Yoga. It is the first of four paths that lead to Truth and one finds one's way along this path through work. Work for the sake of work without expectation of reward. What do you think, Stephanie? Does this appeal to you?" He was smiling across the table at her and she could tell by Else's flurry of giggles that he was teasing her.

"What are the other three?" she asked playfully. "Do I have a choice?"

"The true aspirant is wise to begin with Karma Yoga and the

path of service will lead naturally to Bhakti Yoga, which is worship through love. Then, if he continues along this path, it will lead to the practice of Raja Yoga. This is the yoga of psychic control, a very difficult undertaking and perhaps not suitable for the initiate. The final path is Jnana Yoga, and this is the route of self-analysis and knowledge."

Werner was obviously enjoying the role of enlightened informant. Else was attempting to make her spoon stand up in her oatmeal. "Obviously one's temperament would be a determining factor in making the choice," he continued. "For example, if a person was of a decidedly emotional nature, it might be logical to begin with Bhakti. But of course, I only know what I have read in books–or I should say what Else has read to me–and one must seek a spiritual teacher if one is to embark on such a journey."

"Is this what you and Else are planning to do?" Stephanie thought she saw a flicker of a grimace scoot across Else's face.

"No, no," said Werner, rubbing his beard. "We are merely passing through, you might say. Else and I have come here for a kind of retreat, you know, for refreshment. I think to become a sannyasin or 'take the vows' as they say, would require a great dedication. It must be your life's work in a way, because you must practice meditation and devotion for many hours. I am too curious to spend my life this way." He glanced affectionately in Else's direction. "And my dear wife would probably go right out of her mind. Yes, Else?"

"Yes, Werner, you are the most sensitive of men," she answered. They seemed to be very playful with each other this morning and Stephanie wondered what it must be like to be so absorbed in another person that your whole existence was defined by being part of a couple. Else turned to her and said:

"We have also been reading about Karma as penance for sins. It is almost like the Catholic Church. If you admit your sins and repent, they will be washed away."

"That's true, Else, but it specifically refers to minor offenses," said Werner. "If you truly repent of yelling at your husband, for example, this sin will be forgiven."

"Chauvinist," she said. "Yelling at your husband is not a sin; sometimes it is necessary to get his attention."

"Ah yes," sighed Werner, "a necessary evil."

Stephanie laughed. "But you know," Else continued, "they really believe some holy men are above sin. They can do anything they like, even murder millions of people, and they are not responsible."

"Well, I think it is more complicated than that," said Werner. "A truly enlightened Jnani, as he is called, cannot do a wrong action, but I think this is somehow tied up in the definition of 'wrong action.' There is a quotation in the Gita, the holy book, that says 'The fire of wisdom reduces all actions to ashes.' When I read that, I believe they are talking about another plane of existence, perhaps. Something we mere mortals cannot comprehend. That, my dear, is why we need a guru to teach us and interpret these scriptures. Otherwise, you can use them to justify anything, even yelling at your husband."

His smiling face, with its blind gaze and smooth skin, was beatific in the moment, reminding Stephanie of the portraits of Jesus painted during the Renaissance. Else was nodding her head in agreement and Stephanie realized that even though it was Else's eyes through which they both saw the world, Werner was the one who assimilated it, put it all together and made some kind of sense of it. Else reacted to what she saw but Werner absorbed her reactions, internalized them and translated them back to her in a reasoned format.

Stephanie squeezed a few drops of lime juice over a slice of papaya and tried to sound unconcerned when she spoke. "I was curious about that person you mentioned yesterday, Else. What was his name, Vishnu?"

"Yes, Vishnu," said Else, licking her spoon. "Horrible, really, that such a thing should happen. I mean, nobody even knew he was ill and the next thing we knew, he was dead."

"Yes, it's shocking, isn't it." Stephanie noticed that Werner didn't comment. Possibly he sensed she was fishing for information. "Where did he come from? Maybe he was already sick when he got here. I heard he was only here for a month."

"Yes, that's right," said Else, "only one month. And what a month it was. I mean, things felt quite different around here for a while, didn't they Werner?" Else didn't seem to notice that Werner didn't reply. She kept talking. "Ma Vera in particular seemed very–what's the word I want–agitated by his presence. You should have heard the way she spoke to him." At this point Else's tone became almost conspiratorial as she bent her head closer to Stephanie. "Some people were even saying he was her illegitimate son from a love affair she had with an Indian after the Partition. Can you imagine!"

Werner could stand it no longer. "Else. For shame. That is common gossip and has no foundation in fact. If you believe that to be true, you should not be afraid to say it to Ma Vera herself."

Stephanie desperately wanted to hear more and jumped to Else's defense before Werner could silence her. "But why would people make up something so outrageous if there was absolutely no reason to think it might be true?"

Werner realized he was outnumbered and let Else continue.

"Well, for one thing, if you overheard them talking to each other, it didn't sound like they were strangers. It was as if they knew things about each other from the past and they seemed to have a lot of hostility between them. They bickered constantly."

"But it seems to me," said Stephanie, trying to ignore Werner's disapproval, "that if they were mother and son, there might be some affection between them. Or do you think they had a falling out?"

"I think it was a matter of them having gone their separate ways and not having much affection for each other. I have a feeling Ma Vera disapproved of what Vishnu had become. But that's what I mean. There seemed to be some kind of history between them."

"Speculation, pure speculation," muttered Werner, his eyes aimed at the ceiling as if he were trying to explain to the gods that he was not part of this conversation.

"Why do you think she disapproved of him?"

"Well," said Else, glancing at Werner, "he was not a very nice person. Werner thinks I have no right to make such a judgment of someone I don't even know, but I really didn't like the man. He was very bossy, you know, and acted like he owned the place. He told Deva Mother they could make lots of money if they made the ashram more appealing to tourists. He said they should make the rooms more comfortable and charge more money. He said they should advertise. They should give classes in free love–he said sex would attract more Westerners–like that Guru Rajneesh, the one who went to America and bought all those Rolls Royces. Can you imagine? He wanted to turn the ashram into a cult with Guru Father at the head." Else had worked herself into a state of indignation partly to close the gap between her appetite for gossip and Werner's disapproval.

"How did Ma Vera react when he died?" Stephanie asked. "I mean, if he was her son, no matter what the feelings were between them she would probably be pretty upset."

"And she was," said Else. "We hardly saw her for days after and she barely spoke to anyone. Of course, I'm sure she felt some guilt also for the way she treated him when he was alive. I'm sure she had regrets."

"This is enough, Else," said Werner, pushing his chair back and rising. "Stephanie, you must understand, there is absolutely no proof of these allegations and neither Vishnu nor Ma Vera are here to defend themselves. I for one do not believe a word of any of it. And," he said, turning to Else, "my wife knows perfectly well it is unwise and unkind to pass such things along."

"Yes Werner, you are right," said Else, her voice soothing but lacking contrition. "It is merely gossip and Stephanie knows it.

She is free to judge for herself." She wagged her fingers in a good-bye gesture to Stephanie before picking up their tray and leaving, Werner close behind with his hand on her arm.

Stephanie finished her tea and watched the last few diners leave the cafeteria. They all seemed to have a curriculum or agenda of some sort that sent them off in pursuit of their next scheduled activity. It was rare to see anyone just wandering around during the day. For all the meditation and devotion that Werner had talked about, there seemed to be a lot of work going on as well. Work that everyone took part in at some point. Ann had written about it in her letters, suggesting that it was not altogether voluntary. Each member was required to give service to the ashram as part of his or her contribution to its upkeep. If I stay much longer, thought Stephanie, I'll have to start earning my keep.

She returned her tray and went off in search of Ma Vera. Remembering that Ma Vera was keen on gardening, she took the path toward the river that led to the vegetable garden at the south end of the property. The morning sun was already harsh and glaring, hitting her unprotected face and eyes with a fiery intensity. She instinctively raised her hand to her brow and held it visor-like over her squinting eyes. The air felt dry, but she could feel the sweat forming between her breasts and behind her knees. She remembered how Ann had loved the heat that penetrated the earth, baking the ground until you could smell its warmth. But she had hated the heat of the city, its tarry odor a combination of melting pavement and trapped exhaust fumes.

I can see why she would love this place, thought Stephanie. There's a kind of innocence about it that protects it from the contamination of the outside world. Maybe that was why Vishnu had met with hostility from Ma Vera and the others. He had represented the pollution and corruption of the modern age by suggesting that there was potential for profit in this sanctuary. He was trying to make a buck for himself among a group of people for whom the idea was the basest and most destructive thing possible. How sad and humiliating for Ma Vera if he really was her son.

She spotted Ma Vera checking the progress of pole beans with fierce concentration. "Good morning," she said, hoping her approach was noisy enough to warn the older woman of her arrival.

"Good morning, Stephanie," said Ma Vera with a perfunctory nod of the head. "You should wear a hat if you intend to be out in the sun during the day. I'm sure Manu can find you one somewhere."

"You're right. It's pretty brutal. But I guess you're used to it."

"Yes, I am. I like the way it warms my bones. I don't think I could tolerate the English climate anymore. God willing, I won't ever have to."

"How long have you been here?"

"Do you mean India or at this ashram?" Ma Vera asked, still poking at the beans.

"Both, I guess," said Stephanie, "if you don't mind my asking."

"I came to India in 1947 as part of that group of people around Mountbatten who were charged with deciding the future of this country. I wasn't one of the deciders, of course, I was a clerk or secretary, I guess you'd call it. And I remember we used to type from morning till night; there seemed to be an endless number of briefs and documents that had to be written and rewritten. It was a massive undertaking that had to be completed in something like three months. Anyway, when that was over, I managed to find enough work to keep me going for the next seventeen years. I liked India, you see. I never ran out of things to see and learn. I came to the ashram nearly twenty-five years ago and decided this was where I wanted to stay."

"You never married?" asked Stephanie, hoping Ma Vera was in the mood to talk.

"No. Never met a man I wanted to spend my life with," she answered. "Is that what you came all the way out here to ask me?"

"No," said Stephanie, laughing. "I was wondering if there was anything I could do while I'm here, to contribute to my keep."

"They always need help in the kitchen. I assume you can peel a potato."

"Yes, I have some minimal domestic skills."

"Good," said Ma Vera with a brusqueness that startled Stephanie. "I'll show you around and let you get started."

And so Stephanie missed her chance to ask about Vishnu. She had hoped there might be an opening in the conversation where she could insert his name, but something in Ma Vera's attitude discouraged her.

chapter seventeen

M a Durga! I have brought you a volunteer!" said Ma
Vera as she and Stephanie entered the cookhouse.
The kitchen was a single rectangular room, fifteen
feet by eleven, with a series of open grills fueled by charcoal and
wood fires that were being tended by a large, stout woman whose
light brown skin gleamed with sweat in the steamy room. Several
large pots were either on the boil or simmering gently on the
grills, giving a distinctly wet feel to the room.

The smell of onion and curry spiced with coriander and
cumin and a hint of cinnamon, clung to the walls and hung in
the air in each particle of moisture. The fragrant, humid room
was an earthy reminder of a sensuous reality and a sharp contrast to the aridness of the rest of the ashram. All the doors and
windows were wide open but the lack of any breeze subverted
even the suggestion of ventilation.

"Good," said Ma Durga, wiping her hands on the cloth tied

around her ample belly. "I need a hard-working *señorita* today. That *loco* over there is more trouble than he's worth." She pointed to a figure sitting on a low stool in one corner, clumsily peeling carrots. He looked up and made a crazy face at them and Stephanie saw it was Manfred, the German remittance man.

"I should explain to you that Ma Durga likes to pepper her conversation with Spanish occasionally," Ma Vera told Stephanie, taking a peek at the contents of one of the bubbling cauldrons. "She was once cook to the Mexican Consul in Bombay and fancies herself a world traveler. We call her "*La Señora*" because sometimes she gets temperamental in a very Latin way."

"Where does she come from?" asked Stephanie, noting Ma Durga's flat nose, sharp black eyes and glossy, coal black hair.

"Ten miles from here on the other side of the river," said Ma Vera. "But her reputation as a cook is known across the country. Isn't that right, *La Señora*?"

"Si, that is correct. I could work anywhere in the world if I wanted. But I love it here. My heart is with Mother India. I shall never leave her bosom." She picked up a lethal looking cleaver and pointed it at Stephanie. "Take this," she said. "I need someone to chop those carrots."

Stephanie blinked away her surprise and took the cleaver by the handle. It was heavier than she expected and its cutting edge had been sharpened with precision to a smooth, thin wedge.

"I'll leave you to it, then," said Ma Vera, with a disapproving glance in Manfred's direction. "Mind your fingers, Stephanie."

Ma Durga laughed and hoisted a bucket of peeled carrots onto a well-scarred chopping block in the center of the room. "Half-inch rounds," she said. "No bigger or I shall hear about it." She placed an empty pot beside the bucket and indicated that the sliced carrots should go in it. Stephanie took one of the roughly peeled carrots and started slicing. The knife slid through the woody flesh with no resistance. Watch your fingers, she thought. Watch your whole damn arm.

The three of them worked in silence for a while, the sounds of chopping, slicing and scraping interrupted only by the arrival of the young man, Ashok, who began to prepare the flour and water dough–for the flatbread called *nan* that was served with all meals.

By this time Stephanie was feeling confident enough to slice the carrots three at a time. But for every three she sliced, Manfred managed to supply only two more, so progress was slow. She wondered if she should initiate a conversation with him, but Manfred spoke first.

"So you're the Canadian who's come to take her mother back to Canada, I hear," he said, looking up at her from a cross-legged crouch on the tiny stool.

"Yes," she replied, "and you're the crazy man from Germany whose father is a doctor."

He laughed in one short, sharp burst. "A Nazi doctor," he said. "Get your facts right."

"Sorry," she said. "A Nazi doctor."

He smiled. "So now we understand each other. It's much easier to talk with all that introduction shit out of the way. Don't you agree?"

Stephanie nodded. "Yes, much easier."

"So I'm sorry that your mother is dead. She was a very kind lady."

"Thank you. It's nice of you to say."

"Nice!" he said, the word bursting from him like buckshot. "No, I am not nice. But I try to be honest. When your father is a Nazi, that is how you rebel." He attacked an unpeeled carrot with renewed vigor. "The Nazis could be nice if it suited them. But they were never honest. Never."

Manfred's expression of defiance discouraged further discussion. His thin, brown hair hung straight down to his shoulders and was kept in place by a strip of woven cloth tied around his forehead. His eyes were a colorless gray with faint blue shadows smudged under them. He was rangy and thin, as if he ate and slept only when he remembered to and that wasn't very often.

He's an original, thought Stephanie. A bit like a lost soul from the sixties, but he couldn't be more than about thirty-five. Or maybe a burned-out twenty-five.

"So, have you figured out what's going on around here?" Manfred asked, pointing a carrot at her as if it were a gun. Stephanie stared at the tip of the carrot.

"I don't know what you mean," she said.

"I mean all this holy shit," he said, resuming his peeling. "You don't really buy it, do you?"

Stephanie noticed that Ma Durga and Ashok exchanged glances but didn't speak.

"Well, my mother was more into it than I am," she said carefully. "I don't really know that much about it."

"It's all a crock," he said. "All this pious bullshit. You know, they talk about freeing the soul and uniting with a higher consciousness, but this place is all about rules. Rules and more rules. That's what they really want. Safety, security, a sense of superiority." He was practically spitting he spoke with such vehemence.

"So what are you doing here?"

"It's not a bad life if you ignore the religious crap," he smiled. "It's cheap. The food is good. And nobody bothers you too much. The Mother gets on my back sometimes, but it's a small price to pay. Isn't that right, *Mamacita*!" he shouted at Ma Durga. "The Holy Mother carries a big stick! Ha ha ha!"

Ma Durga looked at Stephanie and tapped the side of her head, mouthing the word "loco." Manfred seemed to be enjoying the role of certified nut.

"Then don't you find it dull sometimes?" Stephanie asked.

"Yes, sometimes," he said. "But then I go away for a while. To the big city. There's plenty of excitement in Bombay if you want it."

They worked in silence for a while, the only sounds the scraping and chopping of carrots and the slap-slap of the bread dough in Ashok's hands. Ma Durga was slicing pineapple and offered Stephanie a chunk. She bit into the fruit and enjoyed its juicy sweetness in her dry mouth.

Her attention was suddenly drawn to the door as the tall, angular form of The Mother strode purposefully into the room. Although she had made no sound, The Mother made her presence known the way a change in atmospheric pressure foretells storms. There had been a feeling in the air.

"Manfred!" she said sharply. "I'm warning you for the last time. If these rumors persist, I will no longer consider them to be unfounded gossip. You will be expelled from the ashram and I will be forced to report you to the police, in which case you will be arrested and deported. Do I make myself clear?" Her voice was icy cold, her face frozen in outrage.

"Heil Hitler!" said Manfred, standing to attention and clicking his bare heels together. The Mother's expression didn't change as she turned and left the cookhouse.

"What was that all about?" asked Stephanie when she found her voice.

"Ah! That holy bitch has it in for me," he said, tossing a half-peeled carrot back in the bucket. "Nazi whore!" he muttered as he stomped out the door.

Stephanie looked at Ma Durga and Ashok, who were apparently as stunned as she was.

"Drugs," Ma Durga whispered, nodding her head knowingly.

Was that the rumour? thought Stephanie. It was easy to see why people might think so. Manfred's appearance, for one thing. Hippie garb, sunken eyes and grayish pallor. And his behavior, erratic and irreverent. Definitely out of place amid the quiet piety of the sannyasin. But was using drugs enough reason for The Mother to have him arrested and deported? Or was Manfred a dealer, using the ashram as a front for his operation? Could be, thought Stephanie. Anything's possible.

She finished peeling and chopping the rest of the carrots in time for lunch and spent the afternoon scrubbing potatoes. When *La Señora* finally released her, she went looking for Manu, who helped her locate her mother's things in an upstairs storage cupboard.

There wasn't much but in among the cotton shirts and underthings she found a collection of snapshots of herself and her father from the time she was a baby right up to the present. Ann must have looked at these pictures often; their edges were smudged and they had the limpness of overly handled paper. There was the one of Steph when she was four years old, the first time her parents had taken her to see the Nutcracker ballet. She was dressed in royal blue velvet and shiny patent leather, her smile as serene as a pampered princess.

And the one of her father and her fishing off the end of the dock at the cottage. She had been eight, long and skinny, teeth still too big for her mouth and hair in a constant tangle. Her father had been in his prime, handsome, elegant even in his plaid shirt and blue jeans, smiling affectionately into the camera.

There was the Christmas they had spent with Ann's parents in Winnipeg in 1974; her high school graduation shot, Stephanie flanked by Grandmother and Grandfather Hobart; oh God, even the naked baby shot with a grinning Uncle Jay holding her up to the camera. Ann had written on the back: "Posterior for posterity: Stephanie, age one month."

She felt the tears well up in her eyes and quickly put the photographs away. I can't do this, she thought. I should be at home with Dad and Uncle Jay. I haven't even spoken to them and they must be frantic. What was I thinking when I agreed to stay here for a few days? I should have gone straight back to Bombay and got on a plane. I must have been deranged thinking there was something to be gained by staying. Mother died of a fever and that's the end of it. So maybe people didn't realize how sick she was; maybe they could have done more. It's too late to do anything about it now. Whatever gave me the idea there was more to it than that?

Eventually she fell asleep, curled up like a fetus, her hands clenched like fists against her chest.

She was standing on the end of the dock looking into the water. The day was very bright, the sun white hot, but the water was unusually black, as if the bottom were a smooth slab of slate instead of the usual stony sand. She could see the big northern pike gliding gracefully through the water, the white sunlight hitting their scales like laser beams. She thought she could hear someone playing the piano across the water, but she couldn't make out the melody. It had a kind of mournful wailing quality, rising and dipping in languorous arpeggios. She looked up and saw the figure of a woman standing in a small boat, waving to get her attention. She realized it was her mother and fear gripped her as she saw the boat begin to rock dangerously. "Sit down," she tried to say, but she couldn't hear her own voice.

She heard her mother call to her: "Stephie, Stephie! Don't leave me out here! I'm afraid! I'm afraid!" She watched in horror as the boat tipped and her mother fell into the black water, a vortex of white foam swirling around her like a gauze shroud, drawing her deeper and deeper into the dark water.

chapter eighteen

Stephanie awoke the next morning covered in a clammy sweat. The small room already felt very warm, the air still and uncharacteristically quiet. She felt uneasy as she reached for her watch hanging from a nail above the bed. Nearly eight o'clock, a time when people could usually be heard in the ashram corridors or outside going about their daily activities. That's odd, she thought, as she picked up her clothes and towel and stepped out into the passageway that led to the bathrooms. Maybe this is a non-activity day, like a Sunday. But the silence felt heavy and unnatural, like the aftermath of an explosion when all you can hear is the ringing in your own ears.

After a quick bath, she hurried down to the cafeteria, passing no one as she crossed the courtyard to the east side of the ashram building. The dining room was practically empty, a smattering of people sitting alone or in pairs, hunched over cups of tea. She spotted Werner and Else near the center of the room finishing their breakfast.

"What's going on?" she asked when she reached their table. "Where is everybody?"

"They are at the temple," said Else. "Haven't you heard?"

"Heard what? I just got up and wondered why it was so quiet."

"Deva Mother is dead," said Werner solemnly. "She died in the night of a heart attack and Guru Father has requested a day of meditation and chanting for her soul."

"You're kidding," said Stephanie. "I just saw her yesterday and she seemed perfectly healthy."

"It was quite unexpected," said Else. "Guru Father is devastated. He told everyone at darshan this morning that he heard her cry out in the night but that she died within minutes of his reaching her. He stayed praying over her body until sunrise when he went and told Ma Vera. Everyone seems to be in a state of shock."

"I can't believe someone else has died in this place," said Stephanie. "Doesn't it kind of give you the creeps? I mean, maybe it's normal in India, but I'm not used to it."

"Don't they say that things always happen in threes?" said Else.

"Superstition," muttered Werner. "There is no basis for thinking there is any relationship between these events."

"Yes Werner, you are right," said Else, "but people are by nature superstitious and must have ways of explaining these things to themselves."

"But that's not really an explanation," said Stephanie, not wanting Werner to think she agreed with Else. "They all died from different causes and at different times. They all just happened to be in this one particular place when they died. That's just coincidence."

"Yes, of course. Stephanie's right," said Werner to his wife. "An unfortunate coincidence, but a coincidence nonetheless."

"Freud said there is no such thing as coincidence," said Else defensively.

"Are you sure he said that?" asked Werner, suspicion creasing his brow.

"Of course I'm sure," said Else. "Who else would have said it?"

"So what are you thinking?" he asked. "What is all this supposed to mean?"

"I think there is bad luck here," she replied. "I think this whole place must have bad Karma."

"Ach! Bad luck," said Werner scornfully. "More superstition."

But Else was not convinced. Her expression remained stubborn and she continued to eat in silence.

"So, Stephanie," asked Werner, attempting to salvage the conversation, "what will you do next?"

She thought for a moment before answering. "I think I'll go into town and try once more to phone my father. I'll be leaving in the next day or so and I want to let him know." She looked around the nearly empty dining room. "I guess today isn't a good day to get things settled."

"No, I think not," said Werner, his eyes lost in a sightless stare.

They finished eating and Stephanie rose to take her tray back. Else stood up at the same time and said, "Werner, I'll take the tray back first and then we'll go. Okay?" He nodded and she followed Stephanie to the food counter.

"They say The Mother and Manfred had a big fight in the kitchen yesterday," she whispered to Stephanie as they emptied and replaced their trays. "I hope he didn't do anything foolish," she said, throwing Stephanie a worried glance over her shoulder.

"What on earth do you mean?"

"You know what I mean," Else whispered and drew her index finger across her throat.

"You must be kidding," said Stephanie, not knowing whether to laugh or ignore her.

Else nodded her head. "He's just crazy enough. He might do anything." She put her finger to her lips as they got closer to Werner. Else touched his arm and he rose to join her. Stephanie looked at Else and shook her head to indicate she didn't believe it.

"Bye Stephanie," said Else. "See you later."

Stephanie caught the next bus into town, wanting to get away from the eerie solemnity of the ashram. She had seen a few people on her walk to the main road, but they had been deep in thought, a couple apparently weeping, dabbing at their eyes with pieces of white cloth.

She took a seat near the back of the bus and was glad to be on the moving vehicle even as it lurched and rocked, spewing black fumes in its wake. That place is beginning to give me the creeps, she thought. And it's starting to freak Else out, too. It must be the isolation. After a while you lose your perspective on things. She can't really believe that Manfred killed The Mother because they had an argument. Besides, Manfred had said that he was used to her "carrying a big stick," and it was a small price to pay for a pretty good life. And Guru Father had seen The Mother having a heart attack.

I can't believe I'm even thinking about it, she told herself. It's too preposterous. Else has a melodramatic temperament and when things get too dull for her she has to invent something to keep life interesting. God knows there's enough going on without having to invent more, she thought.

She looked out the window to take her mind off things. The day was already drenched in heat, the weather having changed in the few days since she had arrived in India. The sky was a pale, opaque gray, the sun a burning white disc. She had taken Ma Vera's advice and found herself a straw hat with a wide brim.

She saw a few sari-wrapped figures bent over rice plants, their feet sunk ankle deep in muddy water. If this were a hundred years ago, she thought, I would probably be riding in some sort of horse-drawn wagon, but I would be looking at exactly the same scene. Except for this bus, nothing within my sight has changed in all that time. The constant hum of insects. The chorus of rooks, caw-cawing like punctuation marks on the day's activities. That same sun burning a hole in that hot gray sky.

Water being drawn from that very well. How had this pocket of the world escaped the juggernaut of the twentieth century?

Her eyelids were heavy and she felt them drop slowly to close out the brightness of the day. For an instant she felt herself being embraced, almost smothered by the airless heat. She saw again the image of her mother falling from the boat, the gauzy spume swirling around her as she sank beneath the surface of the black water. "Help me! Help me! I'm afraid."

The bus lurched suddenly and Stephanie's neck snapped back, her eyes opening, her breath trapped in her throat. She stared around her and realized that the bus had arrived at its destination and the passengers were getting off. Her mouth was dry and she felt a little sick to her stomach, as if she'd swallowed some of the black smoke belching from the back of the bus. She took hold of the seat in front of her and pulled herself to her feet. She swallowed hard to stop her stomach from rising to her throat and felt the blood pounding in her head. Oh God, don't be sick, she thought. Please don't be sick.

She got herself off the bus and took a deep breath, but the air was dense and hot like the inside of a clothes dryer. She saw a statue of Mahatma Gandhi about ten yards in front of her and took several slow steps toward it. She sat down on a ledge around the base of the statue and waited for the nausea to subside. She desperately wanted a drink of water but was afraid to drink the town water in case it wasn't boiled.

She wondered if Dr. Gopal Singh would be in his office and if she should take a chance on walking that far. If he's not there, maybe that other homeopathic doctor will be in, she thought. The nausea was beginning to subside but the blood was still pounding between her ears. Maybe he'd give her an aspirin or something. She stood up and started walking in the direction of the doctor's office. It was already past mid-morning and the sun was approaching its zenith. I should have waited till later, she thought, after three o'clock.

She walked slowly, placing one foot gently in front of the other to minimize the shock waves to her pounding head and soon recognized the small bungalow that housed Dr. Gopal Singh's practice. She climbed the two steps onto the porch and opened the screen door to his waiting room. She felt the cooler air touch her skin and was relieved that the glare from the sun had not followed her into the dim recesses of the house. A few of the doctor's patients were waiting to see him, so she took a seat by the door and closed her eyes to relieve the pressure of the headache.

She didn't know how much time had passed when she heard the doctor's enquiring voice. "Miss Hobart?" She opened her eyes and smiled weakly. Several people still waited on the wooden benches lining the walls. "Please. Come into my office."

He closed the door behind her and she took a seat in front of his desk. She explained what had happened to her on the bus and told him about the fierce headache that was raging in her skull. He checked her pulse and took her blood pressure and temperature.

"I think it's probably a combination of motion sickness and heat exhaustion," he said. "Not serious, but I recommend you stay out of the sun during the middle of the day and don't try to do too much. You're not accustomed to this kind of heat. You've just come from a colder climate and your body has not adjusted." He poured some water from a thermos into a small glass and gave her a couple of round white pills to take. "Those are for your headache. Just aspirin. Don't worry. And I'll give you some Gravol in case you feel ill on the bus again." He took a small square of white paper and folded it around some tablets, making a neat little packet that held the pills securely.

"I must pay you," said Stephanie, taking the packet. "Thank you very much." He nodded his head to one side in a customary gesture of acquiescence. "Two rupees," he said.

She gave him the money and rose to leave. "I suppose you know about Deva Mother," she said.

"Yes. I was there this morning to sign the certificate."

"Was it a heart attack?" she asked. "Could you confirm it?"

"The cause of death was elevated arterial blood pressure. A massive heart attack."

"Did she have a bad heart?"

"Not that I was aware of. But Guru Father was present at the time of death and what he described was a heart attack. She may have had an embolism or blockage in one of her arteries that caused a dramatic rise in blood pressure. Sometimes these things happen without warning. Guru Father has a mild heart condition, but he is able to control it with digitalis. Unfortunately, Deva Mother gave no indication that she was unwell and never consulted me for an examination. Perhaps if she had, we might have caught it in time."

"I see," said Stephanie. "So there won't be an autopsy this time either."

"There is no need," said the doctor. "I am satisfied with the eyewitness report." He opened the door to indicate the consultation was over. "Please feel free to consult me again, but I'm sure you'll be feeling much better by tomorrow. Just remember what I said."

"Thank you, Dr. Singh," she said. "I'm sure you're right."

The headache had not yet begun to subside but her insides had settled back in place, so she headed for the post and telegraph office, keeping to the shady side of the street. It took two tries to put the call through, but finally after four or five rings she heard her father's sleepy voice on the other end of the line.

"Stephie? Where are you?" she heard him say through a faint buzz.

"I'm still staying at the ashram, Dad," she said, trying not to shout into the line and attract the attention of the post office patrons. "Did you get my letter?"

"No," he said, "no letter. But I got your telegram. Are you all right?"

"Yes, I'm fine. How are you?"

"I'm all right," he said, but she could hear the sadness in his voice. "You know I got their cable when you were already halfway there."

"Yes. They told me they sent it. I was too late." She listened to the buzz on the line and waited for him to say something.

"Do you feel up to making the trip home soon?" His voice sounded lonely and hopeful at the same time.

"I should be home in a few days, Dad. Can you manage?"

"I'm okay, baby, really. Jay's been here every night and Lily's been bringing casseroles over every day. I'm being well cared for. It's you I'm worried about."

"I'm fine. Honestly. The people at the ashram are very kind. They were very fond of Mother and they've been looking after me so well. I'll tell you all about it when I get home. Don't worry. I'll call you from Bombay and let you know what flight I'm on."

"Yes, do that. Do you need money?" He was beginning to sound anxious.

"No, I'm fine. I have plenty of money. I'll call you as soon as I get to Bombay. Probably in a couple of days. Bye Dad."

"Bye Stephanie. Be careful."

"I will. I promise. Bye."

chapter nineteen

Allan Lloyd was having difficulty concentrating. No matter how hard he tried to force the thoughts from his head, his mind kept wandering back to them. He wanted desperately to join his fellows in their low, mournful chant, wanted desperately to commune with them in silent meditation. But something kept nagging at his brain like a gnat buzzing around his face. He looked over at Ma Vera, sitting cross-legged like the rest of them, and saw she was staring at the floor in front of her, her brow creased with grief, her lips closed in a straight line of pain. What was she thinking, he wondered. It was obvious to him she was not praying for The Mother's soul as Guru Father had requested. She was wandering in some private wilderness of reminiscence, possibly recalling twenty-five years of friendship she had shared with The Mother.

She's lost two friends very quickly, he thought, a new one and an old one. Ma Vera had become quite close to Ann in the brief months she had been at the ashram and had been distraught at her death. Now she was grieving again, perhaps this time for her-self, and a part of her life that had died with her closest friend.

But it wasn't Ma Vera's grief that was occupying Allan's mind, nor was it his own grief over the loss of a fellow human being. It was a pinpoint of suspicion, no bigger than a grain of sand, that had inserted itself into his consciousness and was grating the way a bit of grit scrapes behind your eyelid. He couldn't seem to get rid of it. It was like a voice in his head telling him something wasn't right. And it was as clear as if someone had spoken the words to him. He believed The Mother had been murdered. And he believed Manfred had murdered her.

He knew in his guts she hadn't had a heart attack; knew from his family-honed tradition of observing people as medical spec-imens. The Mother was not a potential candidate for a heart attack. He couldn't explain it; it wasn't as if he was conscious of looking at people as medical case histories; it was ingrained in him from having grown up in a family of doctors. He had absorbed a habit of observation that took in certain details that other people didn't notice: skin tone, the whites of the eyes, mus-cle coordination, the condition of fingernails and hair.

He had been bothered by the inconsistencies in Ann's symp-tom map and he had stood by and done nothing. This time he was going to follow his instincts. I am who I am, he thought and that's not going to change. If something's wrong, I'm going to find out what it is and if that son-of-a-bitch Manfred is behind it, I'm going to see that he pays.

He could feel the anger beginning to well up inside of him. I have to act, he thought, or this rage will destroy me. I thought I could walk away from it when Barbara died, thought I could go to another place and leave it behind. Now I'm not so sure. It's too much a part of me, like Guru Father says: "A man cannot wear his flesh and bones like a suit of clothes. Nor can he change his heart and soul to be more fashionable."

At first he hadn't really believed that. He had thought he

would change, thought he could change. But changing and forgetting were not the same thing, he was beginning to realize. He might forget the intensity of the pain or the depth of the rage, but he could not change what they had done to him, nor could he change the way he responded to them. That was fundamental to his nature and that was what the Guru Father had been trying to tell him.

Stephanie had caught the afternoon bus back to the ashram, passed on lunch and gone straight to bed. The headache had begun to subside but a fuzzy, disoriented sensation lingered even after a couple of hours of sleep. She woke up hungry and went to the cafeteria for some supper, but ate alone, the dining room half empty and dotted with strangers. She went for a short stroll in the garden, hoping the slightly cooler evening air would clear her head. The devotees were still closeted, some in the temple, others in their rooms, observing the meditation order that had been imposed by the Guru Father. The tourists and transients like herself remained unobtrusive and respectful of the mourners.

The absence of human voices and activity seemed to intensify the sound of the night insects. Their high-pitched keening was like the chorus in a Greek drama, adding to the emotional undercurrent of mourning. If I had come here for peace and quiet, she thought, I'd probably be going crazy. It's never really quiet here. This place is as identifiable by its sounds as it is by its sights. Perhaps that's why Werner can experience so much of it without actually seeing it. There's a palpable activity in the air that you can almost reach out and grab. If I had a tape recorder with me, I'd want to record it and take it back as a souvenir.

Back in her room, she tried to read but had difficulty keeping her mind on the words. The roaring silence kept distracting her, drawing her listening ear into its feverish activity. It made her restless but she didn't have the energy to get out of bed.

She finally drifted into an uneasy slumber on the perimeter of real sleep, a kind of half-sleep that confused reality with hallucination. She was convinced she heard a gentle knocking on her door; believed she saw Allan Lloyd enter her room; thought she heard him say her name; could swear he was shaking her shoulder, trying to wake her. But her sleeping mind told her that was not possible, she was in her bed asleep and was just dreaming.

"Stephanie, wake up. It's me. Allan." She could feel his breath on the side of her face as she listened to his hoarse whispering. She tried to turn onto her side, but she felt his hands on her arms as he shook her gently.

"Wake up, Stephanie. Please. I need your help."

Help me. Help me. She saw her mother fall from the boat. Saw again the white swirling water wrap itself around her. Watched helplessly as her mother disappeared in the vortex.

Stephanie sat up suddenly, gasping for air, a scream stifled in her throat and unable to utter the word "Mother" that was trapped in her mouth. Now fully awake, her heart pounding in her ears, she realized she was looking at Allan Lloyd just as she had dreamed him, sitting on the edge of the bed, his hands holding her arms.

"How long have you been here?" she asked, looking at the darkness beyond the open window. It must be the middle of the night."

"Just a few minutes," he said. "I knocked several times but you didn't answer. I'm sorry if I scared you. I didn't know what else to do." He was watching her intently as if to make sure she understood. "Are you all right?"

"Yes," she answered, taking a deep breath. "Yes. I thought I was dreaming." She looked at him for a moment. "What do you want?"

He realized he was still holding onto her arms. He was suddenly embarrassed and he released his grip, looking away toward the door that he had so carefully closed behind him. "You're gonna think I'm crazy," he said, shifting his gaze to his hands, which were now clasped in his lap. "But there's something I have to do and I want someone with me. You're the only one that I would trust to do this and not tell anyone."

She sensed the tension in his body, heard it in his voice. She wanted to comfort him and dispel the lingering sadness he seemed to be grappling with. But why had he come to her room in the middle of the night? What was it that couldn't wait until morning?

He told her he didn't believe The Mother had died of a heart attack. Call it instinct, he said, call it an educated guess; call it paranoia. But something's not right. He told her he suspected murder and that he thought Manfred might have done it. He knew she would think he was out of his mind, but he had to prove himself right or wrong. And if he was right, he wanted an ally.

"So what do you want me to do?" she asked, thinking she must still be dreaming.

"I want to examine The Mother's body to see if I can find anything to confirm my suspicions. But it has to be tonight because she's being cremated at sunrise."

Stephanie didn't say anything for a couple of minutes. This wasn't what she had expected.

"I need you to stand watch for me and if I do find anything, I'll want you as a witness."

"You're not going to cut her open are you?" She knew as soon as she said it that it was ridiculous. But if Else had suspected Manfred and now Allan suspected him, maybe there was something to it.

"No, of course not," he said, "although I wish I could. I'll just be able to do a superficial check. If he did kill her, I'm sure it wasn't something he planned, so there might be some sign of violence, something external that could prove she was murdered."

"But why would Manfred want to kill The Mother?"

"Look, Manfred was dealing. I'm sure of it. And The Mother was going to report him and have him arrested."

"Is that any reason to kill her? I mean, they'd probably just deport him, wouldn't they?"

"Are you kidding? They'd lock him up and throw away the key. We're not talking marijuana here. More than likely he was dealing heroin, in which case he wouldn't have had a chance. There's too much international pressure on the Indian government to stop the heroin trade." He looked at Stephanie expectantly.

"Okay I'll go with you," she said. "If you really think it's necessary."

"Thanks," he said and she heard the relief in his voice. "We might as well do it now."

"What time is it?"

"Two a.m. We haven't got much time. Prayers will begin in a couple of hours."

They walked hurriedly along the path that led to the temple. Everyone appeared to be sleeping, probably exhausted from the long day of chanting and meditation. Even the night sounds were subdued, as if only a skeleton crew of insects were working the night shift.

"If there are any external signs of violence," Stephanie whispered when they came within sight of the temple, "then wouldn't the doctor have seen them?"

"I don't believe the doctor got within ten feet of her. He wouldn't dare question the word of the Guru Father. The most he would get is a cursory look through the door to see her lying on the bed covered with a sheet."

"You mean the Guru Father lied to the doctor to protect Manfred?"

"Guru Father probably came in when she was in the throes of dying. He may have thought she was having a heart attack and so that's what he told the doctor. I doubt that he suspected anything else and the doctor would have no reason to think anything else."

"Then maybe he never examined Vishnu or my mother either when he wrote up the death certificates."

"More than likely," said Allan. "Remember, the ashram and the Guru Father are very important around here. The whole area benefits, not just from the tourists, but also from the sanctity the ashram bestows. No one wants to rock the boat."

They had reached the temple and Stephanie saw it was lit from within by the glow of a hundred candles. Allan quietly opened the door and they stepped inside. She could see the body of The Mother draped in a pure white shroud, lying on a bier in front of the altar. Thousands of flowers strung in garlands were piled on top of her and around the bier. The waxy smoke from the candles and the incense and the fragrance of the flowers combined to give the air a sickly sweet pungency.

"You wait here," Allan whispered, "and watch for anyone coming along the path. I'll be as quick as I can."

She focused her eyes on the path but could only see about twenty feet ahead of her in the moonless night. She forced her eyes to focus further, foot by foot, and occasionally turned to look at Allan to relieve the strain. She saw him examine The Mother's head and neck with a small flashlight and a few minutes later watched as he carefully began to remove the garlands from the upper part of her body. After about ten minutes she heard him call to her in a hoarse, excited voice.

"I think I've found something."

She hurried over to the bier, her heart beating in her throat. "Look here," he said and focused the tiny flashlight on a point at the base of The Mother's throat. She saw a small bruise and what appeared to be a tiny pimple at its center.

"It's a puncture mark," whispered Allan. "Someone's pushed a needle into her jugular vein." He was breathing in short, shallow bursts and she felt her skin prickle from the horrible excitement. "Quick, help me cover her up again."

They worked fast to replace the shroud and the flowers and Stephanie felt a combination of fear and disgust that she tried to force from her thoughts. When they were satisfied that everything was back in place, they walked swiftly and silently towards the temple doors. In the instant Allan opened the door, Stephanie saw a flash of white moving along the path some twenty feet away.

"Someone's coming," she whispered as she grabbed the door and silently swung it shut again.

"This way," said Allan and grabbed her hand. They ran on tiptoe to the front of the temple, past the bier and the altar and slipped behind a screen depicting scenes from the life of the god Krishna.

Stephanie heard the temple door being opened and closed and listened to the slow footsteps of someone approaching the bier. For a few moments there was no sound at all in the temple except the sputtering of candles and the rushing of her own blood in her ears. Allan was still holding her hand and his body was tense. She could feel his breath near her face.

Stephanie thought she heard the low hum of someone chanting, but as the sounds became louder and sharper, she realized she was listening to someone moaning and sobbing. She looked at Allan and saw him lean over and peek around the edge of the screen. He straightened up and whispered close to her ear.

"It's Guru Father."

Her eyes widened in surprise. She had never even seen the Guru Father and now she was an unwilling witness to his most private grief. He continued to weep with deep, groaning sobs that shocked her with their intensity. She felt Allan's hand tighten around hers and she turned again to look at his face. She could see tears glistening on his cheeks in the dim glow of the room. She reached up with her free hand and touched his face. He winced as if in pain, closing his eyes tightly to hold back the tears. In that moment she felt the utter desolation of the Guru Father's grief and Allan's shame at being witness to it.

In time the sobs subsided and they heard the Guru Father leave the temple and close the door behind him. They waited a few minutes and Allan, still holding her hand, led her back through the temple and out the door.

The night was very still and the air felt cool after the stifling atmosphere of the temple. They both took deep breaths of fresh air and tried not to think about what they had done. "Oh God," she heard Allan moan. "How could I?" Then she saw him crouch behind a bush at the side of the path and begin to retch. She waited for him to finish and when he emerged he was shaking.

"I'm sorry," he said. "I'm really sorry." His face was etched with the disgust and shame he was feeling.

They walked in silence and parted wordlessly at the bottom of the stairs that led to her room. She went straight up to the third floor bathroom, locked the door and took her clothes off. The water felt unpleasantly cold on her clammy skin. She kept filling the metal bowl and dowsing herself until she began to shiver. She pulled her sleeveless dress back on over her drenched body and made her way down the hall to her room. Once inside, she wrapped herself in the thin cotton bed sheet and crawled onto the bed. It would soon be daylight and the body of The Mother would be burned to ashes and returned to the earth.

chapter twenty

hrough the mist of the pre-dawn light, Stephanie watched as the flower-laden body of The Mother was carried by white-clad sannyasins to the funeral pyre. The entire population of the ashram had risen early to attend the cremation and those who had mourned most deeply during the previous day appeared weary and dazed from their almost non-stop chanting and praying.

Ma Vera and Manu stood together, their hands clasped, their heads bowed. Ma Vera appeared barely able to stand on her own and seemed to be supporting herself by standing close to Manu. Her face was creased with suffering and her eyes swollen with the tears that she occasionally wiped with the shawl of her sari. Manu kept glancing in her direction as if expecting Ma Vera to fall over.

Allan Lloyd stood grim-faced and alone, eyes dry, hands clenched at his sides. Stephanie spotted Werner and Else standing near the foot of the pyre. Werner wanted to be close so he could hear the crackle of the fire and feel its heat. They had assembled by the river to watch the Guru Father set the burning torch to the ghee-soaked pyre whose flames would consume The Mother's body.

Stephanie watched as the procession drew nearer. She saw the Guru Father following slowly behind the bearers who carried The Mother's body on a pallet on their shoulders. He held his head high and kept his eyes focused straight ahead, fixed on the flower-draped body. Stephanie found herself studying the man whose pain-filled weeping she and Allan had unwillingly witnessed the night before. He was older than she had expected, over eighty, but his body appeared strong and he stood erect with a soldierly bearing. His hair and beard were long and white, his skin a pale brown with the yellow pallor of someone who spent most of his time indoors. He wore only the white kurta and wide pants common to the male devotees and a white oblong shawl that was draped over his shoulders to protect him from the early morning dampness.

She knew that The Mother had been the business end of the ashram, but she couldn't help wondering about the relationship between her and the Guru Father. Had there been a spiritual bond—The Mother hadn't struck her as a particularly spiritual person—or was it a more personal relationship, maybe even a marriage? Doubtful, she thought, too many complications—color, caste, religion, and the stigma of intermarriage. Most probably it was nothing more than the business arrangement it appeared to be. But then, why was the Guru Father's grief so profound? Surely Deva Mother was replaceable as a business agent. And certainly a man of the Guru Father's beliefs would not mourn death as the end of life. Wasn't it his role to celebrate The Mother's passing to a higher plane of being?

Stephanie was beginning to feel the lack of sleep. Her eyes were burning and her mind kept going round in circles. She forced herself to stop thinking and observe the solemn ritual.

She watched as someone handed the Guru Father a bundle of flaming sticks. He held the blazing torch for a moment and then slowly lowered it to the oil-drenched stack of wood that supported The Mother's body. The pyre ignited immediately, casting a yellow glow on the white robes of the mourners surrounding it. The Guru Father slowly circled the funeral mound and set the entire perimeter alight. Stephanie could feel the heat from the fire even though she stood a hundred feet away from it. The pyramid of flame was reflected in the semi-still waters of the river that flowed beside it. A cone of black smoke drifted skyward from the center of the blaze and the air was filled with the pungent and sickening smell of burning butter and flesh.

Stephanie realized at that moment that her mother's funeral must have been like this. She was drenched with sweat and tears stung her eyes, both from the smoke and an overwhelming sense of sadness and exhaustion. She thought she would suffocate if she didn't get away. She knew now that her mother's life and death were forever bound to this place and that she had lost her to something she couldn't understand.

As she climbed the stairs to her room and fell onto the bed, all she could think about were Allan's words, "I don't think she should have died."

"Werner's been looking for you, Stephanie." Manu, looking drawn and tired, had spotted her sitting under a tree drinking mango juice. "I've just left him in the pottery house and he said if I saw you to ask you to join him there."

Manu's smile was cheerless and Stephanie saw that her eyes were dull and red-rimmed. The atmosphere around the ashram was still somber and what activity there was seemed to be happening behind closed doors or conducted in whispers. Stephanie had slept after the cremation ceremony for The Mother and had found some bread and a bottle of mango juice to fill her empty stomach. *La Señora*'s kitchen was temporarily shut down and lunch preparations would not be starting for another hour.

She walked around to the north end of the ashram building to the pottery room. A small square bungalow had been constructed especially for the making of clay cups, pots and dishes, most of which were used in the ashram kitchen and dining room. Occasionally a visitor to the ashram would try their hand at an interesting glaze, but for the most part, the product was sturdy and serviceable and provided a make-work project for aspiring sannyasins.

She found Werner shaping a bowl from fat noodles of clay that lay on the table in front of him like glistening, overfed worms.

"Ah, Stephanie," he said when she hailed him, "so glad to see you." He picked up another of the clay worms and worked it into the rim of the bowl. "I have not mastered the wheel," he said, looking at a spot somewhere over her left shoulder. "I much prefer to work it with my hands. A bit laborious but much more satisfying."

Stephanie pulled up a stool and sat opposite him at the table. She picked up one of the fat ropes of clay and began winding it into a cylinder, shaping it with her fingers.

"Where's Else?" she asked, comparing her clumsy effort with Werner's smooth handiwork.

"She's having a rest. We got up very early this morning to attend the cremation of The Mother and Else did not get enough sleep."

"What about you?" she asked. "Not tired?"

"No," he said, chuckling. "I don't seem to need as much sleep as Else. To be fair, though, I'm sure our life together is much harder for her than it is for me."

"How do you mean?"

"Well," he said, dipping his fingers in a bowl of water and smoothing the surface of the clay, "she takes so much of the responsibility for both of us. Making the arrangements, inquiring, purchasing, banking. You know. And she must also see for both of us. We share all decision-making of course, but Else is the 'lookout' for the two of us."

Stephanie smiled. "I suspect you have pretty good radar your-self, Werner. You're an observer of life, even without the use of your eyes."

"You are right, Stephanie," he said with an ironic grin. "I have my own way of seeing. And I think perhaps I see things that others miss."

"Such as?"

Werner finished shaping the bowl with a caressing motion, cupping his hands around its perimeter and gently following its slope from base to rim. Satisfied that it met his exacting stan-dard, he set the still pliable vessel aside and clasped his clay-cov-ered hands in front of him. Stephanie noted that the bowl, a medium-sized serving dish, was perfectly shaped, its surface unblemished.

"Such as," he began, giving it some thought, "I believe your mother was frightened by something in the weeks before her death. And since the death of Vishnu, I have smelled fear in the air here."

"Fear?" she said. "You think my mother was afraid of some-one?"

"Someone or something," he said. "She didn't confide in me but I perceived a change after the death of Vishnu. There was a tension in her voice that had not been there before. I am very sensitive to people's voices, Stephanie. It is one of the means by which I grasp reality."

"Maybe she was just upset by a sudden death on the ashram."

"Perhaps. But there is a difference between agitation and fear. I believe she was afraid." He waited for Stephanie to respond, and when she didn't, he continued. "I sat with her on one of the last days of her illness and at one point she entrusted me with some-thing that I now believe you should have." He reached under the table and pulled a small, spiral-backed notebook from his knap-sack. "It was her diary," he said, handing it to Stephanie across the table. "I only know that because she told me so. I have shown it to no one, not even Else. It was given to me for safekeeping and I could not betray your mother's trust."

"Why did you wait so long to give it to me?"

"I had intended to give it to you before you left, I assure you," said Werner. "But I wanted to do it privately, when no one else was around, and that is not so easy for me. I assume your mother gave it to me because she knew I would not be able to read it and divulge its contents. I respect that confidence and believe she would want me to pass it on to you unread."

Stephanie took the red-covered notebook from Werner and ran her fingertips over its shiny surface. It was just a cheap school notebook Ann had probably picked up to make notes in. Stephanie opened the cover and saw that the first entry was dated January 20th, which meant that Ann had begun the diary shortly after arriving at the ashram.

"Thank you Werner," she said, closing the book. "I'm very grateful."

"Yes, of course, Stephanie," he said. "But it is rightfully yours to have." He pushed his chair back and stood up. "Now, if you wouldn't mind, I would appreciate it if you would guide me to the sink so that I may wash my hands and then, if you would assist me back to my room, I will collect Else for lunch."

Stephanie ate lunch quickly and met Werner and Else briefly on the way back up to her room. Else's face was puffy from sleep and there were still creases from the pillow pressed into her right cheek.

"Manfred's disappeared," she whispered. "Nobody's seen him since yesterday." The expression on her face said, "I told you so."

Stephanie went up to her room and sat in front of the open window, leafing through Ann's diary. At first she was uncomfortable opening it and reading her mother's intimate thoughts. She knew she wouldn't have wanted anyone reading her diary, if she'd kept one, but she hadn't been able to shake the uneasy feeling Werner's comments had generated. She soon found herself looking for clues in the pages of neatly written notes. Clues that might tell her what Ann had been afraid of. "I feel as if I have been preparing to come to this place my whole life," Ann's first diary entry began. "Although I sometimes feel anxious and inadequate, I believe this is where I will find peace and truth."

Then in early February she wrote, "I have found some kindred spirits here and it's so much easier to say what's in my mind. The ones who are like me–Allan, Ma Vera, even lovely little Manu were all misfits in their worldly lives. And when I recognized myself in them it was like being diagnosed with a curable disease instead of something fatal. What a wonderful relief! Now I don't have to hide my symptoms or make myself pretend they don't exist. I can rid myself of the stigma of feeling different and rejoice in the freedom to be myself!"

In mid-February she wrote, "Praise the Lord and pass the curried peas! Today I was able to sit in the lotus position for one full hour and meditate without once thinking about the pain in my legs! Allan says it's a real breakthrough (I think there may have been a touch of sarcasm in his tone, however) and Ma Vera says it's definitely easier for thin people than for the chunky types like her. Anyway, I'm proud of myself and told them I'd be standing on my head, unassisted, before the next full moon."

But by the beginning of March the tone of the entries was different. There was a tension in the writing, like the change in Ann's voice that Werner had detected. "There are good days and bad days," she wrote. "I look at her and wonder if she knows what I'm thinking and when she looks at me I feel a chill, as if someone had poked me with an icicle."

Stephanie leafed back through the pages to see if her mother had recorded some event that might be a clue to her change of heart. Clearly she had had a falling out with someone, but Ann had chosen not to write of the episode in her diary. Nor was it clear who she was referring to. The unnamed woman was always "she" and Ann seemed to be increasingly obsessed with analyzing her feelings about this woman. Could it have been Ma Vera, Stephanie wondered? Who else would have been capable of upsetting her to that extent?

"I can't erase the sight of her from my mind and I know these awful thoughts will destroy me if I don't start to control them. She must know I haven't told anyone. Nobody else has any idea that this is going on. I haven't revealed a thing."

By March 15th she was writing, "Maybe I've imagined all this and nothing happened and she isn't freezing me out the way I feel she is. Can it all be a figment of my imagination?"

The entries became shorter and more obscure and Stephanie began to wonder if her mother had been on the verge of a nervous breakdown. The illness that had killed her may have begun to wear her down psychologically as it weakened her physically.

One of the last entries, dated April 15th, shortly before Ann died, made Stephanie shudder as if she were remembering a bad dream. "When I think of poor Vishnu," Ann had written, "dying so suddenly and in a way so violently, I feel like I'm being sucked into a black hole. I feel like I'm drowning."

chapter twenty-one

Stephanie went looking for Ma Vera after dinner. She had not seen her since the early morning hours of the cremation and was concerned about her. Once she ascertained that Ma Vera was not in her room, Stephanie decided a systematic search of the grounds was the best way to find her. She started in the kitchen where *La Señora* advised her that Ma Vera had not been seen all day.

"Here," she said, "if you find her, give her this," and handed Stephanie some vegetable samosas wrapped in a piece of cloth. "And take this too," she said, pouring tea into a jar and twisting the lid on tight. Find her, Ma Durga's eyes said. I am worried about her.

Stephanie left the kitchen by the rear door, walked past the still-warm ovens and headed towards the spinning and weaving room at the northeast corner of the property. She asked the few people she passed if they had seen Ma Vera, but nobody had. It didn't occur to her that Ma Vera might not want to be found. Stephanie was genuinely concerned about the old woman and besides, she wanted to talk to her.

Ma Vera wasn't in the spinning and weaving room, nor was she in the pottery house or the animal stalls at the north end of the ashram. After taking a wide zig-zagging walk through the front gardens, Stephanie concluded she must be in the temple. She decided she would wait for Ma Vera outside the temple. She didn't feel right about entering the place of worship when she knew there were devotees inside. Eventually Ma Vera would emerge and Stephanie would be able to talk to her. She positioned herself on a stone bench where she could see who went in and who came out of the temple. She could see the still smoldering pyre from the early morning funeral. She placed the packet of food and tea beside her on the bench and waited.

Inside the temple, Ma Vera sat alone behind the screen depicting scenes from the life of Krishna. She didn't want to sit with the others just now, even though they were deep in meditation and prayer. She felt her thoughts might contaminate the purity of their contemplation, as if somehow her sadness and rage might send out jolts of negative energy.

Dear God, she thought, why have You deserted me? Why have You taken so much away from me when I have so little left? Must I taste only the bitterness of ashes in my last years? I tried to stem the tide of my bitterness; I tried to forgive. But these are not easy things for me to do. If I had known it would take the rest of my life, perhaps I would have started earlier. Then I might have found some peace before I died. Why is it we can never escape our past, perhaps never even make amends? Did You intend all along that I should suffer like this in my dotage?

She had been sitting cross-legged for too long and now she winced with pain as she tried to straighten out her legs. Finally she lay back on the planked wooden floor and tried to relax the spasms of pain that shot through her back. Slowly she felt the tension begin to ease in her muscles. What a pitiful creature I am, she thought, blaming God for my troubles. This is what old age does to us. It fills us with rage and makes us turn against our Maker. Nothing lasts, she thought, closing her eyes. Nothing is meant to last.

Stephanie waited until she was sure the last devotee had left the temple. She had watched the sun go down and had seen the embers on The Mother's pyre glow yellow, then orange, then deep red as the light faded on the horizon. She must be in there, thought Stephanie. She gathered up the samosas and tea and walked slowly toward the temple, hoping the door would open and Ma Vera would emerge before she got there. But she saw no one. Feeling the chill of recollection, she reached for the handle and slowly opened the door.

The temple looked empty without the flower-covered bier at the center, but the heavy scent of incense and burning wax was still present. Her eyes swept the room, adjusting to the dimness of candlelight. Stephanie couldn't see anyone in the temple; the only sound was the crackle and sizzle of hot wax from a hundred molten candles. She wanted to call out for Ma Vera, but the hushed gravity of the air sealed her lips.

Where are you? she thought, as she crept softly into the room. Her eyes rested on the panels of the screen at the far end, the images of the boyish Krishna barely visible in the candle glow. For a moment she hesitated, but only for a moment. If she's not there, I'll give it up and talk to her tomorrow, thought Stephanie. Like an intruder, a thief sneaking around in someone's bedroom, Stephanie peeked around the screen. Ma Vera was lying flat on her back on the floor, her hands folded across her breast and for a moment Stephanie thought she was dead.

"Ma Vera," she whispered, her voice barely audible, even to herself. "Are you all right?"

She heard the intake of breath whistle in the old woman's nostrils and then the low groan that emerged from her throat as she half opened her eyes.

"Yes," she said, as if affirming much less than the question asked. Yes, I can hear you. Yes, I was only sleeping. She groaned again when she tried to move.

"Oh God, what have I done?" she said. "I can't move." She tried to roll over on her side but the bulk of her torso kept her pinned to the floor like an overturned tortoise.

"Try bending your legs," Stephanie suggested. Eventually, she managed to help Ma Vera prop herself up against the wall. Her movements had been stiff and painful and she rubbed her joints, grimacing and cursing her stupidity. When Stephanie offered her the samosas and tea from *La Señora*, she accepted them gratefully, closing her eyes and groaning with relief after the first bite. "I don't even remember the last time I ate," she said. "Yesterday, I guess."

Stephanie watched in silence as Ma Vera ate the samosas and drank the tea. She looked as if she had aged ten years in the last few days; her tanned, leathery skin had lost some of its tautness and seemed faded and dull.

"You must be very tired," said Stephanie.

"I'm exhausted," she said, squeezing her eyes shut and resting the back of her head against the wall. "I can't even seem to find solace in prayer. I feel as if God's taken his phone off the hook." There was a half smile on her lips, but her eyes were tired and sad.

"I'm sure it's only temporary," said Stephanie, immediately realizing she'd said something profoundly stupid.

"Everything's temporary, my dear," said Ma Vera. "We want so desperately for it to be otherwise, we go to any lengths to convince ourselves it isn't so. The Christians invented Heaven so they would have everlasting life. The Hindus base their entire belief system on the notion of reincarnation in order to explain the endless cycle of death and re-birth. We try to convince ourselves that someone's in charge of this mess we call life. That there's really a master plan that makes sense of it all."

She stopped for a minute to think about what she'd said, as if the idea were completely new to her. "I shouldn't talk that way," she said quietly. "God might hear it and take it out of context."

Stephanie smiled at the old woman's slightly wicked candor. We never lose that primitive instinct to appease the gods, she thought. Touch wood. Cross your fingers. I didn't really mean it.

"You've known The Mother a long time, haven't you?" ventured Stephanie, when Ma Vera remained silent.

"Longer than you think," she answered, taking another sip from the jar of tea. "We first met in 1947. She was married to one of Mountbatten's junior aides at the time. I was a secretary. We weren't of the same class, of course, but those were extraordinary times and we became friends." She closed her eyes as if remembering the events from forty years ago. "She was very beautiful then, you know."

"I thought she must have been," said Stephanie.

"She was," Ma Vera continued. "How I used to envy her." She smiled. "So fair and slender, with those marvelous bones. She was terrified of the sun. So afraid it would ruin her lovely porcelain skin. She always wore wide-brimmed hats and never went outdoors in the middle of the day." Ma Vera chuckled to herself. "I, of course, turned brown if I sat in a room with a window. I used to bathe my skin in lemon juice to try and get rid of the color. Fat bloody chance." Stephanie smiled at the thought of Ma Vera's girlish vanity.

"She was very unhappy then," Ma Vera went on. "I think that's why we were able to become friends. She needed someone to talk to and I was more discreet in those days. Listened and kept my mouth shut." She looked at Stephanie, a hint of irony in her eyes, a touch of cynicism in her smile.

"Why was she unhappy?" asked Stephanie.

"Her marriage," replied Ma Vera, with the heavy conviction of the long unmarried, "was a source of great heartache and pain. Her husband was a deeply insensitive, pompous, overbearing, self-inflated individual. The very kind of Englishman one cringes to think of. A very shallow man who preferred the company of other vain and stupid men. I didn't like him," she added, as if she hadn't already conveyed the message succinctly enough.

"But surely she must have known that before she married him," Stephanie countered.

"He came from a very good family, you see," Ma Vera stated, as if that explained everything. "It wasn't exactly an arranged marriage, but it was an 'expected' marriage. He was considered a very good catch and Thelma was the last of her sisters to be married. That was her name. Thelma. I haven't thought about that in years."

She looked into the empty tea jar and carefully twisted the lid back on. "English marriage customs, especially among the well-to-do, are quite baffling, even to me, and very different from your romantic American notions."

Canadian, thought Stephanie, but decided not to say it.

"She realized very soon after the marriage that it had been a mistake. She was appalled at the thought of spending her life with him. Utterly horrified." Ma Vera shuddered, as if she had narrowly escaped the same fate.

"Did she have any children?"

"With Anthony? No. I think she developed migraine headaches just to avoid sleeping with him." And then, as if to make amends for her indiscretion, "Oh the headaches were real enough. I'm sure they were from the stress. Of course, I couldn't tell her to leave him. She had nowhere to go. It would have been such a scandal." Ma Vera seemed uncomfortable at the thought and shifted her weight to one hip. "It just wasn't done in those days, you see. It wasn't done."

"How did she come to be here, then?" asked Stephanie.

"I didn't see her for many years after the Partition," Ma Vera said, ignoring Stephanie's question. "It was a dreadful affair, you know. Hindus and Muslims killing each other. Women and children slaughtered. Whole trainloads of people massacred. Entire villages wiped out. That terrible migration of displaced people. And all because that despicable man, Jinnah, insisted on his precious Pakistan.

"He wasn't even a good Muslim, you know," she said, a look of stern disapproval in her eye. "Smoked, drank, ate pork. He was a dying man. If only they hadn't set that ridiculous, impossible deadline of three months. Three months! To do all that work. Maps had to be redrawn, armies and supplies divided, right down to the last knife and fork. It was impossible. Really impossible." She shook her head.

"Surely Mountbatten knew Jinnah didn't have long to live. One wonders what might have happened if there had been more time. But then who could have predicted that awful bloody aftermath. It still upsets me to think of the carnage. The waste." Her voice had dropped to a barely audible whisper.

"Perhaps it was inevitable," she sighed. "Perhaps the die was cast when the first British ship sailed into Calcutta four hundred years ago. Maybe it played out the only way it could. We weren't really their oppressors, you know," she said. "They were killing each other long before we got here. And constantly being invaded. We only tried to keep the peace. For the trade. Spices. Cloth ..." Her voice trailed off.

She began to rub her knees in anticipation of standing up. She had said all she intended to say.

"I'm afraid you'll have to help me up," she told Stephanie. "I never should have sat here so long."

It took some maneuvering and a fair bit of strength on Stephanie's part, but Ma Vera eventually stood, if not straight, at least ambulatory. She leaned heavily on Stephanie's arm and limped painfully toward the door. As her limbs became looser and less obdurate, she stood straighter and more apart from the younger woman. They walked without speaking along the path to the main residence. In the air the faint, acrid smell of charred wood remained. The hum of the night insects sounded slower, deeper than usual to Stephanie. More like a dirge.

chapter twenty-two

I always wanted more children," Ann wrote in her diary, "always thought I'd have them. When Stephanie was born, my whole world became focused on this tiny, precious being. No one prepares you for the head-over-heels falling in love experience, the utter and absolute infatuation with another human being that consumes your days and nights after the birth of that child. Or for the absolutely devastating despair when you realize that child depends so completely on you, and you alone. Certainly my own mother didn't. She raised us with such moral fervor that a sense of duty always overshadowed, in fact, swept away whatever gooey emotions might be attached to her mothering. I think she was so afraid we might turn out bad, she didn't dare slacken her vigilance in case we chose that moment to break free of the bonds of good behavior that had been so carefully wrapped around us.

"She never dared to have fun with us and I think that was a mistake. I think Jay suffered for that more than I did. I tried to make up for some of that loss by enjoying my own child, watching her little life unfold and her personality develop unfettered, I hope, by the heavy hand of moral rectitude. Jay never had a chance to make right the perceived wrongs. He chose not to grow up and he equated the freedom of childhood with irresponsible, thoughtless behavior as an adult. I'm not sure he's been able to reconcile what he interpreted as a lack of love with the unsentimental meting out of punishment by our mother that was the expression of her deepest fears for us.

"No mother is unafraid for her children. Every mother blames herself when something goes wrong. I'm sure my mother thought her intentions were the finest, the noblest of any. Yet, how does a mother communicate to her child that she is doing what she believes is best for them? How does she deal with the agony of knowing that her child has lived a life to spite her? Can she ever learn to accept it and know in her heart that there was nothing she could have done?"

Stephanie found Allan in an empty classroom, sitting at one of the tables, staring straight ahead at the empty blackboard. She crept into the room and sat on a chair opposite him but said nothing, waiting for him to acknowledge her.

"So," he said finally, as if they were in the middle of a conversation, "where do we go next?"

"I wish I knew," said Stephanie. "What is it we have to discover?"

"The truth," he said, simply, as if it were an object that had been temporarily misplaced. "Why did they die? Who was responsible, if anybody? What can we do about it?"

"Wait a minute. What are you talking about? How did we get from a puncture mark on The Mother's neck to 'they'? Who are 'they'?"

"Three people have died, Stephanie. Vishnu, your mother and Deva Mother. Don't you think the possibility exists of a connection?" Allan had been giving a lot of thought to that connection, but so far he had come up blank.

"A connection?" she echoed, trying to catch up to him. "What possible connection could there be between Vishnu and my mother, or my mother and Deva Mother for that matter?"

"I don't know," he said. "For the life of me I can't see one except that they were all here and they're all dead."

"Coincidence, Allan," was all she said. "I mean, do you think someone was putting something in the drinking water?" She realized she was being sarcastic and immediately regretted the remark. He looked at her with the patience of someone who has learned to tolerate the unfunny.

"I'm sorry," she said.

"Don't be. I know it sounds paranoid and far-fetched. And there's absolutely no basis for jumping to that particular conclusion. I guess I wish there was some reason for it all that made sense. A nice, neat theory that tied it all together."

She looked around the bare, whitewashed room with its simple wooden tables and chairs and its chalk-speckled blackboard. "If I didn't know better," she said, "I'd say you were reading too many murder mysteries." She smiled and reached across the table for his hand. He placed his palm on hers and smiled.

"Okay," he said, "let's start with coincidence. Manfred's missing."

"So I heard," she said, noticing how warm and dry his hand was. "Is that a coincidence?"

"I don't think so," he replied. "But you already know my theory about Manfred." She nodded. It would be a long time before she forgot the events of their night in the temple and his certainty that Manfred had murdered Deva Mother.

"Allan," she said, choosing her words carefully, "if Manfred did kill The Mother—and I'm not saying I believe that—why would he draw attention to himself by running away? Why would anyone suspect there was anything wrong? Everyone believes she had a heart attack. He must know that by disappearing hot on the heels of her death like that, he's only inviting speculation."

"Maybe someone saw him do it. Maybe he thinks it's only a matter of time anyway before the finger gets pointed at him and so he decides to give himself a head start."

She sat back in her chair and tried to think of a reply. Maybe, she thought, maybe. Maybe he panicked. Maybe he was crazy and paranoid and a killer. Or maybe he didn't do it.

"I talked to Ma Vera last night," she said, "about The Mother."

"Oh?" said Allan. He pushed a lock of hair off his forehead and it reminded her of Paul. She hadn't even called him. Hadn't thought about him until now.

"Did you know they met in 1947?" she said. Allan shook his head. "She told me that The Mother had been married and that the marriage wasn't happy. She said The Mother confided in her that she had made a terrible mistake."

"So does that mean The Mother was divorced?" he asked, thinking about something else.

"I never actually found out," she said. "Ma Vera got off on a tangent about Partition and we never got that far." She tapped her fingers on the wooden surface of the desk. "What's her relationship with the Guru Father?"

"Whose?" he asked, distractedly. "Ma Vera's?"

"No, Dumbo," she said, smiling, "The Mother's."

"Oh," he said, embarrassed. "I have no idea. As far as I know she runs the show and he is the show."

"Do you think they have a personal relationship?"

He shrugged. "Beats me. I never saw them together much. To tell you the truth, I never noticed her that much." He looked at Stephanie as if to say, Is this important?

"I was just wondering," she said. "I'm a naturally curious person, okay?"

"You're just looking for dirt so you can put it on your television show."

She smiled. "Who's the one looking for murderers?"

Allan laughed and sat back in his chair, clasping his hands behind his head. She watched the tension go out of his face for a moment.

Stephanie thought, This is a side of him I haven't seen before. He's distracted, letting his guard down, letting me get closer. He's so vulnerable, though, I wonder how far he'll go before he pulls back. She was surprised to find herself thinking about him this way, as if he were someone she was dating, rather than someone who had chosen a kind of priesthood for his vocation.

"Did you know my mother kept a diary?"

"No," he said. "Did she?"

"Yes. Werner gave it to me. She gave it to him for safekeeping when she got sick." After a moment she said, "There are some disturbing things in it."

"Oh?" he said, his attention suddenly riveted on her. "Like what?"

"Something was very definitely bothering her. I can't tell what from the entries she wrote. They're kind of oblique, like she was afraid to put it in writing." Allan's expression had changed. He was no longer distracted, but tense and alert, anxious to hear what she would say next.

"She keeps talking about a woman that she apparently had a falling out with. At least she believed the woman was 'freezing her out'–that was her expression–and then she began to wonder if she was just imagining the whole thing."

She watched Allan's face, but his expression hadn't changed. "Werner believes she changed after Vishnu's death," Stephanie went on. He says he heard a tension in her voice that hadn't been there before. Do you think that's true?"

He exhaled heavily, as if he'd been holding his breath, and ran his hands through his hair. He thought back over the last few months of Ann's life, the time in which he'd known her. He'd been so self-absorbed in those months he wasn't sure he could remember. What was it she'd said to him, after Vishnu's death? He was sure she'd made some comment that had surprised him. It had seemed so out of character. What was it? He pleated the fabric of his kurta between his fingers, creasing the tiny folds until they looked like an accordion. It was something about vengeance, he remembered. What drives a person to take revenge on another person? She couldn't understand that impulse that some people had.

"Do you agree with Werner?" she repeated.

"Yes," he said finally, "I do."

There had been something on Ann's mind and he had failed to notice it. Something a blind man had spotted and he had not. Oh God, he thought, I go around thinking I'm so sensitive, so caring, and all I'm doing is unloading my shit onto people and not bothering to take anything back. I didn't take her seriously when she said it, didn't pick up on it at all. What if she was trying to tell me something and I just shut her out?

Vishnu's sudden death had shaken them all up, so at the time, Ann's reaction didn't seem so strange. But now that he thought back on it, there was something different about the way she reacted to it. It was much more personal in a way. She was agitated, tense, and her tension caused him to close himself off from her. He hadn't wanted to deal with another problem; he just wanted life to get back to normal.

Stephanie was getting up to leave. She had to get to town, to the bazaar. There were some things she needed and she just wanted to get away for a few hours. She could still smell the burning funeral pyre, even though the fire was long out. It was like the smell of paint, still there in your nostrils even after it had dried.

She saw that she had lost Allan again to his thoughts. She wanted to ask him if he thought Ma Vera could have been Vishnu's mother, but she decided this wasn't the time. She would have to wait until he was back on planet earth again.

"Gotta go," she said. "Things to do."

chapter twenty-three

The bazaar was a daily affair that was set up early every morning and disappeared every evening like a tribe of Bedouins folding their tents. Stephanie had heard about the bazaar from travelers staying at the ashram who had told her she could get Crest toothpaste and Dove soap there–probably black market–as well as American manufactured Tampax and hair conditioner. Check it out, they said, you can even get good pirate tapes of The Eurythmics and Madonna.

The bazaar covered a square block two streets behind the post office and was comprised mainly of folding tables or just a piece of cloth spread on the ground with items displayed on top of it. Stephanie found the Crest and the Tampax without any trouble and quickly turned her attention to the other items for sale that had found their way into this small corner of the world.

Back issues of *Vanity Fair* magazine, all of which she had read, were instantly fascinating in their incongruous environment. One vendor's entire inventory consisted of old campaign buttons inscribed with anything from "Go With Goldwater" to "Indira for India." Could anyone support himself with such an enterprise, she wondered, even in India? And what of the surgical rubber gloves displayed on the next table? Plastic sunglasses and rubber flip-flops she could understand. There would be a market for those anywhere. Even waxed dental floss had its uses. But Lady Clairol Ash Blonde hair dye? To cover the gray?

Stephanie debated whether to try a masala dosa that she saw being prepared on a flat, black griddle a few feet away. The dosa maker was very skilled, the large round pancakes he produced as thin as tissue paper. The steaming, spiced mixture he poured into the center disappeared into the folds of the thin crepe and made Stephanie's mouth water. She couldn't resist.

The potato mixture was a lot spicier than she expected, so she ate in small bites, savoring the taste as the fire seared her tongue. It was much more interesting than anything she'd had at the ashram. She was so involved in eating that she didn't notice the small brown finger poking her arm until it happened a second time. Assuming the boy was a beggar, she shook him off and resumed eating. When he persisted she wasn't sure what to do. If I give him a *paise*, she thought, they'll all want money. But on the other hand, here I am enjoying this food and he may not have eaten all day.

"Memsah'b," he said. "Memsah'b," interrupting her again. "Come, come."

Oh no, she thought, he wants to take me to his father's shop and I'll feel obligated to buy something. Why couldn't he just be a beggar?

"Please, come," he repeated, still persistent, but she detected a note of anxiety in his voice this time. He kept poking her arm and pointing down the block to a row of shops and restaurants. She wanted him to know she was annoyed and had no intention of going with him. "No," she said sharply and showed him the sternest expression she could muster.

"Please, memsah'b," he pleaded, obviously unable to communicate with her beyond the three words he had already used. She could see the distress on his face and wondered if this was his usual game with tourists. Maybe his father will beat him if I don't go into the shop, she thought. Should I feel guilty about that?

Finally the dosa maker intervened, uttering a few sharp words to the boy. He replied in a desperate, pleading tone, going into a lengthy explanation that the dosa man nodded in response to. He turned to her and said, "You go," pointing where the boy had pointed. "Friend," he said, nodding his head from side to side in confirmation.

She gave the dosa maker a look that said, If this is a scam, I'll be back to have it out with you. But he kept nodding his head with the same anxious expression as the boy.

"All right," she said, "show me." The boy began to move crab-like through the bazaar, keeping one eye on her and one eye on their destination.

"It's all right," she said. "I'm not going to run away."

She followed him for half a block and then watched as he entered a dirt-floored, plank-walled chai shop where the proprietor prepared tea by pouring boiling water through a well-stained cloth filter filled with tea leaves. He smiled at her and demonstrated his skill at pouring the steaming, boiled milk into the tea in a long arc that created a bubbly froth at the top of the metal cup.

A tea shop, she thought. His father owns a tea shop. The boy was signaling her to enter the narrow, dark shop. He kept pointing to the back where she could see a shadowy figure sitting alone at a table. She nodded to the chai walla that she would have some tea and followed the boy into the nether part of the shop.

"You are a tough customer," she heard an accented voice say.

Manfred!

"Please, sit down," he said, as the proprietor put the tea on the table. "I must talk to you."

He lit a bidi, the rolled tobacco leaf cigarette favored by low-caste Indians and she saw his hand shake as her eyes became accustomed to the dim light.

"How are you?" she asked. She looked at her tea and noticed that the chai walla had given her the skin from the boiled milk. She made a face to express her revulsion.

"It's an honor, when they do that," said Manfred, noticing the reason for her discomfort. "You are privileged."

"Really?" she said.

Yes, he nodded.

She turned to find the proprietor and when he beamed a smile at her, she bowed her head and placed her palms together in the gesture of namaste. The proprietor seemed very pleased.

"Now I guess I'll have to drink it," she said to Manfred. He smiled and nodded again.

"So, how are you?" she asked again, watching his face.

"That depends," he said. He blinked his eyes quickly and took a deep drag on the bidi. She realized he was nervous.

"On what?" she asked.

"The Mother is dead, right?"

"Yes."

"And people think I had something to do with it, right?"

"There are some rumors."

He was gnawing on the skin around his thumbnail and she noticed it had started to bleed.

"I didn't do it, you know. I'm not a killer. I do a lot of crazy things, but I'm not a killer."

"The Guru Father says she had a heart attack," Stephanie said.

"Yeah, well then she probably did."

"Is there any reason to think otherwise?" she asked, wondering why it was so important for him to explain himself to her.

He sat back and took a couple of gulps from the metal mug of tea in front of him. Stephanie took a small sip of hers and realized it was quite good. How am I going to eat that skin, she wondered, touching it with the tip of her tongue.

"Okay, so I was dealing drugs," he said finally. "The old bitch was right about that." He drummed his fingers on the table and watched Stephanie try to drink her tea without swallowing the skin.

"I had a reason," he continued. "I was trying to get enough money to get out of this place. Back to Europe." He seemed almost embarrassed and turned to look at the wall.

"Why would you want to go back to Europe?" she asked. "I thought you hated it there."

"I do," he said, "but, well, there's this French chick I met at the ashram and she went back to France. And you know how it is, I just want to see her again."

"You're in love," said Stephanie.

"Yeah, sure," he said scornfully. "I'm in love. Okay?"

"It's okay with me."

He fidgeted in his seat like a schoolboy.

"So anyway," he said, "why would I kill the old bitch? I was going to leave the country anyway and what could she do to me without making bad news for the ashram? Eh?"

Stephanie thought about it. "Then why are you so paranoid?" His nervous behavior was making her uncomfortable. And that damn skin in her tea.

"Look," he said finally, with a decisiveness that alarmed her, "I think there's something weird going on at that ashram. I think there's some kind of nut case there who's offing people."

"What are you saying?" she asked, confused by his hard-boiled jargon.

"This is the way I see it," he said, patiently. "It's just too bizarre that three people in a row are dead in that place."

"Why couldn't it just be coincidence? There's no possible relationship between the three." Wasn't this the same discussion she'd had with Allan a few hours ago?

"Ach! Bullshit!" he said. "If you look for it, I bet you'll find a relationship. It's no accident that those three died."

"They didn't even die the same way," she said.

"What's that got to do with it?" he demanded. "I've seen a lot of weird shit in my time but nothing as weird as that place. I mean it. If you know what's good for you, you'll get the hell out of there. There's no way I'll ever go back."

Stephanie could see the tiny beads of sweat that had formed on his top lip. She didn't know what to think.

"You think I'm in danger there?" she asked.

"I think everybody's in danger there except the one with the trigger finger. I wouldn't spend another night in that place. I'd feel safer in a goddam crack house." He wiped the sweat from his lip on the soiled sleeve of his kurta and re-lit the bidi with a small wax match. He inhaled the tobacco deeply and coughed, expelling the bitter-smelling smoke. He seemed agitated yet at the same time relieved to have got something off his chest.

"Manfred," she said, "are you sure you don't belong in a treatment center?"

He looked at her sadly and shook his head. "Look," he said softly, "I get these feelings, okay? I'm not just some crazy dopehead. They ... ever since I was a little kid ..." His voice trailed off.

"You mean you're psychic?" she said.

"Well, I don't like to call it that, but, I know things. You know, I get these feelings and they sort of warn me about danger. I can't explain it," he said, almost pleading with her to believe him, "but even if I can't say what's going to happen, I know it's going to be bad."

Stephanie finished drinking the tea and examined the white blob at the bottom of her cup.

"I don't know whether I'm glad I talked to you or not," she said. "You're telling me my mother was murdered."

"Yes, I guess I am," he said. "And Vishnu and The Mother."

"What about the police?"

"The police?" he said, his eyes opening wide. "You think I'm going to go to the police?" He chuckled softly. "Sweet angel baby, no, no, no."

"I guess not," she said.

"I guess not," he repeated. "Look, do yourself a favor. Go home to your father or your boyfriend or your grandmother and forget you ever came to this place."

"What if I go to the police?"

"Simple," he said. "They won't believe you. And then you'll tell them about me and they won't believe you even more. And of course, I'll be long gone and you'll just look stupid."

"Why wouldn't they believe me," she asked, "or at least be interested?"

"And rock the Guru boat?" he said. "They think everybody there is a nut case anyway, but they're not going to take a chance and upset a holy man, especially when he brings tourists here."

She looked at the piece of skin in her cup and felt utterly defeated. Maybe he was right. Maybe she should just go home and forget about everything. Would her mother have wanted her to endanger her life just to find out the truth? A useless truth that wouldn't change anything? Wouldn't bring her back? But what if Manfred was right and there was somebody with a loose screw at the ashram? Could she forgive herself if somebody else died?

A tiny groan escaped her throat.

"Give it to me," said Manfred.

She looked at him and was about to ask him what he was talking about, but he grabbed the cup from her hand and swallowed the piece of skin before she could protest. She stared at him for a minute and he put the cup down in front of her.

"Thank you," she said.

chapter twenty-four

All the way back on the bus Stephanie went over and over her conversation with Manfred. Was he just a crazy dopehead? Paranoid and freaked out? Was he psychic? Did he really "know about" things like he said? Or was he doing a number on her just to scare her? He was capable of that, she thought. He wasn't to be trusted. What did he care whether she knew about all this or not? It made no difference to him whether somebody else died. Even if everybody in the place died. No skin off his nose.

Ugh, she thought. Skin. The way he'd swallowed that thing made her shudder. In a way, it was kind of gallant, though. He'd saved face for her, solved her dilemma and kept her from being embarrassed in front of the chai walla.

He's a strange one, she thought. He had confided in her, telling her about his "feelings." Either that or he was making a sick joke. When they left the chai shop, he had shaken her hand. "Goodbye Stephanie," he said. "I think we won't see each other again."

She couldn't help but like him, in a way. He was like the wild raspberries they used to pick behind the cottage. Sour little things, with those hard, tiny seeds that got caught between your teeth until you had to pick them out with your fingernail. But at the same time, you kept wanting more because of the little burst of sweetness when you crushed them against the roof of your mouth with your tongue. Manfred was a wild raspberry, all right. Or was he just wild? And could she trust him?

Just imagine for a minute, she thought, that someone at the ashram is killing people. My first question would be, Why? No, my first question would be Who? My second question would be Why? If it were possible to find out Who, then Why might become obvious. No, that doesn't make sense because, if my mother, Vishnu and The Mother are the victims, there is no obvious link between them. Nobody seems to know that much about Vishnu, so that makes him a bit of a wild card. If Ma Vera is his mother, as I suspect, then maybe my mother found out and told Deva Mother and Ma Vera killed them both. But then, who killed Vishnu? Maybe he really did die of natural causes.

That's ridiculous, she thought. Why would Ma Vera care if a couple of women–both her friends, incidentally–knew about an illegitimate child she'd had over forty years ago? What were they going to do? Call the *National Enquirer*?

The bus was approaching the stop near the ashram. She got up and made her way to the front. One thing's for sure, she thought. I'm no detective. If Manfred is a few rungs short of a ladder, I'm going to look like Super Idiot Woman if I start going around claiming there's a murderer on campus. On the other hand, she thought, there's something about that guy that gets under my skin. I can't just forget about him.

Back in her room after dinner Stephanie pulled out the red notebook that had been her mother's diary and began reading with more care some of the passages she had previously only skimmed through.

"I am feeling so much better," Ann wrote at the end of February. "My energy is phenomenal. I feel as if I could go without sleep for a week. They tell me this is quite normal, but the idea is not to go without sleep but to achieve a state of absolute relaxation, without dreaming, in order to derive the most benefit from less sleep. Wouldn't it be wonderful to be able to get by on three or four hours of sleep a night? I might even have time to do some reading!

"I can remember meeting a woman once who told me she only slept four hours a night no matter what she did. She went to the doctor and he told her not to worry about it, some people didn't need as much sleep. As long as she felt good and was healthy, there was no problem. Except for her there was a problem. She didn't know what to do with all the extra time! She would go to bed at eleven every night and get up at three and be utterly bored. She told me she did crossword puzzles to keep herself occupied. What a waste! Most people complain there aren't enough hours in the day and here's a woman who has extra time and doesn't know what to do with it. I believe God gives us the life we must live for a reason. There is a lesson in that woman's life both for herself and for the rest of us. It's an old story, isn't it? We covet something that the possessor doesn't appreciate or wishes he didn't have."

A few days later, her tone had changed. "I didn't like the look of him and I told him so," she wrote. "'You should be in bed,' I said. 'You've got a fever.' 'I can't,' he told me, 'I've got to finish these accounts.' If I'd known he'd be dead in twenty-four hours I would have been more persistent, but I just didn't realize one of those tropical fevers could take you so quickly. I saw her give him some tablets, so she must have been concerned as well. But after, when I asked her what she had given him, she was very abrupt. 'Something for the fever,' she said. Well, you'd think I was blaming her or something."

Ann went on then to describe Vishnu's cremation which took place the morning after his death. It sounded to Stephanie like a much smaller, hastier version of the ceremony that had surrounded The Mother's death. Ann merely described the events as she saw them, not fully comprehending the meaning behind some of the ritual. She offered no comment on the proceedings.

An entry about five days later gave the first hint she might not be well. "I had some stomach cramps last night," she wrote, "and all day today I had a very strong desire to stay close to a toilet. It is the one thing I hoped would not happen while I was in India. I suppose it's unrealistic to think it wouldn't. But I have been so careful. I can't imagine where I picked it up. Unless it was that peas and cheese stuff we had for dinner. I thought it tasted kind of funny. I wonder if anyone else is feeling off today. It doesn't seem to be a subject much discussed around here. I wonder if one could broach it in spiritual terms with one of the instructors. 'Swami Premananda, Can one say the belly speaks of a man's sins when it is in distress?' Hmmm. Maybe there's a future in writing ashram witticisms. Speaking of future, I hope this stomach thing clears up soon. No diarrhea yet, but I can't believe I'll be lucky enough to escape it."

Subsequent entries indicated her mother's illness was worsening. "I don't know which is worse," Ann wrote, "the nausea that travels a constant route between my stomach and my throat, or the terrible washed-out weakness I feel after a visit to the toilet that has been prompted by a single searing cramp in my gut."

As Stephanie read in great detail the agonized entries Ann made referring to both her physical and mental states, she began to come to the horrifying realization that her mother had begun to connect her own illness somehow, in her mind, with the death of Vishnu.

"What does she think I saw and who does she think I'll tell? I'm convinced she's holding something against me, yet her actions would convince anyone otherwise. She brings me powders to take every day that she says Guru Father himself has prepared. She tells me they are very concerned that I don't seem to be getting better. But there is a coldness in her eyes and in her voice that actually frightens me. Can the fever be affecting my brain?"

What could she have seen, thought Stephanie, that had come to be connected in the feverish confusion of her thoughts, with the changed attitude of the woman referred to only as "she"? What was Ann afraid of? "Am I becoming too weak to act?" she asked in a later entry. "Can I face the trip home now that I've told Stephen I'm coming? Oh please, God, don't let me lose my resolve. I must get out of here."

She leafed back through the pages and re-read the sections referring to Vishnu's illness: " ...I just didn't realize one of those tropical fevers could take you so quickly. I saw her give him some tablets, so she must have been concerned as well."

Oh my God, thought Stephanie, as everything came together in her mind like a blow to the head: the tablets! Whoever gave Vishnu the tablets must have killed him, and knowing Ann saw her give them to him, must have killed her too. Only more slowly, more painfully, so it looked like a natural death. She was so weak and helpless she couldn't save herself once she realized what was happening.

Horror filled Stephanie's heart at the thought of her mother lying there helpless under the attentive care of a murderess. She felt sharp sobs began to cut at her throat. Tears fell, hot and unchecked from her burning eyes. A long, low moan emerged from deep in her body as the full realization of her mother's terrifying last days hit her. She looked through tear-blurred eyes at the page before her and tried to wipe the salty drops away. The line under her finger read, "Dear God ... why didn't I ask them to come and get me ..."

Stephanie couldn't remember stumbling along the semi-dark corridor to Allan's room. Didn't remember knocking on the door or pushing it open and kneeling by the bed, weeping with the utter abandonment of a lost child.

Allan knew there was no point in asking what was the matter, no need. He recognized the anguish of a broken heart. He lifted her onto the narrow bed and lay beside her, holding her, soothing her, sharing her desolation. In time, her sobbing stopped, but she was not consoled. He held her tight and felt her heart beat against his chest, felt her breath warm on his neck.

After a while he began to kiss her softly and when she responded, he felt a need so overpowering he wanted her to smother him with her body, to take him so far inside of her he would lie forever in the darkness of her. They made love with slow, sad desperation and when he climaxed and heard one last sob emerge from her throat, he buried his face in her breast. We are both lost, he told himself, in a world where there is no reason for anything. Where death is the only relief from the agony of living.

chapter twenty-five

If Paul Anderson hadn't arrived at the ashram the next afternoon, Stephanie might have lost her resolve and left for home. She felt as if she had no will of her own any more. She had let Allan make love to her, had even encouraged him. When she left his room early that morning, there was a new understanding between them. They'd lain awake half the night and she told him what she'd discovered in her mother's diary. It confirmed his suspicions and he felt helpless and full of the anger he had tried so hard to lose. She fell asleep at one point and woke to hear him sobbing.

Now, alone in her room, she felt guilty for having laid her own burden at his feet. She knew she had destroyed something he had been so carefully trying to build for himself. Perhaps faith. Perhaps a sanctuary. Or maybe just a lie that convinced him life was worth living. It wasn't anything he said that told her this. He had been kind and loving, but she had felt the sadness, the sense of desolation that was a permanent part of him and she knew she had added to it. She felt empty, exhausted, like Sisyphus, forced to push a huge rock up a hill, only to have it roll back down again. She didn't know if she had the will to bring about a resolution to the matter. Why didn't I come sooner, she asked herself. Why didn't I insist on coming as soon as we heard she was sick? Where was I when she needed help so desperately?

And then, miraculously, Paul had arrived, like an apparition, his edges blurred by the wavy haze of heat that hung like a gauzy curtain in front of him. He saw her grief-stricken face and didn't wait for her to ask why he had come.

"You took too long to come back," he said. "I was worried."

She crumpled into tears and he put his arms around her, knowing he was right to have come, not knowing yet why he was right.

She took him up to her room and showed him the diary, poured everything out to him that she had learned and that she feared had happened. He said very little, just listened. When she finished her story, he asked only one question.

"Have you told anyone else?"

"There's one other person who knows," she told him. "And he's suspected for a while."

They talked for a long time. "I want you to come and stay at the hotel with me," he said. He was staying in a small tourist hostel on the edge of town.

"No, I'd rather stay here," she said. She'd made up her mind. "I can't leave without finding out what happened."

"I agree we have to find out what happened," he said, "but you might be in danger here."

"I'll be all right," she said. And then added, "Allan's here."

"Who's Allan?"

"Allan Lloyd," she answered, her eyes focused on Paul's chin. "A friend of mother's. The one I told you knows the whole story. He'll look out for me."

She felt a twinge of regret that she hadn't told him everything, but it was too late now; she'd already taken a step toward betrayal and there was no turning back. Besides, there was Allan to think of as well. Was it fair to either man to know too much about the other?

"How's my father?" she asked.

"Up and down. Although he always says he's fine when I ask." That sounds like him, Stephanie thought. Never betray your true feelings.

"He couldn't understand why it was taking you so long to come home," Paul continued, watching her face. "When I told him I'd decided to come over here, he insisted on giving me money. I didn't feel right about taking it."

"You should take it," said Stephanie. "It makes him feel less helpless. It's the only way he has of being useful."

He realized she was probably right. She understood her father better than he did. But it still rankled that the gesture was an easy one for a rich man to make and a difficult one for a poor man to accept. She would never understand the part of him that needed to assert his independence. To her, it was more important that her father feel useful than that he, Paul, feel unencumbered by obligation. She had said it casually, without thinking, but he realized it was remarkably perceptive of her and this surprised him. Normally she would have offered no explanation for her father's behavior; she would have simply told him it was foolish not to accept the money.

Had the events of the last ten days changed her? Or was she just more vulnerable because of them? More likely the latter. Paul didn't think people really changed that much. They might soften around the edges with time and experience, but he believed your basic nature stayed with you all your life. It wasn't so much that he wanted Stephanie to change–he loved her, after all–but she was capable of hurting him in ways she wasn't aware of. He just wanted her to be more sensitive to people's weak-nesses. The way Ann had been. But Ann had been born that way;

she didn't have to learn about the vulnerability of human nature. She felt it, could see it the way some people can see auras. Stephanie hadn't been born with that ability; she would have to learn it the hard way.

"I think I should talk to the police," he said.

"I'm sure it won't do any good. I think Manfred was right. They won't take it seriously because they don't want to rock the boat."

"I still think I should try. It's a start, anyway."

He took her hand and tried to pull her toward him. He wanted to kiss her but she turned away. "Not now, Paul," she said. She was distracted after the intensity of their earlier conversation, as if by emptying herself of information, she was empty of emotion as well. But in a way, it was like it had always been between them. Connected. Disconnected. Together. Apart.

Stephanie invited Paul to stay for dinner at the ashram. She showed him the layout of the place and he was anxious to see what kind of people were staying there. He didn't really expect them to be kooks and airheads, nor did he think they would be shamans and fakirs, walking over hot coals and reclining on beds of nails. But he was surprised how ordinary most of them were. He found the degree of self-absorption disconcerting and he told Stephanie this. She lifted her eyebrows in surprise and said she hadn't noticed.

While they ate, she pointed out the few people she had come to know. "That's Ma Vera," she said, as the older woman took a seat three tables over. She was pale and drawn, and seemed sad and distracted.

"She's been here about twenty-five years and she was a close friend of The Mother's. They met in 1947 during the preparations for Partition." She relayed to him the conversation she'd had with Ma Vera after The Mother's cremation.

"She seems to be taking it very hard," she said. She also told him of her suspicions regarding Vishnu's maternity, adding, "But

I really have no evidence. It may just be my imagination."

Manu had joined Ma Vera but very little conversation seemed to pass between them. "I really don't know that much about Manu," she told Paul, "other than that she's usually quite lively, once she overcomes her initial shyness. This seems to be her home, but I have no idea where she came from."

She pointed out Werner and Else, nodding in response to Else's wave. "Werner's the one who gave me Mother's diary," she said. "He's been blind since his teens but has a kind of third eye that he perceives the world through. Else painstakingly describes everything she sees to him and then he takes it and puts it through his own inner machinery and gives it his own interpretation. They're quite amazing, really." Paul laughed as he imagined Werner and Else as some kind of circus act, with Else tossing balls to Werner, who caught them and then juggled them in the air.

"How do you like the food?" she asked, noticing he was eating at a slower pace than normal.

"Kind of bland," he said, poking at it with his fork.

"Bland" was the all-purpose descriptive Paul used whenever he didn't like something. Everything from Mexican salsa to chocolate mousse would be described as bland if Paul didn't care for it. She had to smile. In this case it was almost the right word. Something had gone out of *La Señora*'s cooking since The Mother's death. Perhaps this was her way of mourning. Stephanie told Paul about the kitchen and how it operated under the firm, but eccentric hand of Ma Durga.

"She adds a bit of color to the place, normally."

Paul brought her up to date on the latest gossip on the home front while they finished their meal. He told her that Dave Abbot, her boss, had hired a very young, very shapely freelancer to fill in while she was away. "He smiles a lot these days," said Paul. "But I'm not sure how much work is getting done."

"Oh great," said Steph, groaning, "maybe I won't have a job when I get back."

"Oh, I have a feeling old Dave will be very glad to see you," said Paul, smiling. "The novelty of the ingénue should just be wearing off and Dave's patience will be starting to wear thin. I understand she's not much of a speller."

Good old Dave, thought Stephanie. Amazing what a pair of long legs could do to even the most liberated of men. Dave liked the occasional diversion, but politics and television were his wife and mistress. She realized she missed her work, even missed Dave, and hoped Paul was right about the freelancer.

"Hello Stephanie. May I join you for a moment?"

It was Manu who had approached so quietly Stephanie hadn't even noticed.

"Of course," she said. "Please." She indicated the empty chair beside her. "Manu, this is Paul Anderson, my friend from Canada. Paul, this is Manu." She saw the expression on Paul's face soften as he looked into Manu's large, black eyes. He half rose from his chair as she sat down. His eyes never left her face. Stephanie noticed for the first time Manu's earthy sexuality. She's very beautiful, she thought.

"Have you seen Allan?" Manu asked Stephanie, her eyes darting uncomfortably back to Paul, who was staring at her.

"No, not today."

"I'm a little concerned," Manu continued. "It's not like him to disappear for a whole day and no one seems to have seen him. Do you think he might be under the weather?"

"I doubt it," said Stephanie. She was pretty sure Allan was hiding out. She began to feel guilty again about what had happened between them. "I'm sure he's all right," she added, almost to herself. She wanted Manu to leave.

"I hope so," the young woman said. "I don't want to go traipsing around after him or he might get annoyed with me." She smiled an embarrassed smile in Paul's direction.

"Oh, I almost forgot," she said suddenly, turning back to Stephanie. "Guru Father would like to see you in his chamber after the evening meal."

chapter twenty-six

Stephanie was surprised to discover that the Guru Father's private quarters were very comfortably furnished. She had expected a certain amount of austerity in keeping with his role as spiritual father. Like Paul, she hadn't expected a bed of nails to furnish the room; nor had she expected the comfortably upholstered couches and hand-woven carpets that lent a slight air of seduction to the inner sanctum. Perhaps they're gifts, she thought, from grateful disciples. The dense fabrics had absorbed the scent of incense over the years leaving a dry, stale fragrance hanging in the air. A dim light emanated from a small lamp on a round, cloth-covered table beside which the Guru Father sat, serene, yet sad, an open book on his lap.

"Come in," he said in the Anglo-Indian accent that had become so familiar to her ears. "Sit, sit."

His voice was clear, strong and soft, all at the same time. It had a strangely hypnotic effect, soothing and comforting, yet exerting control over the listener's emotions. Stephanie had heard voices like it before. Good politicians sometimes had it when they needed to be especially persuasive. Diplomats in her father's circle of friends certainly had it. And, above all, men of God, honorable or otherwise, had it. She took a seat opposite him on one of the sofas.

"Will you take some tea?" he asked. "I have an extra cup."

"Thank you," she said, more out of courtesy than a desire to drink tea. His manner was courtly and seemed to demand formality from his guest. The tea was sweet and black, she noted, not the herbal tea that was served in the dining room, nor the spiced, milky tea that you got in the bazaar.

"We have been witness to great tragedy in recent months," he said, dispensing with any social preliminaries other than the offering of tea. She wondered who he meant by "we." Was he referring to just the two of them; or was he speaking of everyone in the ashram?

"Sometimes when this happens, we are unable to understand God's message to us," he continued. His eyes held hers in a sad, intense gaze. "I fear you are missing your mother very much."

How extraordinary, she thought, that he's taken the time to speak to me about this in the midst of his own grief. Was he reaching out to her to find some comfort for himself?

She returned his gaze but didn't speak.

"She was a friend to us, as you know," he went on, "and a valued member of our society. We believe that God has taken her from this present life for His own purposes. You know when I speak of God, I speak of the God Principle, that which governs all life. His wisdom and His love are beyond our reckoning and we must learn to trust them. We are but mortals, destined to live out our lives according to His will. We may not interfere with His plan for us anymore than a fish can change the tides of the sea."

But what if she was murdered, thought Stephanie. Doesn't that mean that someone interfered with the plan? Or was that part of the plan? Did God intend for my mother to be murdered?

"I hope, my child, that you have found some comfort among us."

She had to clear her throat to find her voice. It felt as if it had been locked away in her windpipe for days. "Everyone has been very kind to me," she said. She realized she didn't know what to call him. Was he addressed as Guru Father? Or simply, Father? She had no idea.

"Deva Mother was also very dear to us," he said, his gaze dropping to the book on his lap. His fingers seemed to caress the edge of the pages. "She shall be missed."

The silence sat between them like a spectator. There were questions she wanted to ask him but none of them was of a spiritual nature. What was your relationship with The Mother? How did you come to be in this place? Who was Vishnu? Was he Ma Vera's son?

She wasn't sure why she felt so constrained. He was human, after all. He could tell her to mind her own business if he didn't like the questions. But he seemed to be not of this world, here, in this sanctum with its very real carpets and couches and books. Even though she saw the fatigue and sadness in his eyes, saw that his knuckles were knotted with arthritis, and that his fingernails were long and in need of a trim; even though he was flesh and blood and hair and bones, she could almost believe that his spirit superseded all those things and was the very essence of his being. And so, she didn't ask her questions but merely nodded in acquiescence and drank her tea.

He talked to her for a long time about the God Principle, faith and Karma, and how we had to learn to accept our Karma as the determinant of our fate. It reminded her of her mother's letters.

"If God had not wanted us to struggle with the duality of our natures, he would have made us all angels and be done with it." It is this struggle to achieve oneness with the Absolute, he told her, which is man's most difficult, but most rewarding endeavor.

"If it were too easy," he said, "we would not value it so highly."

Who among us, he asked her, has not wished for an answer, a sign, that God exists and that all our pain and suffering is for a reason? But there are signs everywhere, he said. All of life is constant witness to the miraculous cycle of birth, death and rebirth. We are part of a process of endless becoming. We act and we are the act itself, inseparable from it as heat is inseparable from the fire. If you take away a man's soul, is he still a man, or merely a beast of burden? And what of the beast of burden? Is it fair to say it is no more than a strong back and four legs? It is one of God's creatures, after all. What right have we to assume anything? What right have we to second-guess God?

At times he seemed to ramble, talking more to himself than to her. Stephanie wasn't sure she was connecting all the dots, but she knew he was speaking about the importance of faith. Occasionally, he would look straight into her eyes and speak boldly.

"God does not expect us to be perfect. I am not perfect. But my faith is perfect. That is all He asks."

How did you achieve that, she wanted to ask. Did you sit under a tree until you had a vision? Did God actually speak to you? Did you convince yourself that's what happened? Are you trying to convince yourself even now?

Not fair, she thought. I'm being cynical. Just because I can't conceive of perfect faith doesn't mean it doesn't exist for some people. Was that what my mother was trying to achieve? Did she need to know with certainty what others are content to assume? Was she so desperate that she had to travel halfway around the world to find the answer? Was it worth her life?

Stephanie felt very tired all of a sudden. The Guru Father's voice had taken on a kind of droning quality that made it strangely hypnotic. She had stopped listening to the words and could hear only the sound, like a chant or a drumbeat. Steady. Rhythmic. One. Two. Three. Four.

She could feel her body relaxing, first her shoulders and

arms, then her hands, then her legs and feet. Even her eyelids felt heavy. She had no idea how long she'd been sitting there, listening to the Guru Father's voice. Didn't care. Perhaps she'd even fallen asleep. After a while she noticed that the voice had stopped talking. The room was very quiet; even the outdoor noises coming through the open window seemed muffled by the carpets and furniture, as if they had to penetrate the stuffing before they got to her.

She looked over at the Guru Father and saw that his head was down, his chin resting on his chest. His breathing was almost imperceptible, but she could see the regular up and down motion of his chest. He's sleeping, she realized. He's put himself to sleep. He looked old and frail, as if he were made of paper.

She stood up quietly and tiptoed to the door. It must be very late, she thought.

And then she saw it. A silver-framed photograph of The Mother. Much younger, much softer. Smiling through a moment frozen in time, thinking some long forgotten thought. He had put the photograph on a shelf where he could see it from his chair. It was clearly a studio photograph, posed and perfectly lit. Stephanie bent to look at it closer and saw that it was signed. She forced her eyes to focus on the faded lines of ink in the dim light from the lamp. Her heart jumped as she saw what the inscription said.

"All my love. Always. Thelma."

Stephanie slept soundly that night. In the very early hours of the morning she dreamed she was with her mother at the cottage. They were both wearing white dresses made of thin, gauzy material. The air felt chilly and her mother suggested they build a fire.

"The heat will make us feel one with the fire," she said, and to Stephanie, in the dream, it made perfect sense.

"Of course," Stephanie said, but when she went to help her mother make the fire, she saw that it was not Ann but Deva

Mother who was kneeling on the hearth lighting the wood. The room began to fill with smoke until it was impossible to see. Stephanie managed to find her way outside and she ran into the woods, coughing smoke from her lungs, brushing smoke from her hair and clothes as if it were cobwebs. When she looked back at the cabin, she saw it was engulfed in flames, huge, towering flames that reached up into the sky. The fire blazed not twenty feet from her, but she heard no sound of crackling, nor did she feel any heat. She felt only a cold silence as she saw the cabin reduced to ashes.

chapter twenty-seven

Allan found her the next morning in the kitchen, helping with the washing up.

"Hi," he said, tentatively, picking up a length of white home-spun that was used to dry dishes. He picked up a dish and started drying it. It was a large dish so he was able to take his time, concentrating on the top, bottom and sides of it, making sure it was completely dry before he picked up another one. There were three other people, besides Stephanie and himself, washing and drying dishes. He nodded to them briefly, then continued with his task. The dishes were almost done before Stephanie broke the silence.

"A friend of mind has come from Canada," she said. Why couldn't she say "boyfriend," she wondered. She had never felt comfortable using the word. It seemed so juvenile and she and Paul had an adult relationship. They were completely independent, free to see other people if they chose and not bound to each other by any formal agreement. Besides, Paul wasn't a boy, he was a man. But "manfriend" sounded ridiculous and pretentious. She always introduced him as "my friend, Paul," or even less specifically as "a friend of mine." Paul complained that this sounded like he was a casual friend and not a special friend who was, in fact, her lover. "Well, I don't want everyone to know the details of my private life," she would counter. Nonetheless, she always felt guilty and defensive whenever she referred to him as a "friend."

"Is he staying at the ashram?" Allan asked, trying to sound casual.

"No, he's staying at a small hotel he found on the edge of town. I don't even know what it's called."

"There's only one. It probably doesn't have a name."

"I'm going to meet him there for lunch. Would you like to come with me?" she asked impulsively, hoping he would say yes. She didn't want to be alone with Paul and she wasn't sure she should be alone with Allan.

Allan didn't know how to react to her invitation. He needed to be with her because when he wasn't with her, he found he was thinking about her. He was attracted to her physically, but he didn't feel the spiritual bond he had felt with her mother. His need for her made him feel sad and inadequate, as if he knew they could never satisfy each other.

She put her face close to his and spoke in a low voice so the others wouldn't hear. "He's gone to the police and I thought you'd want to hear what they said."

The police? What could the police do at this point, he wondered. There were no bodies, no evidence, only a couple of people with suspicions. Manfred had disappeared and besides, Stephanie didn't believe he was guilty of anything but the drug dealing he had confessed to. Allan no longer knew what he thought about the whole thing. But he knew he had seen the puncture mark in The Mother's throat. No one could convince him that it was anything but a means to murder. Try and tell that to the police.

"Do you want to come with me?" Stephanie repeated.

"Okay. Sure," he said.

They met Paul in the courtyard of his hotel. It did have a name: Hotel Lakshmi. He was sitting in the shade of a tree reading *A Passage to India* and didn't notice them arrive. By the time he realized who they were, they were close enough for Allan to see the look of dismay that crossed Paul's face before he recovered himself. I shouldn't have come, thought Allan. He's more than just a friend. Then he remembered that Ann had told him about Paul, how much she liked him, how she hoped Stephanie would marry him.

"Hi, Paul," he heard Stephanie say. "This is Allan." Paul got out of his chair and they shook hands, each mumbling something inaudible to the other.

"Can we eat here?" asked Stephanie, looking around, avoiding eye contact with either man.

"Yes," said Paul. "I asked. They serve lunch in a small dining room. Or we can have lunch out here, if you like."

"It's a bit hot to eat outside, don't you think?" she said. "Let's see what the dining room's like."

It wasn't much cooler inside. A ceiling fan stirred the air around like a slotted spoon in a pot of hot soup. "I think this is better," Stephanie said.

The men smiled uncomfortably at each other and waited for her to choose a table. When she was seated, they each waited for the other to sit first. Finally, Allan sat on Stephanie's right, Paul on her left. The proprietor appeared at the table as if from thin air.

He described what was on the menu and assured them he and his brother did all the cooking themselves. He would allow no one else to touch the food.

"We are very good at cooking," he said. "It is our specialty."

Allan ordered a vegetable curry. Stephanie chose the vegetarian thali, a selection of curries, rice and yogurt that was a complete meal. Paul hesitated, unable to decide and Stephanie persuaded him to try the thali. The proprietor offered them a choice of Coca-Cola, Orange Crush and Lime Squash. They ordered one of each.

The only other occupants of the room were two men, probably local merchants, who were nearly finished their meal. They called out to the proprietor as he passed and ordered chai.

"Well?" said Stephanie, looking at Paul. "What did they say?"

"You were right," he answered. "They didn't want to know about it." The proprietor arrived with their drinks and they waited until he was back in the kitchen before they spoke again.

"They just gave me a bunch of crap about the ashram and the Guru and what fine people they all are and basically told me I was mistaken. This kind of thing is common in India, they said. They said I mustn't mind." He smiled ruefully as he remembered the conversation. "I mustn't mind," he repeated.

Stephanie was clearly disappointed. "I guess Manfred was right. He told me the police wouldn't be interested. I thought maybe he was just trying to put me off."

"I'm not surprised they reacted that way," said Allan. "Even if they believed you, I'm not sure they'd do anything about it. There's too much at stake around here. It's quiet now because the hot season is starting, but during the winter, this place is full of tourists. Guru shoppers and utopia seekers. Business would dry up pretty fast if word of any of this got out."

Stephanie found it hard to believe the police would do nothing if they knew people were being murdered.

"If they had clear evidence, they'd have to do something, wouldn't they?" she said. "But right now, there's nothing to show them."

Their food arrived and they ate in silence, each of them lost in their own train of thought. After a while Paul spoke to Allan.

"Do you think all three of them were murdered?"

Allan considered for a moment before answering. "I know The Mother was murdered. I'd be willing to swear that was a puncture mark I saw in her throat. Why or by whom, I have no idea. I find it hard to believe that Ann died for the reasons given by the doctor. I had a bad feeling about it at the time and I believe in my gut that she shouldn't have died from the fever. I think somebody gave her something to accelerate the symptoms, or maybe even something that caused the illness. Again, why or by whom remains a mystery to me." He drank some lime squash before continuing.

"As for Vishnu," he said, "I honestly don't know enough about him or his illness to say. I had nothing to do with him and barely saw the man while he was there. But if Stephanie's right and Ann saw someone give him a lethal dose of something, it could mean they were both murdered by the same person."

"So if we could figure out who killed Vishnu," said Paul, "we would probably know who killed Ann."

"I think we need to find out who Vishnu was," said Stephanie. "Where did he come from and what was he doing at the ashram?"

"Who do you think might know something about him?" asked Paul.

"I'm sure Ma Vera knows something," Stephanie replied. "I've tried to talk to her a couple of times, but I never seem to be able to get around to the subject. Or else, she's very clever at keeping me away from it. What do you think, Allan?"

"I'm sure she knows a lot about what goes on around there. But I haven't a clue how to ask her. She scares me a bit," he said, smiling at them both. "I wonder if Manu knows anything. She's been there a long time. She might be willing to tell me if I ask her."

"I'm sure she'll talk to you," said Stephanie, remembering how Manu had looked at Allan. "I'm sure she'd like to tell you a lot of things." Allan looked uncomprehending and merely shrugged his shoulders.

"What about this guy Manfred?" said Paul. "Do you think he

might know more than he's letting on?" He looked at Stephanie. "What do you think, Steph? Any chance he knows more than he's saying?"

"It's possible," she said. "He seemed to lean toward the mass murderer theory, though. That some psycho was killing people. But he did say that if you looked for it, you'd probably find a connection between the three deaths."

She thought about her conversation with Manfred. He had tried to tell her he thought she was in danger there. *I'd feel safer in a goddam crack house,* he'd said. He was so nervous and paranoid, probably because he was sure everyone suspected him of killing The Mother. *I do crazy things,* he'd said. *But I'm not a killer.*

"I didn't really ask him too many questions," she said. She'd been so preoccupied with that stupid piece of skin in her tea and then he'd thrown her completely by telling her he thought everyone at the ashram was being murdered. She hadn't been thinking too clearly.

"Do you think he might still be in town?" asked Allan. "We could try and find him."

"I doubt if he's still here," said Stephanie. "He wasn't exactly in a mood to hang around."

"It won't hurt to check," said Paul. "Do you know where he was staying?"

"No, but I could probably find the tea shop," she said. "The chai walla might know where he is."

"Let's do it," said Paul. "At least it's a start."

So they were a team, for the moment. All doubts aside; a common mission to bind them. Each had cared about Ann in their own way and each needed to know the truth about her death. Allan, because his own rage would consume him if he didn't find some reason for the horror of life. Paul, because his sense of justice demanded an answer for Ann's sake. And Stephanie because, for the first time in her life, she felt events spinning beyond her control and she didn't like the feeling at all.

chapter twenty-eight

They decided to walk the mile or so to the center of town. Stephanie was fascinated to see, close at hand, the playing out of village life and social interaction. Squat but substantial dwellings lined the road; laundry was spread out to dry; cooking fires burned and children played at games of their own invention. She was already familiar with the sight of thin, sinewy women carrying large bundles on their heads. Now she watched the context in which these women lived their lives.

She was surprised at the amount of discourse and chit-chat that went on among the villagers. Did they talk about the weather and their backaches? Or were they more concerned with the way the country was being run? Was this woman's husband faithful? Was her teenage daughter having a child out of wedlock? How complex were the issues for these people who lived at what to her was subsistence level? They seemed relatively content, not oppressed and certainly not starving.

She was content to walk in silence and speculate on the

undercurrents of life in a small Indian village. Allan and Paul had begun somewhat uneasily to explore each other like two dogs meeting on neutral territory. Friend or foe? Stronger or weaker? Straight arrow or loose cannon? They seemed, in fact, to be getting along, much to Stephanie's relief. They had discovered a mutual interest in baseball and statistics flew through the air as they talked about their favorite teams. Allan had missed the trades and contract signings, winter training and spring season start-up. Paul obligingly filled in the details and brought him up to date.

"There it is," said Stephanie, pointing to the mud-walled tea shop where she'd met Manfred. They were parched from their walk in the blazing sun and agreed to go in and order tea. Stephanie warned them about the possible honor of receiving the boiled milk skin. Paul decided to have a Coke instead. When the tea came, she saw with relief that the proprietor had withheld the honor. Possibly it had been bestowed elsewhere and received with the proper appreciation.

The chai walla had recognized her and greeted her with smiles of pleasure and bows of namaste. He assumed, naturally enough, that she had so enjoyed his excellent tea the other day that she had invited her two friends to share her pleasure. He was disappointed when Paul ordered Coca-Cola but he extended equal courtesy to both of her guests. A customer was a customer.

She tried to ask him if he knew where Manfred was staying but the fact that he spoke no English complicated matters. He seemed to know she was referring to Manfred; she gestured to describe his long hair and knotted headband. But he didn't seem to understand that she was asking where he was. He smiled blankly and nodded his head from side to side, not wishing to offend her. He went to the front of the shop and Stephanie saw him call to a young boy who he then sent off on some sort of errand. Within minutes the boy returned, accompanied by an older man who was greeted by the proprietor in a flurry of excitement.

The two men approached their table and the chai walla gestured to the older man to speak.

"Good afternoon," he said. "My friend has asked that perhaps I can be of assistance. Yes?"

"Ah, yes," said Stephanie with obvious relief. "The day before yesterday I had tea in this shop with a man. I believe he remembers that." The older man conferred briefly with the proprietor who nodded his head from side to side.

"I wonder if he knows where that man is staying," Stephanie continued. "I would like to talk to him."

The two men spoke again, the proprietor gesturing animatedly with both hands. The other man nodded and occasionally uttered "Ah." Finally, he turned to Stephanie.

"He says he has not seen the man since that time," he told her, "but he believes he was staying in a room over the Indra Sari and Fabric Shop. It is not far from here. Come. I will show you."

"You're very kind," said Stephanie. They paid for the tea and Coke and after much bowing and namaste, left the shop with the older man.

He took them to the main square where Stephanie had first arrived in the village by bus, and pointed to an open shop whose sign hung below a shuttered second story window: Indra Sari & Fabric Shop.

"You must go up the stairs and to the right of the shop you will find entrance to the room," he said. They all thanked him in a clumsy kind of unison and proceeded across the square.

The wooden stairs were narrow and rickety and the trapped air in the stairwell was stale and musty. Stephanie went first, followed closely by Allan and then Paul. She called Manfred's name a couple of times but there was no response.

"I'm sure he won't be here," she said. The door at the top of the stairs was closed and she rapped her knuckles against it, calling his name again. When they heard no sound behind the door, Allan knocked again with his fist and said, "Manfred, it's Stephanie and

Allan. We just want to talk to you."

Stephanie noticed that the door had moved slightly when Allan hit it. She gave it a push and it swung open to reveal the small, sparsely furnished room.

Manfred was lying on his back on the wood and rope-strung bed. The needle that stuck out of his left arm was encrusted with a tiny bit of dried blood at its base. His gelatinous eyes stared fixedly at a point on the ceiling but revealed no hint of what he might have seen there. A small, involuntary groan escaped from Stephanie's throat.

"Is that him?" asked Paul.

Allan stared at Manfred's dead face and nodded his head.

"Why?" whispered Stephanie. "Why would he do this?"

He hadn't seemed like a man about to take his life two days ago. He had been fearful and paranoid but not despairing. He'd even admitted to being in love.

"Maybe he was murdered too," said Allan, unable to tear his eyes away from Manfred's face.

The other two looked at him blankly. Another murder? Was it possible?

"I guess we should get the police," Paul said finally. When they didn't protest, he took it to mean they were in agreement. "I'll go," he said. "They know me already."

When Paul left, Allan put his arm around Stephanie's shoulder and said, "Come on. Let's wait outside."

She walked down the narrow stairs ahead of him. "He told me he could sense when something bad was going to happen," she said. "But he never knew what it would be. I wonder if he knew he was in danger."

Goodbye Stephanie, he had said to her. I think we won't see each other again. She felt a quiver of nausea in her stomach and swallowed hard to hold it back.

Paul returned within a half an hour with the local chief of

police, who considered anything involving foreigners to be important enough to deal with himself. He determined death by accidental drug overdose based on the evidence at hand. When Paul tried to convince him this death might in some way be linked to the other deaths at the ashram, he would have none of it.

"No, no," he said. "This kind of thing is quite common among this type of foreign visitor. I know what I am talking about." Clearly he had no desire to investigate further.

"Will there be an autopsy to determine the type of drug?" asked Paul.

"No, no," said the Chief. "That will not be necessary. It was probably heroin. It is readily obtainable and what else would he be using a needle to inject?"

As far as he was concerned, it was an open and shut case. The burdensome part would be notifying the embassy and having Manfred's body shipped home. They watched as he went through the few things in Manfred's pack and put his passport in his front shirt pocket.

When they compared notes later, Allan would say that he saw no needle marks on Manfred's arms to indicate that he was a regular user. Although there had been a spoon and a box of matches on a chair by the bed, there was no bag or vial that would have contained the lethal dose that Manfred had apparently self-administered.

Paul would remember that he had seen an empty arrack bottle lying on the floor just beside the bed. Arrack, he knew, was a potent liquor made from fermented coconut milk. Was Manfred the type of guy who would drink a bottle of alcohol and then give himself a heroin fix, he wondered?

Stephanie would not be able to stop thinking about her conversation with Manfred and the haunted look in his eyes. And she would never forget how he'd saved her honor by downing the skin from the boiled milk.

chapter twenty-nine

Allan and Stephanie left Paul in the village and took the bus back to the ashram. Allan said there were things he had to do and Stephanie was tired and upset. Paul made her promise not to do anything foolish, but what he meant by that, she didn't really know.

"Maybe I'll go hang around the spinning room," she told Allan on the bus. "Ma Vera or Manu might be there."

But it was Werner and Else she encountered in the far corner of the small bungalow that housed the looms and spinning wheels that miraculously transformed the raw cotton fibers into usable lengths of cloth.

"Stephanie! Where have you been?" chimed Else, as if she were greeting a long lost friend. "We have not seen you in days." Werner was smiling and nodding his head in agreement.

Stephanie didn't know where to begin, so she began at the end and told them of finding Manfred dead with a needle stuck in his arm.

"Ach! I knew it," said Else. "Didn't I tell you Werner that he would come to a bad end. That kind," she said, stabbing at the air with her index finger, "that kind always end up like this."

"Perhaps you exaggerate, Else," said Werner.

"Perhaps nothing," she retorted. "I know what I'm talking about. He was a self-inflicted crazy who got what he deserved."

Her indignation had the certainty only righteousness can bring and could not be disputed. Stephanie preferred to sidestep the issue of Manfred's nature, deserving or otherwise. She knew that Else, and possibly Werner, believed Manfred had overdosed on heroin. She didn't have the energy to disabuse them of that notion, a process that would involve going into detail about the possible murders of Vishnu, Ann and The Mother. She might have been willing to discuss it with Werner, but Else's volatility left little room for a rational exchange of ideas. Instead, Stephanie tried to steer the conversation around to more neutral territory.

"A friend of mine has come from Canada," she said. "He's staying at the hotel in the village."

"Aah," crooned Else, "I was dying to ask when we saw you in the dining room, but Werner wouldn't let me." She frowned at her unseeing husband.

"I'm quite sure Stephanie would not have welcomed your prying, Else." Werner's tone was uncharacteristically sharp and both Stephanie and Else turned to him in surprise.

"Not prying, Werner," Else said. "Stephanie is our friend and one naturally wants to know more about one's friends. Isn't that true, Stephanie?"

Caught off guard, Stephanie could only mumble something inaudible. Werner, she could see, was amused.

"Else, my dear, you think because I am blind that you can fool me," he said. "But you are the most transparent of human beings. In fact, if I must say it, you are the perfect wife for someone such as myself. I know the expression on your face from the tone of your voice and I know the degree of manipulation you wish to achieve by the pitch. What man could ask for more?"

Stephanie saw, to her surprise, that Else was blushing.

"Werner," she said, with more embarrassment than annoyance in her voice, "Stephanie will think I am an idiot. Don't listen to him, Stephanie. He's only trying to make me feel foolish. But of course, it never works. Now," she said, indicating Stephanie should sit beside her, "tell me about your handsome friend."

Stephanie and Werner laughed in unison and she heard Werner mutter, "I give up," as he resumed his task of winding thread from a large spool onto smaller spools for hand sewing. He was methodical and meticulous, each new spool an exact duplicate of the one before.

Stephanie helped Else clean and sort the balls of raw cotton that would eventually become thread for the weaving looms. She described her relationship with Paul in the most non-committal terms possible while Else pressed for more details like a lawyer in cross examination. Are you in love with him? Do you want to marry him? Do you live with him? Stephanie's answers were vague and evasive but this did not stop Else from forming her own conclusions.

"You are just afraid of losing your independence," she said. "But a good man will not take that away from you because he will value his own independence as much. If he loves you, then he must trust you and let you have your freedom. And you must do the same for him," she added. Werner remained silent.

Else continued to carry on a one-sided conversation, which Stephanie followed with only one ear. Her mind was on Manfred and her own bewilderment at his death following so closely after the others. Was it possible he had been murdered, as Paul had suggested? Nothing could convince her he had killed himself; she was more ready to believe he had accidentally overdosed, as the chief of police claimed.

She listened to Else's voice droning on and felt as if she could fall asleep. It was not unlike listening to the Guru Father the night before; the kind of wisdom being dispensed was not dissimilar. Both were based on a belief in justice; things happened for the better. One's faith in the rightness of these principles was infinitely more important than one's perceptions or experience. What they believed, in fact, became the reality and they perceived and experienced the world through the filter of their faith. She noticed that Else had finally stopped talking. They continued to work in silence for several minutes. Then Werner spoke.

"Stephanie," he said, "how is it you came to find Manfred dead? Did you know where he was staying?"

She told them how she had run into Manfred at the bazaar and gave them an edited version of their conversation. She said he had decided to go back to Europe because he was in love with the French girl. She didn't tell them about the drug dealing or his paranoid conviction that people were being systematically murdered at the ashram.

"He figured The Mother was out to get him," she said, "and decided it was time to leave."

"Hah!" said Else. "And decided it was time to kill her, you mean."

"Such nonsense," said Werner. "If he was going back to Europe anyway, why would he jeopardize his future? Besides, Guru Father saw her having a heart attack. Do you doubt his word?"

"No, of course not," said Else, sullenly. "He believes that is what he saw."

"Let Stephanie finish," he said. "Why did you go back the next day, Stephanie?"

"Well," said Stephanie, "I was in town having lunch with my friend and I just thought I'd check and see if Manfred had left yet. I thought if he was still around I'd ask him what he knew about The Mother and Guru Father. I was curious about their relationship."

"If that's what you wanted to know," said Werner, "you should have asked me. I'll bet I know something not too many people are privy to." A look of satisfaction sat on his face like a fat toad on a lily pad. Else and Stephanie exchanged surprised looks and waited for him to continue.

"I told you people think because I am blind, that I am also deaf and dumb," he went on. "They often say things around me that they would not want anyone to hear."

"Maybe they're not aware you're there," suggested Stephanie. "You can be very quiet."

"Perhaps," said Werner, unconvinced.

"Werner," said Else, losing patience, "what is it you know and why haven't you told me this before?"

"I didn't think you'd be interested," he said, taunting her. "Besides, you never asked."

"Ach!" said Else, disgusted. "This man will make me crazy!"

Werner laughed at the apparent torment he was causing his wife. He was obviously enjoying a rare opportunity to gloat. Stephanie laughed.

"Werner," she said, "stop torturing us and tell us this great secret."

"All right," said Werner. "If I must. But you mustn't interrupt with questions. I'll tell you just what I know."

He told them he had been in The Mother's office folding a new batch of pamphlets that had come from the printer. She asked him to do the job herself, perhaps, he said, in an effort to make him feel useful. He had been alone in her office for some time when he heard the Guru Father greet her on the terrace just outside the open window.

"Their greeting was casual and familiar, neither addressing the other by name. I assumed this was a regular event in both of their days."

He said the meeting consisted mainly of The Mother informing Guru Father of various things, including numbers in residence, incoming, outgoing, that sort of thing.

"I didn't pay much attention to what they were saying, quite frankly. It wasn't very interesting." But then, he said, the tone of the conversation changed.

"I heard him ask her, 'Have you ever regretted it?' And she said, 'No, not any of it. If I hadn't met you when I did, I think I might have killed myself.' 'But what a scandal,' he said. 'I was never going back,' she said. 'What did I care what they thought? My life was all but over when I met you and then suddenly I had a second chance. I was desperately unhappy. What could they have done to me that was worse than what I had done to myself?'"

"And then he said, 'Ah, but to run away with a native, a colored man, in those days. They would never have taken you back.' Then they were silent for a few minutes," said Werner. "'Why are you asking me these things now?' she said. 'Perhaps because I am old,' he replied. 'Perhaps because I need to know.'"

"'I will love you till the day I die,' she said. 'You must know that by now. I have done everything for you.'"

Werner was very still for a moment. "And then," he said, turning his blind eyes in their direction, "I heard the Guru Father get up and leave. They said nothing more."

Stephanie and Else stared at Werner.

Finally Else said, "I don't believe you. You're making it up!"

Werner laughed and then was silent. "Stephanie believes me," he said. "Don't you, Stephanie?"

"Yes," said Stephanie. "I believe you."

"It's as you suspected, isn't it?" he asked.

"Yes," she said. "It is."

Else was clearly confused. "Werner," she said, "I am shocked at you. It's not like you to spread around such information. This is gossip and you despise gossip."

"I am not spreading anything around, Else," he explained. "I have told only you and Stephanie and I trust what I have said will not go beyond this room. It is something I thought Stephanie should know."

Else looked at Stephanie, expecting her to explain. But the younger woman merely nodded.

"You two," said Else, baffled and a little hurt, "have been having secrets."

"Don't be silly, Else," said Stephanie, rising to go. "Werner has just learned how to read my mind the same as he reads yours. See you two later."

"Bye Stephanie," said Werner. Else, for once, said nothing.

chapter thirty

Stephanie found Ma Vera in her room where she seemed to be spending a lot of her time lately. She knocked gently on the door, only half expecting Ma Vera to answer. The silence on the other side of the door was like a presence occupying the room. She was startled to hear a small, tired voice say, "Come in."

Ma Vera was sitting in a wooden rocking chair, the only piece of furniture in the room besides the rope-strung bed and a wooden table. She looked small and old, the years of sun exposure having faded from her skin in a matter of days. Her stoutness and the energy she had exuded seemed diminished, as if some vital fluid were slowly draining from her body, leaving her shriveled and colorless. Stephanie approached her and sat, unbidden, on the side of the bed.

"Are you unwell?" she asked, tentatively.

"Only in spirit," the old woman answered. "The rest of me seems determined to carry on."

Stephanie sat staring at her own hands, which she had folded in her lap like a schoolgirl. She felt like an intruder.

"You've come to ask me something," said Ma Vera.

"Yes," said Stephanie.

"Well? Have you lost your tongue?"

Stephanie looked at the old woman and saw, to her surprise, that the black eyes still burned with a kind of fury. She wished she could offer sympathy but she knew it was not what Ma Vera wanted.

"I want to know about Vishnu," she said.

Ma Vera's eyes widened with surprise. "Vishnu?" she said. "What about him?"

"Was he your son?"

"Hah!" Her laugh was like a bitter cough. "My son?" She laughed again. "God save my soul, no," she said. "Is that what people think?"

Stephanie didn't answer. "He seems to have shown up here out of nowhere and caused quite a bit of trouble," she said.

Ma Vera grunted. "He was trouble from the day he was born," she said bitterly. Then added quickly, "His kind always is."

Else had referred to Manfred as "that kind" and now Ma Vera was referring to Vishnu as "his kind." It was as if no further definition were required. You fill in the blanks. It was paint-by-number character assassination.

"I take it you didn't like him," Stephanie said, hoping she wouldn't have to pry Ma Vera open like a clam.

"No, I didn't like him," Ma Vera replied. "He was a greedy, mean-minded man with the morals of a slave trader. He wanted to take this place, this sanctuary, and turn it into a high turnover resort for the spiritually starved, wealthy rubbish of Europe and America. He envisioned a spiritual sex camp for the rich and bored. A guru supermarket. Put this lovely little place on the map. Charter flights from Bombay. King-size beds. The whole bit. He was very bad news."

"But how could he do any of that?" Stephanie protested. "He didn't own the place. He couldn't just take it over."

"He was an extortionist, wasn't he," said Ma Vera. "Took over the accounting. Insinuated himself into every corner. He knew how to make a threat stick. And what did they know about business? They weren't into it for profit. It was their life. They had built their dream and he wanted to turn it into a nightmare. He was a dreadful man. I cried with relief when he died."

Ma Vera had two patches of red on her cheeks and her breathing had become quick and shallow.

"But I still don't understand," said Stephanie, "what kind of leverage he had."

"Oh, he had leverage, all right," said Ma Vera feverishly. "He could make them do anything he wanted them to." She seemed to be talking to herself, concentrating fiercely on her memories and directing her anger at a point in front of her, as if she were aiming a gun at a target.

"They never had a chance," she continued. "As long as he lived, he was a threat to them. It was God's mercy that intervened and brought about his death. He giveth life and He taketh life away," she said, as if remembering some sermon from long ago.

"What was the leverage?" Stephanie pronounced each word carefully and focused her eyes on Ma Vera's face.

The old woman pulled herself back into the present. Her breathing slowed and the tension in her body began to drop away until she appeared to sag.

"He was their son," she said quietly. "Their love child."

Stephanie felt her muscles relax. Yes, she thought, of course. It would explain a lot.

"They knew very soon after he was born that he was Satan's child," Ma Vera said. "He's what they used to call a 'bad seed.' Born with a cruel streak. It's as if he were their punishment for falling in love and wanting to be together. Because, of course, they had sinned against God in the eyes of many." Ma Vera sighed as if remembering a sad love story she had seen at the movies.

"He never cried as a baby," she said. "His skin was soft and pale, but his eyes just stared at you out of that cradle, as if he were waiting to grow up so he could do what he wanted to do.

"And when he learned to walk, they couldn't let him out of their sight. He used to hurt other children. I mean really hurt them. He'd draw blood and once he tried to choke a little girl just to get something of hers he wanted. Later, it was killing birds and small animals that gave him pleasure. Not glee, mind you, but a kind of deep satisfaction that had a very calming effect on him. Or so it seemed. Can you imagine their suffering?

"I often wonder what their life would have been like if he had been a normal child." She was studying a spot on the floor as if it held some clue that would explain everything. "You see, it was because of Vishnu that he renounced the world and took the path of a sannyasin. It was his penance, in a way. He made a pact with God. If you make my son well and keep him from harm, I will devote my life to You. He kept his end of the bargain. I'm not so sure about God."

Ma Vera seemed defeated by her own sadness. Stephanie wanted to reach out and take her hand and tell her it would be all right. She wished she could offer her some alternative vision. Point her in another direction and say, "See, the sun is shining over there and it will shine again on you someday." But how do you tell a person in the sunset of their life that there will be another day, another sunrise? Ma Vera saw nothing but ashes when she looked around her. The ashes of burned up hopes, the charred remains of long friendships and a lifetime of experience.

"What happened when he grew up?" Stephanie asked, hoping that the old woman would feel better if she talked about it.

"He was sullen and bad-tempered as an adolescent, but he excelled in mathematics and this seemed to give them hope that he might at least find some place in society, something he could work at. Of course, there was always the problem of his temper and his inability to get along with people. He had an insanely perfectionist nature and could be vile if things weren't just right.

"By this time, they were operating a small retreat of sorts. They would offer lodging to individuals seeking refuge and enlightenment. She managed the house and meals and he became a sort of counselor-teacher. He had an extraordinary ability to communicate with these individuals, many of whom were troubled. Misfits, I suppose you'd call them. Perhaps he understood them so well because of his own situation.

"He acquired a bit of a reputation over time, enough to build what you see here. But it was built on heartbreak and pain. The central sorrow of their life was their son and that suffering was never going to end.

"The boy left them when he was around sixteen. Ran away to Bombay. Couldn't stand the piety and the peace and quiet, I suppose. I don't imagine he had an easy time of it in the city, what with his violent temper and his mean ways. He would turn up from time to time when he needed to hide out for a while. Gambling debts and who knows what else. They always took him in and he always gave them trouble.

"He always managed to elude the law, as far as I know. But there were times when they didn't see him for years and they would wonder if he was dead. Wonder and worry. They were always worrying. Was he ill? Was he in trouble? Was he dead? Or worse, was he going to do harm to someone?

"And then he showed up a few months ago with all these plans. He was forty years old and he looked awful. He was a piece of garbage who'd lived a useless, wasted life. If he'd been my son, I'd have disowned him years ago. But they couldn't do that. They felt so guilty and responsible. As if their illicit love had somehow created this monster and they had to deal with it for the rest of their lives.

"So they took him in one more time." She sighed heavily and

with a finality that suggested that the story ended there. But Stephanie knew it hadn't ended there.

"How did he die?" she asked, knowing she wasn't going to get the right answer.

Ma Vera looked up. "I told you," she said. "God was merciful. Of course, if you mean 'What did he die of?' then the answer is, fever. He died of a fever that came on quickly and carried him off like a plague of locusts. If that isn't the hand of God, I don't know what is." Her tone of voice defied Stephanie to contradict her.

Maybe she really believes that, thought Stephanie. Later, in her own room, lying on the bed trying to fall asleep in the stifling heat, she would run the story through her mind again, trying to see it first from Ma Vera's point of view, then the Guru Father's and finally, The Mother's.

Each way the story would be slightly different. The reasons for things happening would vary and the excuses would differ. From Ma Vera's point of view, Vishnu was a bad seed from the day he was born. For the Guru Father, he was a punishment for his sin of loving a married woman, a white woman not of his caste. For The Mother, he was her son and her responsibility until the day she died. They were bound together by the act of birth and she could no more cut him out of her life than cut out her own heart.

Ma Vera said she would have disowned him if he had been her son. But was that true? Can any woman who has given life to a child say, I no longer have a son? And had the Guru Father's life of penance made a difference? Had it done anything to pacify the gods or had it just created a greater rift between him and the son he could neither comprehend nor change? Had he and The Mother failed as parents or simply been the victims of a cruel fate?

She would ask herself these questions again, much later, when her life resumed a more familiar shape. But life would never be the same for Stephanie. There would be scar tissue where once there had been unblemished innocence. There would be no third corner to the family triangle to keep her and her father soft and yielding when their natures started to become hard and unbending. Her children would have no grandmother and her father would have no wife to remember young love in his old age.

But most of all, for Stephanie, there would be no pat answers, no youthful certainty that life was explainable despite its unpredictability.

chapter thirty-one

I don't want to know about this, thought Allan, as he listened to Stephanie tell Ma Vera's story of Vishnu's life. Nobody's born "bad," he told himself, they become that way for a lot of very complicated reasons. Environment. Parental and peer pressures in conflict. Accidents. Humiliations. Who knows what? There was even a group that was promoting the theory that food allergies could make children violent and unresponsive. Put all that together with certain personality traits, perfectionism, say, as in Vishnu's case, and you could come up with a pretty messed-up character.

The notion that Guru Father and The Mother could conceive a child that would punish them for their sin was corny and laughable. It was a form of mumbo-jumbo, like saying AIDS was God's punishment for homosexuality.

He accepted the fact that the Guru Father was a mystic, and granted, he had been raised in the Hindu tradition, but this kind of Old Testament wisdom went out with the Victorians. Stephanie seemed quite able to accept Ma Vera's version of events, but then, Stephanie saw them all as actors in a play and not living, breathing human beings, subject to the same laws of nature as she was. Would she believe her son could be born as punishment for her sins? Of course not.

He wished he hadn't slept with Stephanie. It had really messed him up. All the time he had spent concentrating on his spiritual side, trying to come to terms with his physical pain and his own wretchedness. Now it seemed all undone in a single night. He felt like an American jock, ruled by his hormones, lusting after a woman for sexual release, only to find that the more you scratched an itch, the worse it got. When he looked at the women at the ashram now, all he saw were hips and breasts seductively wrapped in those saris. If Manu looked at him one more time with those limpid, longing eyes of hers, he couldn't be sure he wouldn't grab her and bury his face in her breasts. Sometimes he just ached.

And now Stephanie was shattering his illusions about the Guru Father. How could he go to him now for guidance and spiritual wisdom? Would the Guru Father be credible now that he had a human past? All too human, it seemed, tainted by passion and folly. But maybe it would make him more credible, Allan thought. In a way, they had shared a similar tragedy. The Guru Father would understand the weakness of the flesh. He had suffered a lifetime because of it.

Oh God, he thought, I wish this would just go away. I wish I could just put it out of my mind.

"I still believe she killed him," Stephanie said.

What was she saying now? He had to ask her to repeat it.

"I still believe Ma Vera killed Vishnu," she said. When he didn't respond, she went on. "I mean, she hated him so much. And she even admitted she wept with joy when he died. All that business about God's mercy. I don't for a minute think she believes it. It's just a handy way to end a conversation."

Well, at least they agreed on that, he thought. Now what? "So she kills Vishnu, she kills The Mother and she kills your mother too?" he asked. "Is that what you believe?"

"There's no basis for believing that," she said, choosing to ignore the petulance she heard in his voice. "She loved The Mother; she was devoted to her. And I think she cared about my mother, too."

"So she murdered Vishnu and somebody else murdered the other two?" he said. "And what about Manfred?" He was beginning to sound exasperated. "Stephanie, there has to be some kind of cohesive theory, some logical reason for all these deaths if we're going to call them murder. I know, I know," he said, putting his hands up to stop her. "I was the one who found the needle mark on The Mother's neck. I was the one who was suspicious about Ann. I'm not backtracking, really, but I just can't see any connection between all these deaths."

"Nor can I," she said. "Except that if my mother saw Ma Vera kill Vishnu, then Ma Vera might have had to kill her, too. She couldn't expect her not to tell anyone and she wouldn't want the scandal to destroy her friends."

"And so maybe The Mother saw Ma Vera kill Ann, so Ma Vera had to kill her best friend to keep her quiet, too, I suppose," he said. "I just can't buy that."

They seemed to be going around in circles. Supposition was not fact and until somebody gave them more facts—and who knew the facts?—until that happened, they were going to get nowhere.

What was the probability that there was more than one killer, he thought. And what was the probability of a killer with no motive? Either the killings were the random acts of some psycho—and how random were they?—or there was some key link among the victims they were missing. All four had been residents at the ashram, but not for the same reasons. In fact, if you looked at them, each was there for completely different reasons.

Vishnu had come to take over the place from his parents and transform it into a hotel deluxe for guru shoppers. Ann had come for the purest of reasons; she was seeking peace and enlightenment and thought you could find it by going halfway around the world. The Mother, it turned out, was married to the Guru Father and, strictly speaking, co-owner of whatever there was to own. And Manfred. Who knew what his reasons were for being there? It was a cheap place to stay. The food wasn't great, but it was plentiful. It was a pretty obscure place if you wanted to hide out for a while. If Manfred had been murdered, he was the only one of the four not to die on the ashram premises.

And what were the links between the four? The only apparent one was that Vishnu was The Mother's son. Vishnu and Manfred might have been in cahoots, but would a perfectionist like Vishnu join forces with an unpredictable wild man like Manfred?

And what about the way they had died? Vishnu and Ann had apparently died of fever, but Vishnu had died suddenly and Ann had lingered. The Mother's symptoms had been those of a heart attack, according to the Guru Father, but Allan had seen the puncture mark on her neck. Manfred had apparently died of a drug overdose, but he had also consumed a bottle of arrack some time before his death. Was his overdose self-administered or had someone been there when he died?

Since there appeared to be no guns, knives or blunt instruments involved in any of the killings, was it safe to assume they had all died from some kind of drug ingestion or poison? And could they assume no weapons had been used? The doctor had apparently not examined any of the bodies and three of the four had been disposed of very quickly. Manfred's body was probably being sent home in a box and would his family care enough to have an autopsy performed? They would probably make the same assumption the police chief had made. Now that he was dead, they could stop sending a check every month.

And if a drug or poison had been used, what might induce

fever and heart attack symptoms that had been witnessed by several people? Or were four different drugs used?

He and Stephanie went over the few facts they had and looked again at all the possibilities that didn't add up. The only link, they concluded, was Ma Vera. She seemed to know more than anyone about the individuals and she seemed to have emotional attachments, of one form or another, to each of them. Except for Manfred. Other than the fact that The Mother had disliked Manfred, and Ma Vera had been close to The Mother and therefore might have disliked him for the same reasons, there didn't seem to be any connection between them.

They decided they would have to confront Ma Vera again, although Stephanie expressed concern about her state of mind and her health.

"She seems so old and tired," she told Allan, "and she was so robust when I arrived here. Can a person recover at her age, from the kind of emotional anguish she's been through? I mean, it's obvious she's suffering. I could almost believe she was wasting away."

"She may have a lot more on her mind than we realize," Allan said, "especially if she holds the key to this whole mess."

"Or if she's the perpetrator," added Stephanie.

Paul was due to arrive at the ashram sometime after lunch and they agreed to wait until he got there before confronting Ma Vera one more time. Maybe if all three of them pressured her to speak, she'd admit what she knew. And if she knew nothing more than what she'd already told Stephanie, then at least they would be able to see it for themselves.

After Stephanie left, Allan lay down on the bed and closed his eyes. What am I doing here, he thought? I didn't come here looking for murder, romance and adventure, like some kind of trashy novel. I didn't come here to find the temptations of the flesh or to give free rein to the baser part of my nature. So why is all this happening? Should I be able to ignore all this and somehow rise above it? Is there no way to be around other people and just observe them like they were some exotic species instead of constantly becoming entangled in their lives?

Maybe I should take a vow of silence, he thought. Find some place nobody wants to go to and stay there. I can't believe I came to the other side of the world to get caught up in something far worse than I left. Just like Ann, I suppose. Were we trying to find a life or run away from one? The problem is, you bring all your baggage with you and set yourself up for the same stuff. I guess we both thought we were coming to some kind of paradise. We were so wrong.

He reached up and put his arm across his eyes and felt the tears soak through the thin cotton sleeve of his shirt. Jesus, he thought, does it ever stop? Is there ever a time when you can say, Ah yes, this is the way I want it to be? Probably in the split second before you die, he thought, bitterly. Or, more probably, never.

He rolled over on his side and pulled his knees up to his chest. Classic fetal position, he thought. That's what I've been reduced to. The primal desire to return to the womb. Back before it all started. We should start out old, he thought, and go backwards, gradually getting rid of experience, accumulating innocence and eventually ending up in the safe place we all long for. Then we wouldn't care if life had meaning. We wouldn't spend the whole of it searching for something that might not exist. We wouldn't end up bitter and disappointed. No doubt we'd find a way to mess it up, of course. No getting away from human nature.

But what next, he wondered. Do I stay here and start all over again? Or do I go someplace else and start all over again? Or do I go home and start all over again? It all begins to look the same after a while. It's me I can't get away from. Me, myself and I. They're always with me and they're the ones I'd like to lose. Me, myself and I.

chapter thirty-two

Fortunately they didn't have to look far for Ma Vera and when they found her in the spinning room, she was alone. She had felt the need to do something with her hands and, in the past, the spinning wheel had always provided a soothing, almost numbing activity that allowed her body to be active and her mind to focus without having to think. She had never been one to worry over her problems. She had always tucked her troubles into little corners of her mind and let them work themselves out over time.

She remembered once when she hurt her back, the doctor told her she could do one of three things: "You can take drugs and go to bed; you can go for physiotherapy and exercise; or you can do nothing. Whichever you choose, it will take three weeks."

She felt the same way about problems; it was time that took care of them, not thinking about them or taking drugs to dull the pain. But lately, she had found herself brooding, an activity she abhorred as being wasteful and destructive. Once you slipped into the habit, it was like a drug, easier to take than to leave off.

All she had to look forward to was a lonely old age and most of her memories had become painful. I'll die bitter and alone like my mother, she thought, something I swore I would not let happen. I can see it in front of my eyes like a movie on a screen. And that young woman, Stephanie, asking me all those questions, making me remember things I don't want to think about anymore. God spare me from young people who think there are reasons for all these things that happen. There are no reasons. Reason implies some kind of cause and effect, some rational order to things.

If there's one thing I've come to believe in this world, it's that things don't always happen for a reason. Most things happen for no reason and most of us get through life by running for shelter whenever anything happens. Like those bombing raids during the war. You didn't know when they were going to come. You didn't know where they were going to hit. If you were lucky, you had a quick warning and you ducked into a shelter. That's how I'd describe life, if anybody asked me. One long series of bombing raids, and if you're lucky, you survive, but not without a few scratches and scars. And a few bad memories.

And now she was back again, Ann's daughter. With Allan of all people, and that friend of hers from Canada. What do they think I can tell them? Why don't they leave me alone? I won't tell them any more; there's no more to tell anyway. I've said as much as I'm going to say. Let them ask someone else. Let them ask God.

"Ma Vera," said Allan, gently, "don't you think it would be better if you told us what you know? You can't just let it eat away at you. Surely it's more than any one person can bear."

He looked at Stephanie with a mixture of pleading and exasperation in his eyes. "Please, Ma Vera," she said, "tell us what happened to Vishnu and The Mother and my mother."

"Ohhhhmm," hummed Ma Vera, the sound coming from deep in her throat. "Ohhhhmmm."

"We no longer believe that Vishnu and my mother died of fever, or that The Mother died of a heart attack," said Stephanie. "You don't believe that either. I'm sure of it."

"OHHHMMM," chanted Ma Vera, louder, as if to drown out what Stephanie was saying. "OHHHHMMM."

"Please don't do this, Ma Vera," Allan pleaded. "Four people have died, including Manfred. What if someone else dies? We can't just stand by and let it happen."

"OHHHHMMM." Now Ma Vera was rocking back and forth with the rhythm of the spinning wheel, the thin, ragged thread still running through her fingers.

They looked at Paul to see if he had any suggestions, but he had nothing to offer. The old woman was determined not to talk and he couldn't see a way of making her. Her mouth was set in a grim line and her eyes were shut tight. He was sure the only sound in her head was the deep, rasping intonation that was coming from her innermost self.

"Ma Vera!" said Stephanie, loud enough to be heard over the chanting and loud enough to make Allan jump. "What are you hiding from us? Why don't you finish the story?"

But the chanting only became louder and there were tears sliding out of the corners of Ma Vera's tightly shut eyes and dropping onto her cheeks. Stephanie wanted to grab the old woman and shake her. Her stubbornness was maddening, like a child holding its breath to get its way. So intent was she on getting Ma Vera's attention, she didn't even notice Manu enter the building. None of them saw her until she ran up to Ma Vera and flung her arms around her. "What are you doing to her?" she screamed at them. "She's an old woman! Are you trying to kill her?"

Ma Vera continued to chant, but now her incantation was mixed with a pitiful sobbing as she allowed Manu to hold her and stroke her bent back. She was still holding on to the ragged piece of thread.

Stephanie looked at Allan and Paul, who were equally horrified at what they had done. Stephanie felt awful, as if she'd beaten the old woman with a stick. Allan would have given anything not to be there at that moment and Paul couldn't believe he had stood by and done nothing. Both Manu and Ma Vera were sobbing now, making the three of them feel even more wretched.

"What were you trying to do?" Manu asked hoarsely when she finally spoke.

Stephanie knelt down beside the young woman and spoke very softly. "Manu," she said, choosing her words carefully, "I think something terrible has been happening here. I don't quite know what to say to you." She glanced at Ma Vera as she said this. "But we believe—Allan and I believe—that Vishnu may have been murdered."

Ma Vera had stopped chanting and was now breathing heavily through her nose as she held her lips in a tight, thin crease in an effort to hold back her sobs. Manu looked at Stephanie and allowed her arms to slip from around Ma Vera and fall to her sides. She looked at the old woman and watched as her hunched body shook with sobs.

"She was like a mother to me," Manu said softly, touching Ma Vera's hand, "and you were my dearest auntie." She turned to Stephanie. "When my mother died, I was still a baby, not yet one year old. My father's grief was so great he could not bear to look at me and so he brought me here, to The Mother and Guru Father. They took me in and raised me, and my father renounced the world and became a beggar. He has never returned." She looked again at Ma Vera, who appeared calmer.

"Vishnu, their own son, had left them by then," she continued, "but he would return occasionally and cause them terrible pain. He would call The Mother and Guru Father horrible names and would make nasty comments about the guests who were staying with us. The Mother and Guru Father would always accept this punishment without rebuke and usually ended up giving Vishnu the money he demanded for his gambling debts or whatever scheme he had at the time. They had very little money then, and, of course, they had the added burden of raising me. But they never complained. They just accepted it as God's will.

"But I saw The Mother change in small ways over the years; I guess because of the hardship and also the heartbreak over her son. She never talked about it, but I knew she had come from a rich English family and it must have been difficult for her at times not to think about what she had left behind. But she and Guru Father were devoted to each other and I never heard a cross word between them.

"But something happened to her the last time Vishnu came home. Something terrible, as if all the pain and suffering he had caused her had been festering in her heart all those years and she just couldn't take any more."

Ma Vera had become very quiet.

"Perhaps because he wanted to take everything they had built and turn it into something horrid and commercial; he was going to take the whole meaning of their lives and twist it into some kind of cheap sideshow. And of course, she knew he would finally destroy it and the Guru Father in the process. I guess she just couldn't let that happen." Manu's voice had become so low they had to strain to hear her.

"And so she killed him. She killed her own son." Manu put her hand on Stephanie's arm. "And your poor mother saw it," she said.

"No, no," said Stephanie, her voice catching in her throat. "She only saw her give him some tablets. I read it in her diary. How can you know The Mother killed him?" It was the last thing she wanted to believe.

Manu shook her head and looked again at Ma Vera, who sat rigid as a stone, her dry eyes staring straight in front of her. Manu turned back to Stephanie.

"Just before she died, I was sitting with your mother. Someone was always with her," she said, as if to reassure Stephanie that they had cared for Ann. "She was very close to the end by this time and she had been drifting in and out of consciousness for some hours. But suddenly she opened her eyes and looked right at me.

"'Manu,' she said, and I knew she was lucid. 'I have just remembered something.' 'What is it?' I asked her. Her eyes appeared to be looking inward, as if she were searching the depths of her memory, trying to see it more clearly.

"'It can't be,' she said and her face sort of crumpled with a look of horror, as if she were watching this memory play itself out in her head. 'I remember now,' she said, and she was crying.

"'What do you remember, Ann? Tell me,' I said.

"'She killed him,' she said. 'The Mother killed him.'

"'Killed who?' I asked.

"'Vishnu,' she said, looking straight at me. 'He was sleeping and I saw her put a pillow over his face and hold it there until he died. I saw it, Manu. I forced it out of my memory for a time, but I remember it clearly now.'"

"How could your mother know she had broken my heart?" whispered Manu. "She didn't realize, I'm sure, that Vishnu was The Mother's son and that I, in a way, was her daughter. I'm sure she wouldn't have told me if she had known this."

Manu stood up slowly and turned to face the others. Paul stood a little further back from Allan, who was watching Manu closely. She walked up to Allan and stood in front of him, looking deep into his eyes. Neither of them spoke but it was as if she were saying to him, "Now you know." He nodded his head almost imperceptibly. Then she went over to Ma Vera and helped her stand up. She kept her arm around the old woman's shoulders and the two of them walked slowly toward the door.

Stephanie was still kneeling on the floor. She let her eyes wander over the spinning wheel and examined its most intricate details. She studied its spindles and spokes and noted the fine grain of the wood that had been rubbed smooth from years of use. Even the simple three-legged stool that sat beside it was a diagram of essentials. Sturdy. Utilitarian. Nothing wasted. This is how we make thread, she thought. Out of little bits of fluff. And if the thread breaks, we tie a knot in it and spin the wheel again. It's very simple, really.

She stood up slowly because the circulation in her legs had slowed and her knees felt a little stiff. Paul had come up beside her and offered his arm to help steady her. She looked up at his familiar face, saw his look of concern and was glad he was there.

"Now what?" he said.

chapter thirty-three

There was no doubt in their minds that Manu had spoken the truth. Paul suggested, as a possibility, that she might have implicated The Mother, a dead woman, to protect the real murderer, Ma Vera.

"No," said Allan, with conviction. "She wouldn't do that. If Ma Vera were guilty, she would have said nothing at all. She knows that The Mother is beyond harm now and that she has to tell the truth. I think she also believes you had to know your mother's last thoughts," he said to Stephanie.

"But it doesn't tell me if my mother was murdered," said Stephanie. "We may never find out what happened to her."

"That's right," said Paul. "What are the chances of another eyewitness account? If The Mother did kill Ann, she's taken her secret to the grave."

"I'm convinced that needle mark was the cause of The Mother's death," said Allan.

"Could she have committed suicide?" asked Paul. "After com-

216

mitting two murders, she may have been so overcome by guilt she just decided to end it all."

"I suppose it's possible," said Allan. "She must have had access to some pretty lethal stuff. And known how to use it. Most people would probably give themselves an injection in the arm, don't you think?"

They agreed that was most likely true.

"I guess Ann must have been so horrified at witnessing a murder, she just blocked it out of her conscious mind," said Paul. "Imagine if she had known that The Mother was murdering her own son. She might have had a complete breakdown."

"Maybe that would've been better," said Stephanie. "Then maybe they would have notified us and asked us to come and get her."

"Stephie," said Paul, "it wouldn't have happened that way." He took her hand and rubbed the back of it. "If The Mother knew Ann had seen her kill Vishnu, she would never have let her live, even if she became a babbling idiot. She could never risk Ann's recovering and remembering everything. They didn't even notify you when your mother was dying, did they? They waited until after she was dead before they got in touch with you."

"I suppose you're right," said Stephanie. "I guess I'll always wish things had turned out differently."

They were sitting at a table in the corner of the empty dining room drinking tea. The range of emotions he was experiencing was making Allan feel physically ill. How could he have allowed himself and Stephanie to bully Ma Vera into some kind of confession when she was clearly–at least it was clear to him now–having a breakdown? He berated himself for not having been more sensitive to her state of mind, for not having seen how the once feisty old woman had deteriorated physically and mentally. Even Stephanie had expressed her concern for Ma Vera's health.

He had thought of himself as a sensitive man, but now he realized he had been sensitive only to his own suffering. He had approached Ma Vera as if she were a murderess and shown her no mercy. He had been judge and jury, acting the way he would have expected his father and uncles to behave, with their sense of superiority and moral righteousness that had nothing to do with human sensitivity.

And when Manu had confronted him, wordlessly, it had been a moment of truth, an instant of communication when he realized that to be human is to be deeply flawed and the burden of that knowledge, once affirmed, would never go away. If Manu hadn't interrupted them, how far would they have gone to force a confession from Ma Vera? It frightened and disgusted him to think he might have had no moral limits.

Would they have pushed until she cried for mercy? Until she begged them to stop? Or until she collapsed? Until she died? He was appalled to think that he had no conviction about what he might have done. Maybe he judged himself too harshly in an effort to right all the wrongs, but for Allan Lloyd, a line had been crossed and a burden of shame now sat on his shoulders.

For Paul Anderson, who had remained silent and riveted to one spot throughout the entire episode, it had been like walking into a movie two-thirds of the way through and witnessing only the last terrifying scenes. Up until then, these people had been merely players in a story that had been told to him. But all of a sudden he was seeing real emotions being acted out by living human beings that he thought he knew, but only in the way we think we know the characters in a book.

The story of a mother's tortured love for her son being turned into murder was almost too bizarre to comprehend. The fact that Ann had witnessed this murder and then suppressed it from memory until her last dying moments, was a poignant and heartbreaking element to the story that touched him in the most personal way. When Manu told the story to Stephanie, he had felt a pain in his heart, a physical, stabbing pain in his chest that had almost made him cry out.

Poor, lovely Ann, he thought, who truly believed she would find peace in this life if she looked hard enough for it. Had she died with that last, horrific memory playing itself out in front of her? She had been spared, at least, from knowing that a mother was killing her son, but did she know that she herself was dying at the hands of a murderer? Or did the thought exist only as a terrifying possibility as she felt her life ebbing away?

They might never know and they would live with the awful memory of her last moments as surely as she had died with it. He looked at Stephanie and wondered what these revelations had done to her. Would she bear a burden of guilt forever? Would all nostalgia for her mother now be reduced to one horrifying frame of reference, her needless, violent death? Poor Stephie, he thought, her suffering was just beginning.

There was nothing Stephanie could do to stop the ache in her heart. I'm never going to get over this, she told herself, as if it were a commitment to her mother's memory rather than a fact of emotional damage. For her mother to have witnessed such a heinous crime and then to have been victim of one as well was almost more than Stephanie could bear to think about.

What had Ann done to deserve such an agonizing end? Why had she, of all people, been the one to witness The Mother's despicable crime? Ann had died despairing and afraid. Stephanie thought of all the times she had criticized her mother for being weak, lost patience with her dithering and her mood swings, her headaches and depression. Not once had she sympathized with Ann, or tried to understand what it must be like to be her. Now she would have to live with it. There would be no reconciliation.

Yet she felt nothing for The Mother's despair; a despair so profound it had driven her to take the life of her own son. Stephanie could only imagine The Mother taking away Ann's life, slowly, bit by bit, so as not to seem so much like murder. And then, perhaps, she had killed herself, unable to bear her grief and shame.

I could believe that it happened that way, Stephanie told herself. In time, I could convince myself that it happened that way. But for now, she felt only a terrible and heavy sadness.

"Would you two mind if I go and lie down?" she said. "I just need some time to myself."

Allan felt relief, suddenly, that he would not have to discuss and speculate. It was like a reprieve, for the moment, to be able to go off and think things over. He nodded at Stephanie and Paul and left them.

Paul stood up and offered Stephanie his arm. She allowed him to help her up and she walked with him to the ashram's main entrance.

"I'll come back tomorrow," he said. "Will you think about coming home now? We can leave here right away and make our bookings from Bombay."

She nodded without resistance, too exhausted to really care what he was saying. She watched him walk toward the main road, his long stride more deliberate than usual, his shoulders hunched forward in thought. She turned back to the courtyard and as she passed The Mother's office, she heard a small voice call her name. It was Samina, The Mother's secretary. The slender, dark-eyed young woman, still dressed in mourning white, hastened across the open foyer.

"Stephanie," she said, a nervous catch in her voice, "a letter has come by courier for you. I was just going to take it to your room."

"Thank you," said Stephanie, taking the white oblong envelope. She saw it bore the crest of her father's stationery and she felt her heart quicken in anticipation of news from home. She climbed the stairs to her room, opening the letter carefully and reading it as she closed the door and sat down on the bed.

"Dearest Stephanie," he wrote, "Just a letter from your lonely old Dad to say he misses you very much and wants you to come home soon. Now, if that isn't a pathetic way to start a letter, I don't know what is!" She smiled at her father's typical flip-flop of emotions, not letting too much go, always being sure to hide the pain behind a joke.

"I've been managing with the help of Jay, who insists on keeping me company, and Lili, who of course, makes sure I eat more than I really care to. But I know they're acting out of kindness and their own sorrow and I haven't the heart to send them away. I am keeping busy at work, even though they try and send me home, but what good would it do to come home to an empty house and just sit there? Nothing's going to change, so I might just as well keep occupied.

"I trust Paul is there by now. To tell you the truth, I was relieved when he told me he wanted to go over there and find out what was going on. I wanted to write him a check for expenses, but the silly bugger was so stubborn about it, I told him we'd ante up when he got back. Tell him it's only money and not to be so damned serious about it. What difference does it make to me if it costs a hundred dollars or a hundred thousand? It's my family. Shouldn't he be able to understand that?

"I refuse to do anything about your Mother's burial service until you're back here. I know you told me she had already been cremated and her ashes scattered but we must have a memorial service. And you should be here for it. Besides, I'm sure you want to be. You'd never forgive your old Dad if he went ahead without you.

"I asked Arthur Ross to have his people look into this ashram business for me. I'm sure you'll be interested in what they found. It seems that this Guru Father character's real name is Vikram Chandra Seth. He was born near Agra (that's where the Taj Mahal is, in case you don't know) about seventy or so years ago. Father a small shopkeeper specializing in herbs, spices, colored dyes and rice; father and mother both devout Hindus. Two brothers, one sister, all older, all presumably dead by now. (That's pure speculation, of course.)

"As the youngest, he was apprenticed to learn a trade.

Eventually, he became a qualified chemist, or what we call a pharmacist. Operated a pharmacy of sorts in the bazaar in Old Delhi for some years. Then, in 1947, he closed up shop and apparently took off with the wife of an aide to Mountbatten, with whom he'd been having an affair. (That's how come they know so much about him.) Quite a scandal at the time, as I'm sure you can imagine. Seems they surfaced some years later around where you are now, running a sort of hostel for holy men.

"They apparently had a son, but it is not known for sure if he was their own child. The property where the present ashram is located was donated to them by a grateful citizen who had received their hospitality at one time. The place seems to run on the up and up, depending on donations for the most part, from well-to-do guests and residents (like your Mother, I suppose). By the way, the aide to Mountbatten (in case you're interested) went back to England and filed for divorce after a couple of years. He never remarried, preferring, I suppose, the company of his faithful hunting dogs. He died a couple of years ago.

"That's all the news that's fit to print, my girl. Please come home soon. I know I shouldn't pressure you—you're an independent woman with a life of your own and all that—but just now, you being in that particular place doesn't quite sit well with us at home. Your Uncle Jay said if I didn't beg you, he would. He and Joannie and the kids and Lili and EVERYBODY send their love, me included."

He had written "Dad" at the end of the letter with the flourish of a signature, underlining it for emphasis. He was an important man, after all, not just her father.

chapter thirty-four

She approached the Guru Father's chambers with some trepidation, but summoned her courage to knock smartly on the door. The rat-tat sounded too loud in the silence of the empty corridor. The voice that answered with the familiar "Come in" came from the far end of the room. Stephanie pushed the door open carefully and deliberately. It's not over yet, she thought.

He was sitting, as before, in the large upholstered armchair that seemed so incongruous in this place of ascetic practices. The picture of The Mother, mounted in its silver frame, now sat on the table beside him.

"I thought I might see you again," he said softly. "Will you have tea with me once more?"

"No, not this time." She sat on the sofa, as before, and considered again what she was going to say.

He was wearing a ceremonial robe of some sort and his hair and beard had been carefully combed. She caught the glint of gold thread running through his garment, even though the curtains were drawn against the early evening light and only candles lit the room. His leather sandals were also adorned with a golden filigree and they appeared to be new. He wore a ring with a large blood-red stone on one hand and on the other, a polished wafer of lapis lazuli in a gold setting.

"They were gifts from her," he said, when he saw Stephanie looking at his hands. A silver teapot and china cup and saucer sat on the table next to him.

"She did a terrible thing," said Stephanie, suddenly. It was not what she had been planning to say at all.

"Yes."

They sat in silence as if there was nothing more to say. She heard the soft tick-ticking of an old clock somewhere in the room, but didn't look around for it. She kept her eyes on his face.

"I didn't know, of course," he said, "until your mother told me." His expression was sad, almost tender. "She had no idea she was speaking to me about my own wife and son." His voice dropped and Stephanie strained to hear him. "Or I'm quite certain she would not have come to me."

He spread the fingers of both hands across his lap and appeared to examine the knuckles. "I really had no choice," he said.

She watched as he picked up the delicate china teacup and sipped some of the clear beverage. Then he filled the cup again from the silver teapot. Steam rose in delicate tendrils from the top of the cup.

"I was able to make her forget the distressing incident," he went on, "put it out of her mind, so to speak, with what you would probably call hypnosis. Unfortunately, she remained emotionally distressed but was unable to recollect the cause of her anguish. The tea she drank in my company induced symptoms of an intestinal disorder and I was then able to prepare powders, which my wife unwittingly administered, causing her health to further deteriorate.

"My poor, dear wife was so distraught over the death of our only son, I couldn't bear to watch the pain of her suffering. When your mother, who she thought she was nursing back to health, died as well, it was the beginning of her final breakdown."

He drank from the fragile cup and refilled it with the still steaming tea.

"Again, I had no choice," he said. "I administered digitalis, a medication prescribed to me by Dr. Gopal Singh, while she slept. I did indeed witness her die of a heart attack."

He closed his eyes and breathed deeply, as if composing himself. Stephanie was afraid he might fall asleep as he had the other night. But after a few minutes of slow, measured breathing, he opened his eyes and spoke.

"You are much too young, " he said, with some effort, "to know what it is to reach the end of your life and see everything around you turn to ashes. I could not believe this was happening to me after a lifetime of service to God. Just as Jesus asked, so was I asking, 'Why hast Thou foresaken me?'"

He turned and looked at the framed photograph of The Mother, and he seemed silently to ask her the same question.

"Not one moment do I remember," he said, turning back to Stephanie, "from the time I renounced the life of Vikram Chandra Seth and chose the life of devotion, not one moment," he repeated, "do I remember sinning against God. And yet He punished me continually. And in the end, I became a man without conscience. A man capable of the unspeakable. How can this happen?"

He spoke the words with such vehemence, Stephanie almost wished she could give him an answer. He reached for the cup of tea and drank from it. This time he didn't refill it.

"What about Manfred?" she asked, hoping he would be able to answer.

"Ah," he said, shaking his head, "the foolish German. The son of a Nazi doctor with so much sadness and anger in his heart.

That was a terrible mistake. He did not have to die."

He took another deep breath before going on. "My wife was so disturbed by his accusations, she came to believe he knew things he could not possibly have known." He looked at her helplessly.

"I put something into a bottle of arrack I knew he would eventually consume. I had no idea he would leave the ashram so suddenly and decide to go back to Europe. Of course, he knew nothing and his death was completely unnecessary. Perhaps he would have had a second chance to make something of himself if I had not intervened."

Intervened. Yes, you intervened, she thought. He had spoken so calmly of his three murders that she suspected he didn't yet realize what he had done. But maybe she underestimated him. Maybe it was all too clear to him what he and The Mother had done. Or else, why would he be telling her anything at all when he must have known there was no way to prove it?

He had killed three people out of what he believed to be necessity, in order to preserve what he had spent a lifetime building. And now what he felt wasn't even remorse, but a profound sadness and self-pity that his life and everything he had worked for was lost to him. Maybe he was right to ask how this could happen. But it was too late, she thought. Much too late.

"I know it's impossible for you not to think harshly of me," he began to speak again, "but I will ask you anyway to try and find it in your heart to forgive me. Forgiveness is God's greatest gift to us. And yet so few of us are able to exercise this gift. The great tragedy of mankind, don't you think? We are no better than beasts after all."

This time he picked up the teapot and drained its contents into the cup. No steam rose from it. A dark, tepid pool of liquid sat in the bottom of the cup.

"Perhaps we are not so different, you and I," he said, taking his eyes from the cup and focusing them on her face. "We have both had our world turned upside down. There is so little time left in mine that it will soon sink quickly into oblivion from its own weight. Yours is not even halfway done and will no doubt recover its balance in time and right itself, or it may forever remain inverted. I know this feeling, for I have lived most of my life in such a state.

"But I felt such intense, passionate love for her, I thought I was somehow redeemed by it. It was my only compensation, but it was not my redemption. It was, I guess, my undoing. Unless the seeds for that were planted long before I met her."

He looked again at the rings on his fingers.

"You are a Christian and you must believe I am condemned to hell. I believe I am condemned to live out my Karma. Perhaps they are the same thing. We both suffer and those around us suffer. So you see," he said, his voice suddenly louder, "you must not be controlled by the dark side of your nature. You must not let it win or your whole life will have been for nothing."

She saw that his eyes were shining with a feverish intensity. His face had become quite pale and his breathing was labored. It's almost time to go, she thought.

"Finally you learn," he said, "that you cannot control anything. And that relinquishing control, which you once thought was a way of avoiding the responsibility, does not absolve you. In the end, you see there is no end. In the end, you find that you were doomed from the start."

He reached for the cup of tea and drained the last dregs in one long swallow. He examined the bottom of the cup as if reading his fortune in the specks of leaf clinging to it. Then he carefully replaced the cup in its saucer and turned to her.

"Please leave me now," he said. "There is not much time and I must make one final appeal to God."

His smile had already taken on a serenity that was as deceptive as her own outer calm as she rose to leave. She knew she was leaving him to die, granting him this one last wish to control his final moments. Briefly she wondered if she should "intervene," try and save his life so he could suffer longer for what he had done. Why should she be humane, she thought, and let him die without facing trial and punishment? But she felt only pity for him and an overwhelming sadness.

The anger would come later, when she was back home, and it would last a long time. She would see him sitting before her as he was now, and she would want to hit him again and again and beat him with her fists until he was dead and she was exhausted.

But for now she could only wonder at what he had said and ask the same questions he had asked. How can this happen? When does our resistance finally break down and we give in to forces more powerful than reason? And is that what we spend our lives doing? Resisting the "dark side of our nature?" Is it what we fear most about ourselves? Knowing it exists in all of us, held back only by a fragile and wavering sense of decency, or conscience? She shuddered when she thought how deliberately he had acted in preparing and administering his potions. I had no choice, he said, as if he had been guided by a force outside of himself instead of the fear and dread that were consuming his insides.

Maybe we're not so different, you and I, he had said. It was a thought that would haunt her for a long time. Do I know what I would do if I were faced with such a moral dilemma? Would I do everything possible to save a loved one? Would I stand by and risk discovery or reveal the crime myself and let justice be done?

She had left him to his fate because it was no longer clear to her where the lines should be drawn. If the hypothetical question had been posed six months earlier, she would have had no trouble answering. But now, treading the mucky surface of reality, she was not so sure. She thought of the *homme pendu* in her mother's Tarot cards, the hanging man suspended at the crossroads, unable to choose, fearing to make the wrong choice. I will know when the time comes, she thought. But wasn't this the time? Wasn't she making a moral decision by walking away, or was she making no decision at all? Merely letting events take their own course. Not intervening.

She met no one on they way back up to her room. There was an eerie silence, as if the walls had absorbed death and were slowly spreading its spirit into the air.

I'm not what I was, she realized, and never will be again. I'm like Lady Macbeth, with blood on my hands as surely as if I had used the dagger myself. There can be no more illusions; I have seen the other side. I can no more erase the knowledge of what's happened than he can erase the fact of it. If he burns in hell for eternity, I won't be absolved.

chapter thirty-five

When Paul arrived the next morning with a taxi, Stephanie's canvas bag and the bag containing her mother's few possessions were packed and ready to go. The news of Guru Father's death had slowly spread through the ashram and once again its inhabitants had been plunged into mourning. The atmosphere was somber, made heavier still by the oppressive heat.

She had gone to Allan's room before first meditation, when the sun was just rising above the thick orange haze of the horizon. She told him about her father's letter and her conversation with the Guru Father. She didn't talk about her own sleepless night and her anguish at having to repeat the Guru Father's confession. She told Allan she was leaving, and that she was satisfied she now knew the truth.

Allan said he would be staying on, for a while at least, to see how things panned out. He felt he owed something to Manu and Ma Vera and wanted to make sure they were taken care of.

"I don't know where I'll want to be a year from now, or even a month from now," he said. "I've got a lot of things to think about." He touched her arm and smiled. "Maybe I'll end up being a doctor after all." Then the smile left his face. "But I don't think so."

She put her arms around him and they embraced. "Good luck, whatever you do," she said.

"I'll write to you," he said. "Let you know where I am."

"Yes. I'd like that."

Now Allan knew the truth and it would be up to him to tell the others. Possibly Manu and Ma Vera already knew the real story, and what did it matter what anybody else thought?

Would the ashram survive without the Guru Father, she wondered? Would someone take his place as spiritual leader? What would happen to the property now that there was no surviving family? Should I care, she thought? Only because of her mother, Stephanie realized, because Ann had wanted so much to be able to believe, and because something of her would always be here.

Paul arrived before nine o'clock. She was waiting for him on one of the stone benches in the front garden. She told him briefly that the Guru Father had died during the night and that the ashram was once again in mourning.

"That's not the whole story," he said. "There's more, isn't there?"

"Yes," she admitted, "much more. But I can't go into it right now. It's a long, sad story but it's over now. He told it to me himself."

"Who? The Guru Father?"

"Yes. I saw him last night and he told me everything."

"Does Allan know?"

"Yes, I told him this morning. I thought it was only fair." They were at the main door of the ashram. "Come on," she said. "My things are upstairs. Let's get out of here."

They were coming back downstairs when they ran into Werner and Else with their rucksacks on their backs.

"Are you leaving too?" Else whispered.

"Yes," said Stephanie. "I have no reason to stay any longer."

"Have you heard?" Else said, and dropped her voice still further. "About Guru Father?"

Stephanie nodded and Else continued. "Isn't it awful? I told Werner I won't stay here a minute longer. I don't care how cheap it is, this place gives me the creeps."

"Come, Else," said Werner, "don't be morbid. Let's just leave quietly."

Paul offered to share the taxi and when she saw the surprised look on Werner's face, she realized he must have had no idea that Paul had been standing there. She made quick introductions all around and Werner and Else climbed gratefully into the cab with them.

"So Stephanie," said Else, once they were off the ashram grounds, "were you able to find out anything else in your detective work?"

Stephanie was a little taken aback. How had Else known she'd been snooping around? She was convinced Else knew very little of what had actually gone on but her emotional antennae had obviously picked up something.

"Well, I found out one more thing," said Stephanie, hoping to satisfy Else's curiosity and complete an unspoken bargain with Werner. Else turned excitedly in her seat and Werner was watching her so intently Stephanie almost wondered if he could see.

"The Mother and Guru Father were married," she told them, "and Vishnu was their son."

Else gasped in surprise and Werner simply nodded his head up and down in a knowing way.

"So it's true," said Else and turned to Werner. "You had suspected as much." She looked at Stephanie and said, "Werner told me he suspected that might be the case." Then her face clouded over as she thought of something else.

"How sad," she said. "And now he has died of a broken heart."

"And you were convinced everyone was being murdered," said Werner, a note of scorn in his voice. "I hope you have learned your lesson," he added. Then he turned his eyes toward Stephanie.

"Perhaps that is why your mother was so upset after Vishnu died," he said. "She may have sensed a mother's grief for the loss of a child."

Stephanie looked hard into his clear, sightless eyes. Does he know, she wondered? How much does he really see?

"Yes, perhaps," she said.

They rode in silence for most of the way. Else attempted to engage Paul in conversation, asking him about his life in Canada and telling him about life on the ashram. She kept throwing Stephanie looks of approval, indicating she thought Paul was a good catch. Stephanie smiled and said nothing.

They parted company when they reached the village. Else and Werner intended to continue their journey through the ashrams of India and caught a bus almost immediately that would take them further east.

"We will stay near the ocean," said Else, "now that the hot season is here."

Their goodbyes were hurried, which was a relief to Stephanie. They waved to each other as the bus pulled away, belching a single billow of black smoke when the driver accelerated.

Their bus would be along in an hour, so Paul offered to find cold drinks while she stayed and watched the bags. She was glad to be alone for a while and she asked Paul to try and find some food for the trip, just to be by herself a little longer.

The sun glared down, a flat, white, hot disc against the almost colorless sky. The only shade was from the limp, parched leaves of a nearby tree, so she dragged the bags over to it and propped her back against its knobby trunk. Things were slowing down already, with most people heading indoors to escape the heat. A wretched looking dog, starved and weary, limped past her on three legs. Stephanie sat very still, believing that even the slightest exertion would make her feel much hotter. The only movement she made was to blink her eyes once in a while.

She saw someone walk slowly into her line of vision. He was a holy man of some kind, a saddhu, she knew that. He squatted directly in front of her and they stared at each other for several minutes. He was a small man, she noticed, and very thin. He was nearly naked except for a white loincloth that looked almost like a diaper. His entire body was covered in dust and ashes and his long hair was matted and dusty so she couldn't tell if it was black, brown or white. He didn't look very old, maybe forty or fifty, and his face was decorated with red and white lines that she knew had something to do with Hindu ritual. He carried only a walking stick and a wooden begging bowl.

He began speaking and she stared at him, uncomprehending. He chanting something, repeating the same sounds over and over. She continued to stare at him, listening but not understanding.

He ended as abruptly as he had begun. Then he dipped his thumb into the ashy contents of his wooden bowl, reached over and drew a line across the middle of her forehead. He smiled and she noticed he didn't have very many teeth. Then he slowly rose to his feet, turned and continued on his way. Stephanie watched him until his thin, stooping body was out of sight. She felt alert and relaxed at the same time, as if she had been swimming and the water had been clear and cool and clean. She closed her eyes and listened to the sound of her own breathing.

Someday I'll come back here, she thought.

END

S.P. Hozy

If Only To Say Goodbye

a sneak preview

Publication date: February 2005
ISBN 1-55321-109-X

Chapter One

On May 15, 1976 Joanna Reynolds was visited by a man from the State Department. She had been re-reading one of her favorite books, Daphne DuMaurier's *Rebecca*, and remembering that she had first read *Rebecca* not long after she and Franklin were married. At the time, Joanna identified strongly with the nameless young woman who had married the complex Maxim de Winter, a man with so many secrets.

"Mrs. Reynolds," the State Department official said, "I'm afraid I have some bad news for you. Your husband has drowned in an accident in Thailand."

Looking back, Joanna recalled experiencing only a sense of disbelief. Not grief, not even sadness. All she could think was, hasn't this man read the book? It's not Maxim who drowns, it's Rebecca.

Franklin Reynolds had been in Thailand for nine months as head of Americans Aid Refugees. He had been appointed by a Senate committee formed to solve the Vietnamese refugee problem. After the fall of Saigon and the American departure, boatloads of Vietnamese fleeing the communists became an embarrassment to the American government. People all over the world saw their desperate faces daily on television as they fled across the border into Thailand. The camps set up for them by the Thai government had become a nightmare. Most of the refugees were ill, famished and exhausted. Their babies were dying in the unsanitary, crowded conditions. The wait was interminable and many seemed doomed to a life in limbo, unwanted and hopeless.

Franklin was the perfect choice to head the organization that had been formed to help these people. He was a high-profile mover and shaker who could get things done with a few phone calls and a few words in the right ears. He'd been doing this kind of thing for over a decade. In 1964 he had been part of Lyndon Johnson's anti-poverty drive. He was asked to oversee the presidential election in Saigon in 1967. Then in 1968, he was with the delegation to the Paris Peace talks with the North Vietnamese.

That was the first time Joanna asked to go along with him on one of his trips, but Franklin had bluntly told her he didn't want her there. She had hidden her disappointment; he was so adamantly against her going that she didn't even ask his reasons. She just assumed it would be inappropriate for her to go. But he wouldn't let Joanna go with him to Helsinki in 1969 where he was attending the SALT talks, or to China and Moscow in 1972 where he was part of Nixon's protocol team. There were other, smaller trips to places like Turkey, Panama and Athens, but she wasn't allowed to go on them either. All these disappointments now came crowding back as Joanna thought about their sixteen years of married life and how her husband's powerful personality had defined and dominated them.

In the early years of their marriage Joanna tried to be the right kind of wife to the son of the wealthy, respected Chicago family that owned Reynolds Medical Instruments. Her father had died when she was four and her mother took the insurance money and put it into a small hairdressing salon on the main street of Aurora,

Illinois. Her hard work and determination put Joanna through the University of Chicago where she graduated with a degree in literature. Joanna took her skills to the public library and was hired as a clerk whose job it was to sort and shelve books, stamp them out, check them in and direct people to the washrooms.

That was in 1956. The Eisenhower administration was in charge, Grace Kelly married the Prince of Monaco and Elvis Presley sang "You Ain't Nothin' But A Hound Dog." Life was pretty good.

By the time she met Franklin three years later, Joanna had worked her way up to Assistant Librarian, Literature, and got to go to department meetings, answer reference questions from readers and help kids with their homework. She enjoyed her work, even though a lot of it was routine and repetitive, because it was cloistered and familiar and made her feel useful.

She met Franklin at the library's opening of a new history wing that had been sponsored by his family. Franklin's father was a history buff and had bequeathed his entire library, plus a substantial cash gift, toward the new wing.

At first Franklin was attracted to Joanna's quietness. He said he felt peaceful whenever she was around. He wasn't looking for excitement; he already had plenty of that in his life as a junior partner in one of the city's more prominent law firms. Even in those days Franklin was a crusader. He took up causes the way some people pick up stray animals. Housing for the poor. Medical care for the elderly. He was a rich man's son with a conscience. He loved to tell her about his victories and Joanna loved to listen.

They got married in 1960. His family didn't dislike Joanna but they didn't consider it a match made in society heaven. She wasn't what they'd had in mind for Franklin, but she grew on them the same way she'd grown on Franklin. They were talkers and she was a listener. They acted and she watched. She had good manners and wasn't bad looking. Franklin's sisters taught her how to dress and put on makeup and shake hands with important people. Joanna was an able, if unspectacular, pupil and she was what Franklin wanted. Franklin, as the favorite son, usually got what he wanted.

The man from the State Department finally left after Joanna assured him she'd be all right on her own. She walked out into the familiarity of the backyard, pulled a few weeds and watered the lawn. She and Franklin had lived in the same house in suburban Chicago all their married life. They had landscapers and gardeners but Joanna was the one who decided what should be planted and she took pride in the garden's Oriental simplicity. She always felt peaceful there and believed that Franklin did, too. He liked to spend time there when he was at home. The garden was the safety zone in their marriage, a place where they could be together, because theirs had become a marriage based on separateness and separation. The garden was one of the few things they still shared.

Joanna didn't cry because it seemed to her as if she were living somebody else's life, like watching a disaster on the six o'clock news–somebody else's tragedy. She was going through the motions, giving herself a chance to catch up with the bad news. She knew the unanswered questions were still there, in Thailand on a beach somewhere.

Were things going to be very different from now on, she wondered? She had come to accept Franklin's absences as normal. After it became apparent he didn't want her traveling with him, Joanna started taking courses at the university. She studied philosophy, sociology, anthropology, world religion, anything that took her fancy. She told herself she liked being alone. There was always money in the bank, the bills were paid on time and she didn't ask a lot of questions.

But now it was 1976 and she was forty years old and Franklin was dead, drowned, apparently, while swimming in Thailand. Except, in all the years she'd know him, Franklin never went swimming. He didn't even own a bathing suit. The few times they'd taken a vacation together, he'd refused to go to the Caribbean or anyplace that involved boats. "I don't like the water," he said, "and I can't swim. It's not my idea of a holiday."

So they'd gone to London and Rome instead.

Yet, according to the report, Franklin's body had been found washed up on the beach at Pattaya, a resort town less than a hundred miles from Bangkok. He was wearing swimming trunks and the only mark on him was a bump on the forehead.

In *Rebecca*, Du Maurier wrote, "I suppose sooner or later in the life of everyone comes a moment of trial. We all of us have our particular devil who rides us and torments us, and we must give battle in the end." Joanna didn't know it then, but her battle was just beginning.

Chapter Two

Joanna knew she would need to break the news to Franklin's family and decided to tell Claire, Franklin's older sister, first. She didn't want to tell her over the phone so she drove the five or so miles to Claire's home in Oak Park. It was clear and sunny and the birds were singing their heads off. It seemed in such bad taste.

When Claire answered the doorbell herself Joanna was relieved. It hadn't even occurred to her Claire might not be home.

"What's wrong?" were the first words out of Clair's mouth.

Many people thought Claire was austere and intimidating, but she wasn't like that at all. Claire was one of those intensely proud but shy people who often mask their shyness by presenting a cool, almost haughty demeanor. Joanna was a bit like that herself and always thought of Claire as her spiritual sister. Claire was ten years older than Joanna and had a graceful maturity that Joanna envied. Claire seemed to move with time, not against it. She was what some people call an old soul. She was intelligent and kind and Joanna had always trusted her. Many times in the past she'd relied on her wisdom.

The color drained from Claire's face when Joanna told her. Joanna made her sit down and poured them both a Scotch.

"Are they absolutely certain it was Franklin?"

"Yes, they're sure. It wouldn't be that difficult to identify a man as well known as Franklin. He's been in Bangkok for nearly nine months. There must be a whole network of people he's been involved with."

"But you know he never goes near the water." Claire's hand was shaking as she picked up her glass.

"I know. That bothered me too. But the State Department assured me the Thai police did a thorough investigation. I thought maybe Franklin had finally made up his mind to overcome his phobia. You know if he decides to do something, he does it with absolute determination.

"I suppose it's possible," Claire said. "Franklin has always been so stubborn and secretive. He might do something like that and never say a word about it." Her eyes filled with tears as she said the words, but she blinked them away and took another sip of her Scotch.

"Franklin never told me why he was so afraid of the water." Joanna wanted Claire to talk about him, to remind her of the man she had married and to help her understand what was happening.

Claire looked down at her hands and carefully examined the rings that adorned her long, slender fingers. She was looking back to a day in her childhood that had affected her deeply.

"When we were children," she said, "we had a summer home on Lake Michigan. We were all taught to swim very early on, but Franklin was still too young and he hadn't learned yet."

She told Joanna that Franklin and their sister Ina had been building sand castles under the supposedly watchful eye of their nurse. Maybe the nurse had looked away for only an instant; maybe she'd dozed off for a few seconds in the hot sun. She didn't notice Ina running into the water with a bucket full of sand in one hand and a shovel in the other.

"Her own momentum must have overtaken her," said Claire. "I don't know how else it could have happened. She may have hit her head with the bucket when she fell and got her eyes and mouth full of water and sand. Before anyone even noticed, she was dead."

Franklin probably thought Ina was trying to swim. He didn't know she was dying. The hysterical scene that followed frightened him so badly that he refused to go near the water ever again. The lake had been so calm. It gave no warning of what was to come, yet, in an instant, it took Ina's life away and caused his mother to scream repeatedly, "My baby's dead! My baby's dead!"

"We children had never experienced such a feeling of utter helplessness," said Claire.

Franklin had never mentioned the episode to Joanna. She knew he had a sister who died young, but the family never discussed it. They were all bred to be careful and discreet, and not to talk about themselves or their feelings. Joanna knew it was hard for Claire to tell the story even after all those years.

"I guess you'll need to contact Franklin's lawyer," Claire finally said, steering the conversation in a more practical direction. It was all right to talk about lawyers at a time like this.

"I'm sure everything's in order," said Joanna. "I'll have to call Ed and let him know what's happened. To tell you the truth, I'm not sure what I should do. The State Department said they'd notify me when Franklin's body was being shipped home."

Neither of them could grasp the finality of the situation. There was nothing to look at, no evidence of a death. No body to confirm their worst fears. They were both used to Franklin being away for long periods of time, but if he were dead, surely they would feel some sense of loss.

Claire asked what kind of service Joanna intended to have. Had Franklin and she ever discussed their wishes on the subject? Had they purchased cemetery plots?

"He once mentioned that he wanted to be cremated and his ashes buried in the garden," Joanna said. "I assume there will be instructions in his will." Claire was trying to keep Joanna's mind on mundane matters, away from the unanswered questions that neither of them wanted to think about.

They made up lists of people to be contacted and kept to practical matters. Although Joanna didn't discuss the details with Claire, she knew Franklin had left her everything outright and that his net cash worth was around a million dollars. Even though the Reynolds family no longer owned the controlling interest in the business, they lived comfortably on the interest earned from investments.

Joanna went into the den and phoned Ed Lauder, Franklin's lawyer. He was genuinely upset by the news. He and Franklin had been friends for close to fifteen years.

"I'll have to contact Franklin's office in Bangkok and ascertain whether any personal documents are being held there," he said. "I'll call the State Department and the Embassy in Bangkok to verify the arrangements and get an official death certificate." He would call, he said, and they would get together as soon as he was certain he had all the relevant papers.

Claire made coffee in the kitchen. "Joanna," she said, "whatever you do, don't brood. Don't let yourself slide. It's just too easy. When Robert died, I couldn't think of a reason to keep going. He left me well off, no loose ends, but the bottom line was he left me. And even though there were times when I could have sent him packing, he was too much a part of me to want to carry on without him. I felt I had no right to be alive."

When Joanna got home a few hours later she checked the mailbox. There were a few bills and fliers, but while she was sorting through them she came across a letter addressed to her in Franklin's handwriting.

Her hands shook as she tore open the envelope. The letter was written on blue airmail paper and dated nearly three weeks earlier.

"Dear Joanna," it said, "I've been trying to write this letter all day. I have a lot to tell you, but I can't say any of it in a letter. Things have not gone as I planned and I need to get away from here and sort this mess out. I've neglected my private affairs and made a few unwise financial decisions and now find I've left us rather badly off. I will be coming home as soon as I can extricate myself from my responsibilities here. Please respect my confidence and don't speak of this to anyone. Forgive me for being stupid. I feel I've let us both down. F."

Chapter Three

What was going on? The man she knew to be terrified of the water had drowned; and the man who was always scrupulously careful about financial matters had made a few unwise decisions and left them "rather badly off." Living without Franklin somewhere in her life was going to be an adjustment, but living without Franklin's money was not a prospect Joanna had even considered. She'd always assumed she'd be financially secure.

Now she realized she might be facing the kind of life she was totally unprepared for. She'd married Franklin a few years after finishing college, and except for her brief stint at the library, had no marketable skills or experience. She had only a little money of her own—some unspectacular bonds left to her by her mother that she kept more out of sentiment than financial benefit—and their household goods, some of them fairly valuable, but none of which Joanna wanted to part with.

What if Franklin had left a pile of debts? She might not even end up with the house. Was she going to be a penniless widow forced to scrape by on a pittance? Would she have to declare bankruptcy? Joanna started to cry and hated herself for it. "You're so selfish," she thought. "You're crying for yourself, not for your dead husband or the end of your marriage, but for yourself, because you've lost your life of ease." She felt confused and afraid. Things like this didn't happen to people like them. What was she going to do?

"You bastard," she shouted to the empty room, "you didn't share things with me when you were alive. You didn't tell me things. You wouldn't let me travel with you. And now you've left me nothing. How dare you! How dare you leave me like this!"

Joanna cried out her anger for a good hour before acknowledging that she was angry with a dead person and what was the point? The damage had been done. It was left to her to pick up the pieces and carry on with her life. But she felt different. She felt betrayed and cheated and powerless, and she knew those feelings weren't going to go away in a few hours or a few days.